Your Man Chose Me

D1018405

Your Man Chose Me

Racquel Williams

WITHDRAWN

www.urbanbooks.net

Urban Books, LLC
97 N18th Street
Wyandanch, NY 11798

Your Man Chose Me

Copyright © 2016 Racquel Williams

All rights reserved. No part of this book may be
reproduced in any form or by any means without
prior consent of the Publisher, except brief quotes
used in reviews.

ISBN 13: 978-1-62286-896-4
ISBN 10: 1-62286-896-X

First Mass Market Printing April 2017
First Trade Paperback Printing September 2016
Printed in the United States of America

10 9 8 7 6 5 4 3 2 1

*This is a work of fiction. Any references or sim-
ilarities to actual events, real people, living or
dead, or to real locales are intended to give
the novel a sense of reality. Any similarity in
other names, characters, places, and incidents is
entirely coincidental.*

Distributed by Kensington Publishing Corp.
Submit orders to:
Customer Service
400 Hahn Road
Westminster, MD 21157-4627
Phone: 1-800-733-3000
Fax: 1-800-659-2436

I dedicate this book to my three sons: Malik, Jehmel, and Zahir. Everything I do is to make things easier for all of three of you. I love y'all with everything in me!

ACKNOWLEDGMENTS

First and foremost, I want to give all praises to Allah. Without Him, I wouldn't be able to put out these books. I am blessed that He is leading my path!

To my Mom Rosa, thank you for being there through the good times and the bad times.

To Carlo, I appreciate you for all that you do.

To Danielle, Stacey, Papaya, Ebonee, Ambria, Qiana, Nika, and Fabiola Joseph, thanks, ladies, for always having my back, especially in this industry. I love y'all.

Johnne Johnson, we met by accident, but I am happy we did. Thank you for being the extra set of eyes when I'm working on a book. You are harsh at times, but that's what I need to continue putting out great stories.

To Sharlene Smith, thank you for the long talks when I am at a breaking point. Your words are appreciated.

To Tasha Bynum and Trinity Dekane, ladies, I appreciate the support.

Acknowledgments

To my readers, who I know for sure are there through the good times and the bad times, I appreciate y'all! Taheeerah Brown, Aisha Taylor-Gamble, Myre Childs, Rhea Wilson, LaTanya Garry, Barbara Morgan, Dawn Jackson, Kreation by Kia, Cherri Johnson, Mary Bishop, Kendra Littleton, JoAnn Hunter-Scott, Crystal Handsome, Toni Futrell, Priscilla Murray, Joyce Dickerson, Nola Brooks, Erica Taylor, Yvonne Covington, Evelyn Johnson , Lenika Winfiels, Denise Henson, Tajuana Smith, Alisha Benjamin, Tamika Cowart-Mason, AkiaKiaBoo Porter Dessiree Ellison, Qiana Drennen, Donica James, Cherita Price, RedgirlPettrie, Jane Pennella, Lisa Borders-Muhammad, Alexis Goodwyn, Mellonie Brown, Tonya Tinsley, Shekie Johnson, Antoinnette-Mitchell-Tate, Pam Williams, Tammy Rosa, Rebecca Alexandria, Venus Murray, Shann Adams, Nancy Pyram, Tina Simmons, Patricia Charles, Temmiyyia Davidson, Nicki Williams Kenia Michelle, Jenise Brown, Kysha Small, Suprenia Hutchins, MzNicki Ervin, Trina McGuire, Chyta A. Curry, Drea Bryant, Rebecca Rogers, Paula Milan, Rita King, Stephanie Wiley, Stacey Phifer Mills, Tera Kinsley-Colman and Kesia Ashworth-Lawrence and others.

Acknowledgments

If you support me, and don't see your name, I apologize; please charge it to my head and not my heart.

Shout out to all my readers and supporters, I am definitely blessed!

PROLOGUE

I should have been happy to be alive, but some days a bitch like me often wondered, why the fuck was I here? The bitch who birthed me barely spoke to me and when she did it was always some fucked-up-ass shit. I can't count how many times she called me a bitch or a whore. When I was younger, I used to cry because I couldn't understand why my mama was so cruel to me. It was only when I got older I understood that it was because my sperm donor left her ass for another woman. She had become a bitter bitch and I had become her competition.

Shit got worse when she started dating this old, broken-down nigga. From the minute he laid eyes on me, I knew he was up to no good. I tried my best to avoid him because I could tell the nigga was a pervert. I could tell by the way he smiled at me behind Mama's back.

One day I was sitting outside on the porch, looking at the little kids play next door. I was so wrapped up in my own thoughts that I didn't see when he crept up on me.

"You look good in those shorts," he said to me as he licked his crusty black lips and smiled, showing his set of yellow teeth.

"Whatever! You keep on talking like that and I promise I'm gonna tell my mama on yo' ass for real," I snapped. I was about tired of his old fifty-something ass coming at me every chance he got. I tried to brush him off, but his behavior had gotten erratic over the past few weeks.

One day it had gotten so bad that he tried to grope me while I walked past him; so I sank my teeth down on his arm with all the strength I had in my body, which caused him to slap the shit out of me. I didn't flinch but he did let go of my breast.

"You're gonna give me that young, fresh pussy one of these days, you little bitch!" he yelled.

"When hell freezes over." I rolled my eyes and walked off on him.

I was about tired of him and his eccentric behavior. I walked into the house where Mama was sitting in her favorite chair watching an episode of *Criminal Minds*. I walked past her, but then turned back around. "Hey, Mama, can I talk to you?"

"Girl, what is it now? You see me watching my show." She continued staring at the TV.

"Mama, I need to talk to you about Aubrey. He's been trying to get into my panties for a while now and I'm tired of it."

"Bitch, what the fuck you just say to me? Is your little dirty ass accusing my man of wanting to fuck your little stinking pussy?" She got up and stared me down.

"Yes, that's exactly what I'm accusing him of. You think I would make this up?"

"You know, you have always been jealous of me and Aubrey's relationship, but I never thought you would go so far as to accuse him of wanting you."

"Accuse me of what?" He walked in smiling.

"Tiana claiming you want to fuck her but, baby, I know the truth. She is the one who wants to fuck you. I think she be hearing when you fucking me at night so she wants to get that same feeling."

"Mama, really? How can you sit there and accuse me of wanting that bastard? I'm your fucking daughter!" The tears welled up in my eyes as I pleaded with my mama.

"Get the hell out of here and stay the fuck away from him. You hear me, you little fast bitch!" she spat in the coldest tone.

The walls around me started spinning as anxiety kicked in. I couldn't believe the bitch who birthed me would sit up and accuse me of wanting her no-good-ass nigga. The tears continued to flow as I looked at my mama, shook my head, and walked away. I slammed my room door and crawled under my covers. I couldn't believe what had just happened. All I knew was I had to get away from here and that sick-ass bitch!

CHAPTER ONE

Tiana

People say your past shouldn't dictate your future, but the shit that I had been through definitely molded me to become the person I was today. After that dumbass bitch chose her man over me, I made a mental note to become my own protector by any means necessary.

I learned early on that if I wanted something in life, I had to go after it. A bitch like myself wanted more out of life than most of these other bitches and I was willing to go the extra mile to get it. Call me cutthroat or grimy, but what a person would never call me was a broke bitch.

Days after that shit happened, I packed my bags with the few pieces of clothing that I owned and the $200 that I had saved up. I looked over at the bitch snoring on the couch and tiptoed past her, careful not to wake her up. I closed the door behind me and ran down the driveway. She must've heard me because I heard her hollering, "Tiana, bring yo' ass back here."

I didn't look back; instead, I ran all the way to my homegirl's house. See, Ayana and I had been friends since kindergarten and we were like sisters. She was a year older than me and because of that she had always acted like my big sister. I'm not going to lie; I enjoyed being the youngest.

Life at Ayana's house was the opposite of what I was used to. Her mother was real laidback and never really bothered us, unless she wanted us to run to the store to grab her lotto tickets. Needless to say she acted like a mother to me, unlike the bitch who birthed me.

It didn't take long for me to adapt to my new environment. It was then that I learned that I had to grow up and use the one thing that God had blessed me with: a tight-ass pussy. Don't get me wrong, I wasn't no ho; but I refused to be hungry and go without when I had something in between my legs that could feed and clothe me.

I wasn't one of these skinny bitches walking around. Matter of fact, I was a little on the heavy side but I had a fat ass that made niggas drool every time I walked by. I damn sure thought I was one of the baddest bitches to ever walk the streets of Decatur, Georgia. I wasn't attracted to them little broke-ass niggas running around looking for pussy. I wanted a grown-ass man who could take care of me and who made sure I was set. The thing about older niggas was that they would pay for a young piece of pussy especially if you sucking and fucking them the right way. I swear I was blessed with a nice mouthpiece. I would suck a nigga dick 'til his eyes rolled to the back of his head and toes curled up. I ain't bragging but Superhead ain't got shit on me.

Things had changed drastically for me. I was no longer broke, and being hungry was a thing of the past. I wasn't in love with the niggas I fucked; I just pretended that I liked them enough to make them spend that dough on me. I was cool when they called me their girlfriend or bae to their friends. As long as my pockets stayed on swole, I'd be whatever they wanted me to be.

Even though these niggas were lacing me with their dough, I wasn't no fool. Good pussy will only take you so far and I didn't want to be an old bitch with nothing to show for it.

It was also time to get up out of these people's house. I mean, don't get me wrong, I ain't ungrateful or anything, but the older we got the more I kind of sensed that Ayana didn't like having me around as much anymore.

On my eighteenth birthday I decided to get my own one-bedroom apartment. I had more than enough money saved up from tricking off them niggas. A few months later, I decided to go back to school and get my GED. I wanted to go to college one day to be a psychologist and I knew in order to do that I had to get my shit in order. I simply grew up and got on my grown woman shit!

CHAPTER TWO

Tiana

I don't believe in coincidences, and I think it was fate that intervened when I met Micah. It was my first year in college and he was a sophomore. I kind of knew he was digging me by the way he would stare at me in our English class. I'm not going to lie, I was really digging him too, but I played it cool. I didn't want to come off as being thirsty. God knows I wasn't trying to rush into anything; after all, I had just broken up with my last boyfriend, Lucas. I broke it off with him because I was tired of him trying to fuck me in the ass. Don't get me wrong, I liked it in the booty every once in a while, but that every night shit kind of turned me off. It made me wonder if the nigga was a little fruity.

"Miss Caldwell, are you with us?" my instructor asked as he interrupted my deep thoughts.

"I'm sorry sir, I got lost in thoughts." I smiled at him.

I glanced back and saw that Micah was staring at me. I felt a little embarrassed that the instructor called me out like that. For weeks, Micah had been asking me out. I politely turned him down twice but he never gave up. I have to say he was very persistent. I love a man who knows what he wants so I decided to take him up on his offer.

I heard a car horn honk. I peeped out my window and noticed that he was parked outside. *Shit, this nigga act like he can't come to the door to get me,* I thought as I took another look at myself in the mirror and admired myself one last time. I wasn't no skinny chick, but I had enough meat on my body for the right nigga to grab on to. I grabbed my Michael Kors clutch and sashayed out the door.

I couldn't help but notice his shiny orange Charger. He got out as I approached the car and he greeted me with a hug. "Damn, babe, you look stunning and you smell good. Make a nigga want to tear your clothes off right out here in the parking lot."

"Oh, my. Thank you. I'm not sure if that was a compliment, but thanks anyways," I said as I got into the car and put on my seat belt.

The car smelled like brand new leather and was well kept. I lay back in my seat as he drove down the street with Jeezy blasting through his speakers. I glanced over at him as he bobbed his head to the trap music. I admired his facial features; homeboy was neatly groomed, and his skin tone was velvet dark but smooth like a newborn baby's ass.

He took me to Red Lobster, which wasn't where I really wanted to go, but I went along anyway. See, most chicks would be impressed to go on a date to Red Lobster, but not I. Red Lobster to me was like the hood deli, where all the hoodrat chicks hung out.

After waiting for about forty-five minutes, we were served our food. I ordered the seafood platter while he ordered steak. While we ate my mind was wandering all around. I couldn't help but imagine his strong, muscular hands rubbing down my thighs. Maybe it was the way he was eating that steak that made me imagine him eating my pussy.

"So, Miss Tiana. Do you have a man?"

"Hmm, Mr. Micah. Do you have a woman?"

"I see you want to play games. This is it right here: your man ain't here and my woman ain't here so I guess we're single." He smiled.

I didn't respond. I smiled and went back eating my food. When we were finished, he paid the bill and we left.

"So what are your plans for the rest of the night, love?"

"I don't have any. I think I might study a little until I doze off."

"Damn, on a Friday night? You must not have many friends out here. By the way, where are you from? You have a little bit of accent."

"What you mean? I was born and raised here in Decatur. What, you thought I was a foreigner?" I asked sarcastically.

"Now that you mention it, you do look kind of exotic." He laughed.

"Georgia is my birthplace. I am a Grady baby, to be exact."

"I see. Well, Baltimore, Maryland, is home for me. Mom-dukes decided to move out here after my oldest brother got killed." A sad expression was plastered across his face.

"I'm sorry to hear that."

"Nah, it ain't no biggie. Enough of that though. I'm trying to get to know you a little bit more."

"Do you mean you looking to get some pussy? 'Cause if that's all you want, you looking at the wrong chick." I stared him down.

"Nah, it ain't even like that. I really like you. From the first day I laid eyes on you, I knew I was gonna make you mine," he boasted.

There was something about his cockiness that grabbed my attention. I swear my pussy was throbbing as if it needed a good dose of dick-whipping.

I'm not gon' sit up here and act like I didn't want to fuck. Shit, it'd been awhile and I wanted him as bad as he wanted me. We decided to get a room at the Budget Inn and Suites on Memorial Drive. I was a little surprised that he didn't take me to his apartment, but he told me his roommate was there. I kind of understood.

After we got there, he rolled up a blunt he had and we smoked it together. I'd had weed before when I was younger, but I hadn't smoked in a while. I also drank a cup of pink Moscato that he had bought earlier. It didn't take me long to start feeling the effects of the weed and the alcohol. Straight up, I wanted to fuck. I guessed he felt the same way, 'cause he started rubbing on my thighs. The touch of his rough hands sent chills up my spine and between my legs. I had to use everything in me to stop from coming before he gave me the dick. Things got heated when he got up and knelt down in front of me and spread my legs apart. Something in me wanted him to stop, but then again my body was screaming, *bitch, stop tripping.*

Seconds later, I was stripped butt-ass naked and homeboy's head was buried deep down in my pussy. He sucked harder as I ground down on his tongue. "Aargh," I screamed in ecstasy.

The man made love to my pussy as if he was a pussy artist. He had me screaming all kinds of obscenities as he sucked and nibbled on my clit.

I couldn't hold it anymore so I exploded in his mouth. Even then he didn't ease up; instead, he just licked up my juices and continued sucking.

"Can you make love to me now?" I pleaded.

"I got you, ma," he said.

I watched as he pulled out a condom and placed it on his dick. I was eager to get fucked so I pulled him down toward me. I groaned as he entered my tight, slippery pussy.

"Aargh, you tight as fuck," he mentioned.

I didn't respond. Instead, I bit down on my lip as he worked my middle. I tell you the boy was well endowed and he knew how to use it. He fucked me so damn good that I exploded on his dick multiple times. It didn't take any time for him to cum. I was kind of disappointed by that because I wanted more.

I got up and rushed to the bathroom to wash off. My pussy was sore from him beating my walls down, but I enjoyed every bit of it. I hoped him busting so soon was just a one-time thing because the dick was too good for him not to be able to go longer.

When I got back in the room, he was lying there smoking another blunt so I sat down beside him.

"You good, ma? I hope I didn't damage that good-good," he joked.

"I'm straight. I am little tired though."

"Listen, B, I'm feeling you on some real shit and I would love to make you my girl."

"Really? I thought you said something earlier about having a girl," I quizzed him.

"I'ma keep it one hundred with you. I got a baby mama but we ain't together."

"Really? You got kids? How many?" I wasn't feeling that shit at all.

"Yeah, I got two little girls with shorty. But like I said she ain't nothing but my baby mama."

"I know one thing: I ain't got time for no baby mama drama and all that."

"Listen, B, you gon' be wit' me, not my baby mama or my kids. Just me," he tried to convince me.

Where the fuck is all the single dudes? Just when I think I found Mr. Right, he got to have kids and baby mama.

"Listen, I want a chick like you: beautiful and educated. My baby mama don't want to do shit outside of having babies and partying. Twice she told me that she was on the pill, and she ended up pregnant. After that I was out. I want to get my degree and go places, you feel me?"

"I hear you. I just need time to think about all this. 'Cause I ain't got time for no loudmouth chick coming at me over her baby daddy. God knows I ain't got the patience."

"A'ight, fair enough. Anyway I got to bounce. I got some things to handle."

"Really? I thought we had the room for the night," I said as I looked at him.

"Damn, ma, I'm sorry. I just got some things to handle. I tell you what, I will make it up to you next weekend. We can go away to someplace nice. I'll pick you up and we'll go."

I was kind of upset. I just fucked this nigga and now he had to leave. I remained quiet though because we had just started talking and I didn't want him to think I was a big crybaby.

I got dressed and he dropped me off at home. Before I exited the car, he held on to my hand. "Tiana, I want you and I'm going to get you."

"I hear you," I said before I opened the car door.

He got out, walked me to my door, and stood outside until I went inside. I flopped down on my bed daydreaming about what transpired between us. I was really feeling him and I know I wanted him. To be honest, I didn't give a fuck about his baby mama. I wasn't tryin'a to fuck her and it wasn't like I knew the bitch anyways. I was determined to make him my nigga. I just didn't want to come off as thirsty. I was ready to settle down and he was the perfect candidate.

CHAPTER THREE

Ayana

I was sick and tired of going through a rough life. I mean ever since I was young, I struggled. I can't sit up here and lie and say that Mama wasn't there because she was. Most days her ass was drunk or just going through some mental shit. After my father left Mama, she just slipped into a depression. I felt so sorry for her to the point that I wanted to find that nigga and kill him.

Things got even worse when my best friend/ sister came to live with us. It was already bad on us, but I couldn't turn her away. I knew her step-daddy was tryin'a fuck her and her no-good-ass mama wasn't tryin'a stop it either. How could I say no to her? Even though I ended up regretting that I saved that ho.

See, Tiana was one of them bitches who thought she was the shit. All because she had hair all the way down her back and a little bit of ass. I wasn't jealous but, shit, the bitch thought she was God's blessing to niggas. I ain't see how though, 'cause that bitch was fat and, nah, I don't mean phat. The bitch had some weight on her compared to my size three. There were days when we would be hanging out and one of the neighborhood dope boys would walk up to us and instead of her ass allowing him to choose who the fuck he wanted, she would get up in dude's face. Before you knew it he would be shooting her his number. Then I understood where her mama was coming from; maybe her fast ass was fucking and sucking her mama's man. After really getting to know that bitch, I wouldn't put anything past her.

I would sit back and smile as I let that grimy bitch have her fucking way. 'Cause one thing about it, niggas gon' always be quick to fuck a loose bitch, but when they find a laidback chick like me, they will definitely wife them. I was never in competition with her; I knew my day was coming.

I was happy when her ass finally got out my mama shit and went off to college. I no longer had to live in her shadow. Better yet, I didn't have to pretend anymore that I liked the bitch. I stayed behind to go to hair school, which didn't work out, so I got me a job dancing. I wasn't into staying broke all my fucking life, so I twerked my ass and made good money doing it.

It was one night after work when I met Anthony. He was a handsome brother with long money. I wasn't sure at the time what he did for a living, but I did know that whatever it was there was some major paper involved. Him and his boys would come up in the club and make it rain.

That night, he walked up to me and introduced himself. I told him my name and he told me that he was interested in me. At first I didn't take him serious because I knew that most of the ballers who came through only wanted to fuck after the club closed.

"So, what you trying to do, fuck?" I quizzed him.

"Nah, pussy ain't a thing. I'm trying to get to know you. I've been watching you for a minute now."

"Oh, okay, so what a high roller like yourself want with a stripper chick like me?"

"Shawty, quit talking like that. I want to get to know you. Take you out of this life and put you into a better situation."

I didn't know if that was a compliment or an insult. I was getting ready to snap on this nigga.

I didn't know who the hell he thought he was talking to me like that. "Do I look like I need to be saved? I make good damn money in here. I don't need you to save me, Anthony, or whatever your name is."

"Ha-ha," he chuckled. "Little mama, I didn't mean to offend you. I want you to be my woman is all I'm saying. I got enough money to take care of you, so you don't need to be up in here dancing. That's all."

"Well, you can take your money and find another bitch to save. I'm outta here." I walked off before saying another word.

I was feeling irritated as hell. I didn't want a nigga to feel sorry for me. I wanted a man to be with me because that's what he wanted. I got into my car and pulled off.

Days went by and I couldn't get dude off my mind. There was something about his "in control" attitude that turned me on. I tried not to think about him but the urge was too much to resist. It was only Monday and I didn't have to return to the club until Thursday. Ol' stupid me didn't even ask for his number.

Thursday came so fast and I was eager to get on the dance floor and show my ass. If I was correct, I knew him and his boys would be rolling in around 12:00 a.m.; that had been their schedule for the last few months. I wasn't sure what it was exactly, but him, his boys, and the boss had some kind of business affairs going on.

"I Wanna Fuck You," by Plies blasted through the speakers.

The sound of Plies's voice sent me into a frenzy. I wound, twerked, and flipped on that pole like my life depended on it. Niggas started screaming and throwing money at me, but they didn't catch my attention. I turned around to face the crowd and that's when I noticed him standing in front of me. I smiled as I continued dancing. It was in that moment that I realized I wanted to make him my man. As it turned out, that was my last night dancing at the club.

He took me home and we fucked all night. Baby boy was definitely a freak. From sucking on my clit to licking my ass, he made love to my body and soul. I returned the favor and sucked his dick until his eyes started rolling into the back of his head. I made sure that I fucked him better than any other bitch ever could. I had that nigga screaming all kinds of shit that night. He was so loud that you would've thought he was the bitch.

"Damn, B, you got some good-ass pussy," he screamed.

"Just relax and let me ride that dick," I told him.

In no time he busted in the condom. I slowly eased up off of him. I wanted to go longer, but I guessed he was tired. I wasn't gonna complain. I knew the next time would be better.

At first, he was a little leery of fucking me without a condom. I guessed it was because I was a stripper. Shit, I didn't see the logic, since he ate my pussy on the first night. These niggas had shit backward. They're willing to put their mouth on a pussy, but be putting on condoms to fuck the pussy.

"Can I ask you something?" I asked as I kissed on his neck.

"Sure, babe, what's up?"

"Why we always got to use a condom? I mean, we've been messing with each other for a while now so why can't I feel your naked dick up inside of me? You think I'm dirty or something?"

"Nah, babe, it ain't like that. I mean, I ain't really ready to have no kids right now and I'm pretty sure you ain't either."

Nigga, speak for your damn self, I thought as I continued kissing on him. "I just want to feel your dick inside of my pussy; plus, I'm on the pill so nothing is going to happen," I said as I started grinding on him.

In no time his hard nine inches was up inside of me. I groaned and moaned as our skin made contact. I used everything inside of me to hold my walls as tightly as I could. I ground all the way down on his pole and I watched as he bit down on his bottom lip and he held on tight to my hips. The look on his face gave me every bit of satisfaction. He gripped me tighter and his dick got harder. That let me know that he was about to bust.

"Damn, babe, I'ma 'bout to bust. Get uppppp," he yelled out.

Instead of jumping off, I pressed down on his chest and ground harder on his erect dick.

"Aarghhhhhhh," he groaned out as his dick exploded inside of me. "Shit, I busted in you," he said seemingly upset.

"Relax. I told you I'm on the pill and it's supposed to be safe," I reminded him as I rubbed his face.

"Yeah, I suppose so."

I got up and went to the bathroom. I wasn't going to keep saying the shit over and over. Shit, his dumb ass should've used a condom if he was that concerned.

Everything between us was great, up to the point when I found out I was pregnant. Yes, you heard me right. I was pregnant. I was not feeling too good, so I went to Planned Parenthood and they gave me a pregnancy test.

"Your test is positive, Miss Beasly."

I looked at this white bitch. Did I hear her right? Ever since I was young, I was trying to get pregnant, but the shit never happened. I thought that I might've fucked up my insides after I had that abortion when I was younger. "Are you sure?"

"Yes, ma'am, as sure as I can be," she confirmed.

I left the clinic, happy as hell. I was going to be a mommy and I could not wait to tell my bae. *Oh, shit.* I stopped in my tracks. He didn't want any kids and he thought I was on the pill. I had to come up with something fast before I broke the news that he was about to be a daddy.

CHAPTER FOUR

Ayana

A year later

It's funny how a nigga can be all sweet in the beginning, but as soon as the kids come along they start acting funny. Ever since I had my daughter, Anthony's ass had been showing out. First he became angry that I was pregnant. He even went as far as accusing me of trapping him because of his money.

"Bitch, you lied to me. You told me you was on the pill," he yelled.

"Boy, fuck you. I didn't fucking lie. Take that shit up with the people who make the pills. What the fuck I look like trapping you?" I spat.

"Man, I swear, you better get your ass on that pill or something, 'cause if you don't I am not fucking you raw anymore. I ain't trying to just have kids popping out every fucking year. I want to be able to take care of my fucking kids. This ain't any life for them. I'm in the fucking streets," he lashed out.

"Get a fucking job then. Ain't nobody tell your ass to be in the fucking streets. You chose that life, boo-boo." I swear I was tired of him and his accusations. He acted like I held him down and raped him. If he wanted to be such a great fucking parent, he would give up hustling. Shit, we had enough money to move away and live comfortably. In my book it was all just excuses.

Shit really hit the fan when I ended up pregnant with my second child. He threatened to leave, but I knew he was bluffing. This pussy was too good and that nigga was not leaving his kids so he needed to quit with all that shit.

After I had my second daughter, things kind of got better. We started spending more time around each other. I kind of felt bad that I lied to him about being on the pill. The second time I got pregnant, I put a hole in the condom. I knew that if we had the children, I would be set for life. There was no way I was going back to being broke ever again! Not this bitch.

He also was trying to leave the streets alone. He went and enrolled in Georgia Tech. He wanted to study to become an engineer. I ain't goin' to lie, I was happy that he was leaving the streets alone; but I wasn't happy that the money was going to slow down. I stayed cool though, because he was still doing a little something on the side. I learned that his boys were doing most of the dirty work and he just collected the money.

CHAPTER FIVE

Tiana

After spending the weekend with Micah, my feelings for him had gotten stronger. It was easy because he treated me so good. He didn't think twice when spending money on me and he wasn't cheap either. From the latest designer purses and shoes, if I wanted it, he bought it for me. I wasn't no vain chick, but as a college student I barely had money to get by so I welcomed the change. On our way back from the mall, I was kind of curious about where he worked. I didn't want to be nosey, but fuck it; I needed to know where all this money was coming from.

"Ay, boo, can I ask where you work?"

"Ha-ha, you playing, right?"

"Umm, no. I'm dead-ass serious."

"I don't work. I got some business in the streets if you know what I mean."

I wasn't no green chick, so I knew exactly what he meant. My heart skipped a few beats.

I'd dated a few dope boys in my younger days, but I wasn't into that anymore. I was not one of those chicks who was going to be up late at night wondering what the fuck done happened to my dude, and I definitely wasn't going to visit him in no jail either.

"I know what you thinking and, trust me, I'm trying to get out of these streets. That's why I decided to go to school, so I can make a life for me and my seeds."

I looked at him and I saw the sincerity in his eyes. I knew in my heart I was going to help my man get out of these streets. He was better than slinging rocks; plus, his grades were good, so I knew that he was not only street smart but also book smart. There was a time when I would have loved the fact that he was a dope boy, but all that changed after I was fucking this big-time dope boy name Keshaun. One day they burst into his house shooting while he was fucking me. I was lucky that the fat bastard was on top of me and took all the bullets that were sprayed all around the room. I lay there in fear that one of the niggas would check to see if I was alive. God was definitely on my side because they didn't; instead, they just left. That night, I pushed dude's bullet-riddled body off of me, grabbed my clothes, put them on, and ran to my car. I made a promise with God that night that I would never chase dope boys anymore.

"Well, you're grown but, baby, I want a life with you. I can't do that if you stay in these streets. These streets don't love nobody and the jails have a bed available at all times."

"Damn, ma, you ain't got to get to preaching and shit." He busted out laughing. This was good, because most days he barely smiled and looked like the world was on his shoulders.

"I ain't preaching. I'm just trying to save my man, that's all. We can make it in this life without dope money. We are a power couple," I confirmed.

"I love that, a power couple," he repeated and smiled.

The rest of the ride to my house was quiet. We were both lost in our thoughts. That was until his phone kept vibrating back to back. Whoever it was wasn't letting up.

"Damn, somebody trying to reach you bad."

"Yeah, that's my baby mama, tryin'a argue. I ain't got time for that shit."

Damn, she must be dying or she desperate for some dick.

He cut the music up to drown out the constant buzzing of the phone. I closed my eyes, listening to the soft music of Sade that was playing.

CHAPTER SIX

Ayana

I was sick of this nigga and his shit. It was a few minutes past nine and his bum ass still ain't get here yet. I told him earlier that me and my girls were tryin'a go to Pappadeaux to eat. I dialed his number once again, but still there was no answer.

"Listen to me, you no-good-ass nigga, I know you out fucking with some bitch while your sorry behind should be watching your fucking kids. I swear to God this shit is over. I swear on my mama."

I was beyond pissed when I hung the phone up. I dialed my mama's number, even though I didn't want to bring my kids around all that drinking. There was no way I was going to stay in this house tonight.

"Hello," she mumbled.

"Are you sleeping? I need a favor." I didn't give her a chance to answer.

"Child, what is it?"

"I need you to watch your grandbabies for a little while."

There was a brief pause on the phone.

"I'll pay you," I blurted out.

"Well, what's a little while?"

"About three hours. Me and the girls are going out to eat and their daddy is nowhere to be found."

"All right. I guess I'll get up then. Bring them on over."

I hung up, still fuming with anger. I shouldn't have had to go through this when they got a daddy who should have be here watching them. I swore that nigga was going to pay for all the shit he put me through.

I got to Mama's house in Stone Mountain in no time. I quickly brought them to the door. I didn't have time to sit and chat because I had to go home and get ready. Tonight was important 'cause I barely ever got to see my girls and I missed hanging out with them. I rang the doorbell and waited for her to open the door.

"Hey, babies." She took my youngest, Diamond, out of my arms.

"They already ate and I bathed them. They have snacks in their bag."

I turned around to leave when she grabbed my arm. "Baby, where is that man at and why is he not helping you with these babies?"

"Mama, your guess is as good as mine. I don't know where he at. I've been calling him and he ain't picking up the phone."

"I tell you, you be playing with his ass. You need to put your damn foot down and make him help you take care of these children."

"I got to go." I kissed my babies and ran away from the house. I wasn't going to sit there and listen to her talk about my baby daddy. Shit, I didn't need anyone to tell me that he was a piece of shit. I knew that right after I had Diamond. I wasn't no fool though; I wasn't leaving him so my girls could grow up without having their daddy around. Shit, we were in this for the long haul, whether he liked it or not.

"Hey, guys, sorry I'm late," I said as I joined Meme, Seika, and Lori at the table. These three bitches and I had been rocking since I moved to Lithonia a few years ago. Lately we hadn't really been chilling 'cause I had the kids and they were either working or booed up.

"So what y'all eating?" I quizzed them.

"I don't know. Let's see what they got," Lori said.

"So, Yana, what's going on wit' you? You seem a little stressed out. I hope you ain't tripping over no nigga."

"Hell nah, you know I don't trip no over no nigga. I'm good, just a little tired," I lied. I loved my bitches, but there was no way that I was going to let them know what I'd been going through with Anthony lately.

Our food came and we ate, laughed, and drank alcohol. It definitely felt good to get away from being a mommy for a while. After we were finished, we paid and called it a night.

"It was great seeing y'all tonight. Let's do this again soon."

"Yes, we should," they all said in unison.

I got into my car and pulled off. I checked my phone and noticed that I had three missed calls from Anthony. *I know this nigga ain't have the nerve to call me,* I thought as I threw the phone on the other seat. I thought about getting the kids, but it was after twelve and I didn't want to wake them up. I decided to go get them first thing in the morning.

As I drove down the street, tears filled my eyes. I remembered when shit was good between

Anthony and me. When he treated me like a queen. How could we go from sugar to shit that fast? How could this dude treat the mother of his children like this?

When I pulled up, I noticed that his Charger was parked in the driveway. I swear I wasn't in the mood to fight with this nigga. I opened my door and got out. I kind of stumbled from the effect of the alcohol that I had consumed earlier. I opened the door and walked in. I thought about letting shit fly but decided not to; this nigga needed to hear it. I walked upstairs where he was sitting on the bed.

"Yo, where the fuck was you at earlier? I know yo' ass seen me calling."

"Yo, B, lower your voice, and who you talking to like that?" he yelled.

"I ain't got to lower shit. I was calling you for your fucking kids. You knew you was supposed to watch them. Remember?"

"Yo, I got caught up handling some business."

"Ha-ha, you're a fucking joke. I hope that bitch you was laid up with is worth you losing your fucking kids, 'cause I'm leaving and I'm taking them with me," I spat.

He got up and took a step closer to me. "B, I said I was handling some business, but let's get this fucking clear: you ain't taking my kids anywhere, you hear me? I don't give a fuck if you leave, but they ain't going anywhere. Speaking of kids, where they at?"

"Boy, fuck you. I pushed them out my pussy, so I'll take them wherever the fuck I please. I'm not one of these old dumbass bitches 'round here. You better ask somebody. I'm the bitch who will get your head knocked off."

"I ain't tryin'a hear none of that, B. So, I ask again, where are my daughters?"

"They over they grandma house. You wasn't worried about them earlier, so you can give up the 'worried parent' façade."

"You got my kids over your drunken mama house? You a stupid-ass female."

"Really? You ain't had no problem when she watched them when we went on that cruise to the Bahamas. Boy, shut the fuck up with your dumb ass."

"You right, I am a dumbass nigga for picking up a fucking whore and trying to turn her into a housewife."

Without thinking, I slapped him across his face. He grabbed my arm before I got the chance to dig my fingernails into his skin. I was trying to draw blood from this nigga.

"Don't you ever put your hands on me, B. I ain't never hit a female before, so please don't push me to make you the first," he said before he walked away.

"Fuck you, Ant. I swear, fuck you!" I screamed and ran down the stairs to the living room. The words from that nigga stung me so deep. I couldn't believe that he talked to me in that manner.

That night I lay on the couch thinking of all the ways that I was going to get him back. I didn't give a fuck if he was my children's father.

CHAPTER SEVEN

Tiana

I kind of noticed that Micah was kind of withdrawn. I tried not to intrude because I wanted to be his calm whenever he came around. I wasn't one of those bitches who kept nagging at a nigga. Nah, those the kind of bitches niggas be running from. He wanted peace and quiet, a woman who rubbed his back and helped build up his self-esteem even when he was at his lowest. That chick was me. I made sure that I treated Micah like a king and I barely questioned him about what he did out in those streets. As long as he treated me like a queen, I was good.

I wasn't feeling too good so I decided to stay home. I had never missed a day of class before, so I knew it shouldn't be no biggie. I was feeling nauseated and my head was hurting bad. I wished I could just stick my hand down my throat and throw up; for some reason I felt like it would make me feel better. I cut the TV off, closed my blinds, and crawled back in my bed after I made a cup of peppermint tea.

I heard the phone ringing, and I knew that it was Micah by the Plies's "Good Dick" ringtone that I had set for him. "Hello," I weakly answered.

"Babe, where you at? Why you not at school, yo?"

"I wasn't feeling good so I decided to stay home."

"Damn, why didn't you call me?"

"It wasn't anything. I think it's just something that I ate that might've upset my stomach."

"A'ight, ma, I'm on my way."

"Nah, Micah, go ahead to your class. I'm fine. Matter of fact, I'm about to go to sleep. I feel really drained."

"A'ight, ma, I'll be over there later."

"Okay."

"Ay, T, I love you."

I blinked twice because I wasn't sure that I heard him. *Did this dude just tell me he loves me?* I really didn't know what to say. I mean, don't get me wrong, I loved him too, but I thought I was moving too fast and I didn't want to scare him off by telling him I loved him. To hear him say it was soothing to my soul.

"Love you too, babe," I softly said.

After he hung up, I put my head under the cover with sweet thoughts of my man fresh on my mind. I swear, I was so happy that I took a chance with him. This time around it was different. I was actually in love and it wasn't just about his money. I smiled as I dozed off.

Days went by and the bad feeling wasn't getting any better. I even started to throw up, and the smell of food made me sick to the point where every time I tried to eat I would end up running to the bathroom. After day four, I doubted that it was a bug so I decided to go to my doctor.

"Miss Caldwell, how are you doing today?"

"Not too good, Doc. I think I have a stomach virus."

"Okay, let the nurse take your vitals and we will go from there."

The nurse took my vitals and asked me questions about how long I'd been feeling like this. To be honest, I thought this feeling started about two weeks ago.

"Here you go. I need a urine sample."

"Urine, for what? I think it's something I ate."

"Yeah, it's no biggie. The doctors just ask me to take a sample."

"Oh, okay."

After waiting for about twenty minutes, the nurse called my name. I followed her into the doctor's office.

"Have a seat, Miss Caldwell. Well, congratulations—"

I cut her off before she could finish her sentence. "What are you talking 'bout, lady? What are you congratulating me on?" I eagerly asked.

"You are pregnant."

"What! This can't be true. I've been using a . . ." My voice trailed off as I remembered a few weeks ago when we decided not to use a condom. It was our first time.

"I know you may not be expecting this, but babies are definitely a blessing. I am going to start you on prenatal vitamins and also schedule you an appointment for an ultrasound in six weeks. In the meantime, crackers and ginger ale will help with the nausea. Drink plenty of water and get plenty of rest."

"Thanks, Doc," I managed to utter.

She handed me the prescription and I left the office. It didn't make sense to me at all. I loved fucking, but I never thought about having a child. Furthermore, I was in college and I didn't plan on dropping out to become a mommy. That just wasn't my thing.

During the ride home I kind of entertained the idea of becoming a mommy. I wondered how Micah was going to feel once I told him I was pregnant. I was well aware that he already had two little girls but we never talked about us having any children. Ready or not, this was a conversation that we had to have this evening and not a minute later.

Micah was on his way over and even though I wasn't feeling too good I got up and showered. No matter how bad I felt, there was no way I was going to let him see me looking crazy. A lot of bitches be dressed to a T when they are trying to get with the man, but the minute they get him they allow themselves to fall off. In my opinion, that's one of the reasons why their men stray.

I took a shower and got dressed in my Victoria's Secret pajamas then I brushed my long mane into a ponytail. I loved how straight my hair was. That was the only thing that I had inherited from that bitch who gave me birth. I quickly put her out of my mind because I did not want to fuck my mood up.

I lay on the couch waiting for Micah to come. An hour had passed since he called and said that he was on the way. I dialed his number and it kept going straight to voice mail. I threw the phone on the couch and turned on the TV. I knew *Blue Bloods* was on so I decided to catch an episode.

I must've fallen asleep because the constant ringing of my phone startled me. I searched and finally grabbed my phone. I glanced at the caller ID and I noticed it was Micah. I also glanced at the time and noticed it was after 12:00 a.m. I picked the phone up even though I was feeling salty.

"Hello," I answered with annoyance in my voice.

"Babe, I've been calling you. I'm outside. Open the door."

"A'ight." I let out a long sigh.

I got up and peeped through the window. I saw him getting out of his car. I tried to straighten up my face, but God knows I was irritated. I ain't that kind of bitch who allows a nigga to play little games with me. I wasn't mad about him being late; it was because he lied and said that he was on the way. I was about to set this nigga straight right now.

I opened the door and he walked in. "Hey, babe." He leaned over to kiss my face but I moved out of the way. I locked the door behind him then walked toward the living room.

"Babe, I'm sorry I'm late. Something came up and I had to make a detour. I'm sorry, ma."

"Sit down, Micah. Let me tell you something. I ain't tryin'a put no knot around your neck, but you need to know I'm not the kind of bitch you can play with. If it is just pussy you want then you need to go ahead and make it be known 'cause, truth is, I like you and I'll probably still want to fuck you. But when you sit up in my face telling me how you love me and all that bullshit, it's gon' be a problem if I find out you fucking around. You feel me?" I looked him dead in the eyes.

"T, I'm telling you, ma, I ain't fucking around on you. I love you and I'm trying to be with you, if you allow me to. No shit, ma, you the only chick who can ask me to leave the streets and I'm willing to do it. I love you and, as crazy as it sounds, I want to make you my wife."

I swear if these words were coming out of another nigga's mouth, I would've sworn he was lying. But I saw the sincerity in his eyes and I didn't sense a bit of deception. Even then, I didn't fall for it because niggas were known to be the best liars I'd known. A nigga will swear on his dead mama or his seed when he's tryin'a convince a chick that he ain't lying. I'd had my share of no-good-ass niggas, so this time around I was more careful not to fall for foolery.

"Well, since you talking marriage and shit, I got something to tell you."

"What is it? Spit it out," he demanded.

"I went to the doctor today and found out I'm pregnant."

"What?" he stuttered as he searched my face.

"You heard me. I found out all that nausea was because I am pregnant."

"Damn, babe, that's great," he busted out.

"Really? Boy, you crazy. You already have two kids and we are both in college trying to get our degrees."

"So what? My kids are taken care of and I'm about to graduate next year. I got money to take care of you and my baby." He grabbed my hand.

"What, your drug money? I am not bringing a baby into this world with you still running the streets. I'm not one of those greedy bitches who needs a whole lot. I don't want to lose you to the motherfucking streets or prison. You already know how I feel about that. I don't know if I'm ready to have a baby. I just don't know."

"What you mean, T? You have to have my seed; you can't get rid of my seed. This baby was made out of love. Ma, I will marry you tomorrow to show you how serious I am."

"I'm not saying that I'm going to have an abortion. I just don't know if I'm ready. I want to finish school and get married. I don't want to be nobody baby mama. I want to be a wife."

"And that's what I'm trying to make you. Marry me, T."

"I don't know, Micah. I need time to think about all of this; plus, I don't want to rush and get married. I want a big wedding, on an island somewhere, maybe Jamaica."

"Ma, I promise, if you have my baby I will make all your wishes come true. I ain't bullshitting you, ma."

"We will see. Like I said, I have to think about this. This is a big life-altering experience for me."

"A'ight, that's cool. Just promise me that you will give my seed a chance."

I didn't respond; instead, I looked at him and smiled. I wanted to believe him, but I decided not to listen to my heart and just follow my mind. He pulled me closer to him and wrapped his arms around me.

"Babe, I swear, you are a breath of fresh air in my life. A nigga like me need that especially being out in these streets. And it's a plus that you not just after a nigga because of his money."

"Hmmmm, well, I'm happy that I'm the kind of woman you were looking for. So let me ask you a straight-up question. What's going on with you and your children's mother?"

"Ain't nothing up. She has my daughters and that's all there is to it. I used to rock with shawty real hard but I quickly found out that she was only after my money; and, to be honest, I think she set me up by lying about being on birth control. After my second daughter was born, I decided that I really didn't love her and that I was done with her."

"Oh, okay. That's good that you're still taking care of your children. Some niggas would've bounced on the mama and the kids. I respect that you're standing up for them."

"Of course. I would never leave my seeds. I grew up without my pops and I saw how Momdukes struggled to raise my brothers and me. I can't let my kids go through nothing similar."

It was refreshing to see a young black dude sitting here, talking about taking care of his children with pride. I had no idea what him and ol' girl went through, but I thought she was a dumb bitch if she allowed him to slip through her fingers. I bet, whoever she was, she was regretting that shit right now.

He kissed me on my forehead interrupting my thoughts. I squeezed his hand as he hugged me. Without any words, he eased up from behind me and got on his knees and pulled my pajamas off. He spread my legs wide apart. First he inhaled my fresh scent then he slowly licked my clit and used his tongue to twirl around it. He took his time playing in my pussy with his tongue. I lay back, relaxed and thinking about my future with my baby and the man of my dreams. Fuck that bitch; bottom line was her man chose me.

CHAPTER EIGHT

Ayana

It was another night that Anthony didn't come home. When I tried to call his phone, it went straight to voice mail. I kept calling back to back, but there was no answer. I wasn't no fool. I knew he was fucking around on me. The nigga was weak as fuck, 'cause he had a good woman at home. Instead of him being here with his family, I bet he was out there running around with a dumb bitch. Whoever that bitch was, she needed to know that he came as a package that included me and his fucking daughters. *I ain't going no-motherfucking-where and if that bitch want him, she gon' have to take these ass whuppings I got waiting on her.*

After I put the girls to bed, I went into the kitchen and poured a glass of Patrón. I needed something strong to wash away some of this pain I was feeling. After I drank two glasses, I was no longer feeling self-pity. I felt powerful and like I was in control. I dialed Anthony's number again, but he didn't answer. I wasn't in the mood to leave no voice messages. Instead, I hung up and scrolled through my phone and found Tahj's number. He was Anthony's rival/enemy. A few months ago they had a big beef. I wasn't in it but I knew Tahj from when I worked at the club. He usually dropped a lot of paper on me, so in my book he was an a'ight dude. After that shit went down with him and Ant, I ran into him at the grocery store. It was then when we talked and he told me that if I needed anything to holla at him. I didn't say much. I just smiled and put his number in my phone. I had no intention of calling this rat-ass nigga but tonight I felt the need to call him. I was hurting so bad inside and, not to mention, I was lonely. I pressed send on the phone and waited as it rang.

"Hello," his sexy but rough voice echoed through the phone. I thought about hanging up, but quickly decided not to.

"Hello, this is Ayana," I responded.

"Ayana. Ayana, ummm . . ."

"Anthony baby mama," I helped jog his memory.

"Oh, yeah, my bad, love. I have a bad memory. Charge it to the high-grade weed." He chuckled.

"No problem. I'm just calling to see what's going on with you."

"Ain't shit. Just chilling, you know?"

"I was calling to see if you wanted to chill."

"Is that a trick question? You know damn well a nigga been trying to get at you for a minute now."

"Oh, yeah? Well, I'm feeling kind of lonely and I need some company."

"Hell yeah. Where you at?"

"I'm at home in Lithonia."

He paused when I said that, then he spoke. "Is that a joke? Don't that nigga Ant live with you? What kinds of games you playing?" His sweetness turned to annoyance real fast.

"Yes, he stay here, but he ain't here. Matter of fact, that nigga out fucking some other bitch, so why should I be worried about him? You not scared of him are you?" I knew that statement would grab his attention.

"Yo, you should know me better than that. I ain't scared of that pussy nigga. Shit I'll come through and beat up the pussy for you real quick. Text me your address."

"A'ight, cool. See you in a few."

I hung up the phone and flopped down on the couch. I knew what I did was a violation, but I didn't give a fuck about Anthony right now. He didn't care about me or my fucking kids so why should I give a fuck? I got up, poured me another drink, and got in the shower. I washed my pussy thoroughly and douched. I wanted it right for this nigga, 'cause one thing a nigga wouldn't say was my pussy be stinking.

I got out of the shower and oiled my body down with some baby oil. I wanted that shiny look; plus, I heard rumors that Tahj had a horse dick and, if it was true, I wanted that dick to slip right in.

In no time, I heard my phone ringing. "Hello."

"I'm pulling up. Open the door."

I hung up, walked to my daughters' room, and peeped in. They were fast asleep, which was good. I couldn't risk my oldest daughter, Dominique, telling her daddy that another man was over here; and I didn't want them to hear their mama screaming for mercy.

I pulled their room door all the way closed and ran downstairs. I opened the door and he was standing there looking sexy as fuck. He wasn't the cutest nigga but his swag was on 1,000, which made him a sexy motherfucker in my world. Tahj was the kind of nigga who made your drawers wet instantly.

"Come in," I said and motioned him to come in. I knew he was in dangerous territory and, all along in my heart, I was praying that Ant didn't pop up. I knew it wouldn't end too pretty if he ever found out that I'd had this nigga in the house.

"Hey, love. How you been?"

"I'm good, just going through a little bullshit with ol' boy. Other than that, I'm good."

"Shit, you must love it. You need to get rid of that lame-ass nigga and come fuck wit' a real G."

"You might be right, but you know that's my baby daddy and the girls love him."

"Shit, let that nigga play Daddy. That don't mean you gotta give that nigga the pussy."

"You right," I concurred.

Without saying anything else, I pulled his hand all the way up the stairs. I knew that I was pressed for time so I didn't waste any more time with small talk. I stripped out of all my clothing revealing my freshly trimmed pussy and my big breasts, which stood firm because of the breast implants I got when I was dancing. I saw his eyes pop open. I didn't think my body was what he imagined.

"Damn, love, you ain't wasting no time," he said as he unbuckled his belt. I watched seductively as he took his boxers off revealing that big-ass dick that resembled a horse dick. I saw that them bitches weren't exaggerating when they said that nigga was packing.

We started kissing and rubbing on one another. My pussy was tingling as he rubbed his dick between my legs. I wanted his dick. I was hungry to get fucked the right way. We didn't waste another minute as I slid his dick into my wet pussy.

"Aargh," I groaned out as his dick made its way to my insides. It felt good but it also hurt. Even though I used baby oil, it still felt like I was a virgin getting fucked for the first time.

I closed my eyes as he held my legs apart and dug all through my guts. I wanted to scream out but I couldn't. I feared that if I did, I would wake my daughters up. "Uhh, uhh," I groaned and moaned.

I dug my fingers into his arm as he applied pressure to my pussy. I was low key loving it. I just wished he were a little smaller. He fucked me for about thirty minutes without letting up. I came over and over, spilling my rich, creamy juice all over his dick.

"Damn, love, this pussy on point," he grumbled.

That kind of gave me the courage to throw the pussy on him. I used all my inner strength and matched all the strokes he was throwing. I knew he was trying hard not to cum because he would ease out a little bit each time. I didn't have time for that shit, so I sped up my moves and before you knew it he had pulled out and busted all on my stomach.

"Arghhhhhhhhhhhhh," he screamed out.

I know the pussy is good but I wish he'd shut the fuck up.

He got up off me and sat on the side of the bed. I got up and ran to the bathroom. I grabbed a washcloth, wet it, and brought it back to him. I thought about taking a quick shower, but decided it would be best that I do that after he left.

"Here, use this and wipe yourself off. I don't know what time Anthony's coming home, so you might need to hurry up. You know he'll flip out if he found out that I had you up in here. I don't know what you did to him, but whatever it is he does not like you."

"Fuck that pussy nigga. He 'ont want to really see me. The only reason why I ain't burn his ass already is 'cause of my sister. For some reason she still in love with his ass."

"What you mean? Ant used to fuck with your sister?" I quizzed him.

"Used to? Man, up until to a few months ago, that nigga and my sister was messing around. After the shit popped off with me and him, she promised me not to fuck wit' that nigga."

I stood there shocked as hell, but I tried not to show it.

"Why you looking shocked for? You really thought you was the only one he was fucking? Shit, word on the street is that pussy nigga is fucking one of the bitches he go to school with. So, ma, you need to quit worrying 'bout a nigga who don't give a fuck 'bout you."

"I ain't worried about nothing. I'm good over here, trust that. Anyway, I hope I get to see you again."

"Shit, just hit a nigga up whenever you want that pussy beat up. I'ma holla at you 'bout something in the middle of the week."

"Okay. I'll call you."

I walked him downstairs and as soon as he was out the door I slammed it shut. I was happy he was gone, but I was mad as hell at the information that he'd just disclosed. I knew that nigga was fucking around on me, but every time I asked him, he lied and said that he was faithful. I felt so stupid because I actually fell for that bullshit.

I cut the lights off and walked up the stairs. Tears welled up in my eyes as I thought about him fucking that bitch; she wasn't even all that. Old raggedy-ass bitch. This nigga straight played me and, to make matters worse, the whole fucking hood knew.

I grabbed my cell and dialed my bitch Lori.

"Hello, bitch. You better be dying or locked up calling my damn phone this time of the night," she spat with an attitude.

"Bitch, whatever, lemme ask you a question. You ever hear any rumors that Ant was fucking that bitch Yanique?"

"Nah, why?"

"That's what I just heard."

"Bitch, please, you know Ant got a few dollars so bitches gon' always claim that they fucking him. Don't fall for the foolery; he loves you and them kids."

"Nah, fuck that, I believe it. Tahj just told me that shit and he ain't the kind of nigga to make up some shit like that especially about his sister."

"Bitch, so he just came out and told you that shit? You know him and Ant don't get along, so he might be just trying to throw salt on Ant's name."

"Nah, he told me that shit after I fucked him."

"Tell me you playing. How the fuck did you manage to pull that off? Bitch, you is trippin'."

"I ain't trippin'. That nigga been playing me for too long. I am sick of his ass for real, so I called Tahj and gave him the pussy."

"You know I love you right? Just be careful. I don't want Ant to find that shit out; and don't be too quick to trust Tahj either. He may be just using you to get to Ant."

"Damn, bitch, you gave me a whole speech and shit. We not in church. Trust me, I know what I'm doing." I laughed.

"Well, on that note, I'm taking my ass to bed. Got work in the a.m. I will call you tomorrow when I get off."

"A'ight, bitch."

Her words played out in my head after I got off the phone. I never thought of it like that. I just wanted to get back at Ant. I was tired of being lonely and sitting in this damn house with these fucking kids while he ran the streets without any care in the world. Nah, I didn't feel bad for what I did, not at all!

I went into the shower and washed off, then got dressed and got in the bed. I didn't bother to change the streets either. *Fuck that. If he ever makes it home, he will have to lie on the sheets that I fucked his rival on. Two can definitely play the game,* I thought as I dozed off.

CHAPTER NINE

Tiana

Micah asked me to move in with him. I was kind of reluctant because even though we were together and I was carrying his child, I didn't know how it was going to be. Besides I'd heard several stories about how dudes change up once the babies are born. My best friend/sister Ayana often complained about her baby daddy.

Speaking of Ayana, it'd been a couple of months since we last spoke. I didn't know what it was but in my heart I felt like things had changed between us. After I moved out and started college, I would go by to see her, but each visit she just seemed so distant and I noticed that the bond we once shared wasn't as tight as before. Every time we talked she would constantly mention the other bitches she hung out with. I wasn't jealous or anything but I was sick and tired of hearing about bitches who were clubbing, fucking, and sucking. I didn't want to hurt my girl's feelings so I just sat there and listened. I ain't gon' lie though, I did miss her. I planned on visiting her tomorrow after class so I could give her the good news about my pregnancy.

After class, I quickly walked out and spotted Micah standing with a group of dudes. I walked up and he excused himself. "What up, babe, you want to grab a bite?"

"Nah, I'm about to go see my girl in Lithonia for a little. I haven't been to see her in a while."

"Oh, okay, that's cool. I'm about to head to Atlanta to hang wit' the niggas for a little while. Hit me when you get home and I'll come through. By the way how you feeling?"

"I can't seem to get rid of the nausea and these headaches, but other than that I'm getting used to this pregnancy thing."

"Well, I wish I could go through it wit' you, but if there is anything I can do, just let me know," he said as he rubbed my stomach. The touch of his hand sent electric warmth through my body. This was my first pregnancy and I was happy that I had him to share it with.

"A'ight, later." I kissed him and we parted ways.

On the way to my car I couldn't help but smile. I loved that man and I felt so blessed that he entered my life. He was a street dude and most times they're known for being dogs and players. Not him though; he treated me like his queen.

I dialed Ayana's phone number, which I had stored in my phone. I hoped she didn't change it on me because then I would have had to stop by her mother's house to get it.

"Hello," she answered the phone interrupting my thoughts.

"Hey, sis."

"Hey, you. I didn't know that was you."

"Are you at the same spot? I'm on the way to see you."

"No, I'm not. I'm on Rock Chapel Road."

"Okay, text me the address. I'm leaving the school now and, depending on traffic, I'll be there in about twenty minutes."

"Okay, chick, see you in a little while."

I hung the phone up and saw that a text had come through. I opened it so I could put the address in my GPS. I cut the radio on as I drove on I-20 thinking about my life with my man and my baby. I wasn't sure about having this child but, after today, I was surer than ever. I wanted to have my baby and give him or her the love that I never had. I vowed to be the best mother

I could be, even though the bitch who birthed me was a piece of shit. I promised myself that I wasn't going to be anything like her. I was determined to protect mines by any means necessary.

I pulled into her driveway and was kind of thrown off because here was this beautiful brick house in a nice neighborhood. I knew damn well that she couldn't afford this unless she was back dancing. See, Ayana used to dance at Blue Flame over on the west side and she used to make good money. I never approved of her shaking her ass for money but she was my bitch, so I supported whatever she chose to do. I rang the doorbell as I took a quick glance of the area. All the houses were big and beautiful with nice lawns.

"Hey, chick," she greeted me as she opened the doors.

"Hey, sis, how you been?" I said as I gave her a big hug. I walked into the spacious living room.

"Sit down. I was just about to straighten up."

"No worries. I just came to see you. I miss you. We haven't been talking like we used to."

"I know. You got school and I got children. The story of my life," she said sarcastically.

"How your mama doing?"

"She's fine; she got the kids over there with her right now."

"Really? She don't drink no more?" I quizzed her.

"Tiana, what does her drinking have to do with her watching the kids?" she asked with an attitude.

"Calm down, A, I was only asking a question."

"Sorry, I didn't mean to snap. I'm just under a lot of stress right now. My dude is cheating on me and hasn't been home in three days. I've been calling him and he never answers."

"Really? That's the kids' daddy, right? How long this been going on?"

"To be honest, T, this shit been going on for a minute but I didn't want to see it. Now he just straight disrespectful. He hasn't been home to check on me or the girls. I swear, I can't do this shit anymore."

"Did you talk to him about it? You can't let these niggas do what they want to do, you know that. Put his ass out. You're a strong person; you don't need no nigga to survive. You better put his ass on child support."

"Girl, trust me I ain't stuttin' that nigga. I already got him back when I fucked his worst enemy in our bed. That nigga must not know who he fucking with for real."

I was shocked by her last statement. Damn, I wanted her to get the nigga back, but to fuck another nigga in the bed they shared was just lowdown. I looked at her and all I saw was evil.

No love, just pure, dark evil. I felt bad for the nigga because whatever she had up her sleeve was not good at all.

"Enough about me and my fucked-up life. What's going on with you, Miss College Lady?"

"Girl, nothing, I have another year to go, then I will get my associate's degree in psychology. Then I plan on going to another school to get my bachelor's."

"You go, girl. Ever since we were growing up, you were always the one with the brains."

"I got something to tell you," I blurted out.

"What, bitch, you won some money?" She laughed.

"Nah, better than that. I'm pregnant."

"You pregnant? I didn't even think you were fucking."

"Bitch, bye. I ain't no fucking Virgin Mary. You must've forgot the shit we used to do when we were young."

"That don't count, 'cause I plan on taking that shit to the grave. But anyways, are you serious? Who is the lucky baby daddy?"

"You don't know him; we go to the same school. We have been seeing each other for a minute now. It wasn't planned, but it happened, so here I am knocked up." I smiled.

"Well, congrats, boo, and welcome to mother-hood. I hope your baby daddy is way better than mines, 'cause these bum-ass niggas be sweet as fuck before the babies."

"Well, I think my boo is kind of different. He already has two daughters and he is great with them. His old dumbass baby mama is the one who be acting up. I'm trying to tell him to get custody of the girls and we can raise them. He told me so many stories about the stupid shit she be doing. I swear some of these bitches make it hard for the rest of us."

"Yeah, but you can't really listen to a nigga when he pillow talks. Some these niggas will say anything to get the pussy and they be straight up lying. Just make sure that this is what you want, because being a mama ain't all it's pumped up to be."

"I got you. I just know he is different from these other dudes."

"Yeah, a'ight. Anyway, when am I gonna meet this Mr. Wonderful? What did you say his name was?"

"His name is Micah."

"What a coincidence. Ant's middle name is Micah. I pray he ain't nothing like Anthony."

I didn't respond. I just smiled. She seemed bitter. Whatever that dude did to her, it defi-nitely took a toll on her.

We chatted for a little while longer then I decided to leave. "Well, I'm about to go. I have to go study. How about we set up a date so I can meet my brother-in-law and you can meet yours?"

"I would love that; that's if Ant and I stay together. Call me and we can definitely do dinner."

"All right, sis, take care. We need to talk more. I really miss you and my nieces. Say hi to Mama for me when you see her."

"I sure will. You know she asks about you all the time."

I hugged her and went out the door noticing the sun was still beaming down. I loved warm weather but, for some reason, since I'd been pregnant it kind of bothered me. I was ready to go home and lie down under the AC.

I got into my car and pulled off but, before I could turn, I looked up and I saw Ayana peeping through the curtains. Something didn't seem right with her. I couldn't put my hands on it, but she was so different from the girl I grew up with. I swear I sensed jealousy and nothing but negative vibes coming from her. I drove down the street in total silence as I replayed in my head something that she said: *"What a coincidence.*

Ant's middle name is Micah. I pray he ain't nothing like Anthony." Oh, hell no, I hope not, I thought as I sped all the way to Decatur.

I called Micah as soon as I got to the house. I was too eager to see him. I hoped what I was thinking was wrong, but there were too many coincidences: Micah had two daughters; Ayana's baby daddy had two daughters. And they had similar names. Was she the one he was talking about? Her drunken mother, his baby mama from hell; could it really be my best friend?

"Calm down, it's just coincidence," I tried to coach myself. I rubbed my stomach and walked into the shower. I needed to relax a little and water always soothes my soul.

I must've dozed off because I heard footsteps, so I jumped up and saw Micah standing over me.

"I was trying not to wake you."

"It's fine, I need to get up anyway. I need to talk to you."

"What's up, you good?"

"Yes, I'm fine. I need to ask you a question."

"Ask away."

"What's your baby mother's name?"

"What is this about?"

"I think I went to school with her. What's her name?"

"Ayana."

The walls started to close in. I felt dizzy and my vision became blurred. "I don't feel too good," I mumbled as everything went dark.

CHAPTER TEN

Tiana

I woke up in DeKalb Medical. I learned from Micah that I fainted. The doctor told me my blood sugar was low and that I was dehydrated. I also needed iron pills because the iron in my blood was low. Damn, I went in with one issue and left with a bunch of other issues. I was well aware that I had to take care of myself and my baby.

On the way home I stared out the window. My heart was broken and my whole perfect little life was shattered. How did I end up in this fucked-up situation? I was really pregnant by my best friend's baby daddy. I turned to take a look at him. Did he know? Did he know he was screwing me and my best friend? Tears filled my eyes. I wanted to sink into a hole right about now. This was one big-ass mess that I managed to get myself in.

"Babe, you a'ight? You crying?" he inquired.

"Nah, I'm fine, just a little tired," I lied. I wanted to let him know how much I was hurting. I wanted him to hold me. I loved him and I needed him bad as hell!

When we got to the house, I made some soup and got into the bed. I just needed to lie down, rest my soul, and figure things out.

"Get some rest. I'm going to be gone for a minute. I have some business to handle." He kissed me on the forehead.

After I heard the garage door go down, I dialed Ayana's number. I had a question for her.

"Hello, you got home okay?"

"Yes, I did. Lemme ask you a question. What school your baby daddy go to?"

"Georgia Tech, why?"

"You know that's my school. I'ma keep an ear out for you, see if I hear anything."

"Thanks, boo."

I sank under the covers as tears started flowing. This couldn't be real. There was no way in hell me and Ayana were fucking the same damn nigga and neither one of us knew it. The big question was, did he know he was fucking two best friends? I cried until my eyes started to burn and my head started to hurt. I wished I had someone to talk to, but the only person I could talk to was the woman of the man I was fucking.

CHAPTER ELEVEN

Ayana

I didn't know what breeze blew Tiana's ass over here, but the bitch acted like she was the shit ever since she started college. She must have known that I wouldn't fool with her ass. It was hard for me to keep a straight face when she came over here. The reality was I didn't fuck with that bitch like that. It pissed me off even more when she sat up here acting like the nigga she was fucking was the shit. *Bitch, please.* It was only a matter of time before that nigga saw right through that "made in China" bitch. That bitch would find out soon that her shit stank just like the rest of ours. I couldn't wait for the day when that bitch called me crying the fucking blues. The bitch pissed me off when she started talking 'bout my mama. That bitch must not have remembered that it was my drunken mother who fed her hungry ass and put a roof over her head. I saw her ass cleaned that shit up fast, 'cause I was ready to knock that bitch's head off for real.

I kept calling Anthony's phone because it was now turned on again, but he still wasn't picking up. I got into my car and decided to drive around to all the spots that I knew he could possibly be chilling at. I grabbed my little .25 and put in my purse. I got it while I was dancing at the club. You can never be too careful; especially when you dance, these old lame-ass niggas be trying it.

I got on I-20 and headed to Decatur. I tried to see if I spotted his car anywhere, but he was nowhere to be found. I decided to head to the barber shop on Candler Road; that's where most of the hood niggas hung out at. The barber shop was really a front for the dope shop. All the dope boys be there and all the thirsty bitches be there also.

I pulled up on the side and checked my hair to make sure I was on point. I saw some of them hating-ass bitches standing outside so I sashayed past them and walked into the shop.

I walked over to Big Mike's stall. "Hey, Big Mike, you seen Ant?"

"Hey, Ayana. Nah. I seen that nigga earlier today."

"Oh, okay, thanks." As I proceeded to walk out, that's when Tahj's bitch-ass sister walked in front of me.

"I see somebody looking for their baby daddy." She chuckled.

"Bitch, get the fuck out of my way. Since you fucking him, you should be wondering where he at also."

"No, honey, like you said I'm only fucking him. He's your dick and you're his baby mama so that's your job to worry about him. I only fuck him and get the money."

By the time the words left that ho's mouth, I had jumped on her. I started taking punches at that ho's face.

"Fight, fight," I heard the other bitches screaming; and a crowd rushed over.

That bitch was matching my blows, but I was determined not to lose this fight. I stomped that bitch so hard blood started spilling out of her mouth.

"That's enough," I heard Big Mike yell. He snatched me up in the air and carried me to the back of the store.

"Put me down," I yelled. I was angry and I was ready to finish whupping that bitch's ass.

"Man, chill out! What's wrong with you, out here showing out like this? Ant gon' be pissed as hell when he finds out that you been out here fighting."

"Fuck Ant. All y'all knew he was fucking that ol' raggedy-ass bitch, but y'all kept it on the low. Matter of fact, fuck all y'all for real. Now let me fucking go."

"I'ma press charges on that bitch," I heard that bitch scream.

"Bitch, fuck you. You rat-ass bitch."

"I'll let you go if you promise to go home. Ain't no need for you to be out here trying to go to jail. You got kids, ma."

"A'ight, man, I'm leaving, but if that bitch say anything else, that ass is mine."

He held my arm and walked me out of the shop. That old scary-ass bitch didn't even leap. He let me go and I got into my car. I was so angry that I was shaking. I leaned my head on my steering wheel as I cried. I was hurting so bad, I just wanted to use this car and run over all them bitches out here. *This nigga Anthony done made a fool out of me and now he got the entire hood looking at me like I'm a fool.*

I turned the car on and busted a U-turn and sped off. I saw that bitch through the mirror still popping shit. I wasn't moved. *That bitch better go wash that blood off her face.* My head was hurting from that bitch pulling my weave and I felt a knot on my forehead.

I pulled into my driveway and that's when I noticed Ant's car. I figured news traveled fast so he found his way home. I walked in and he was sitting in the living room.

"So, this what you do now? Out in the streets fighting like you done lost your mind?"

"Boy, fuck you. You've been gone for four fucking days and now you have the fucking nerve to come up in here checking me about a bitch you been fucking?"

"Yo, I told you I was going to be handling some business. I can't afford to sit around here when I got moves to make. You want nice shit and to live in a big house. How the fuck you think you get these things? You don't fucking work," he yelled.

"Boy, whatever, you ain't the first dope boy I fucked with. You not hustling twenty-four hours a day. You have to wash your ass and change your clothes, so where the fuck you do that at?"

"You know what, Ayana, this shit is getting old. I'm tired of doing this! The bitching and the accusations, I want this to end, B, for real. I just want to be in my kids' lives; that's all I want."

"What the fuck you saying? You done? Who is this bitch who makes you want to walk away from your family? Is the pussy that fucking good for you to say fuck us?"

"It ain't about that. I am not happy, and you're not happy. Why should we keep going through this bullshit? Now you out in these fucking streets fighting like you ain't got no damn sense."

"Boy, like I said, you just mad 'cause I stomped a hole in your bitch's face. The next time you try to play me for another bitch, please make sure that ho is something to look at. You the only one who want a bitch half the hood done ran through. I pray to God you put on a condom when you was running up in that ho."

"Yo, I ain't tryin'a hear all that. I ain't never fuck that bitch. I put that on my seeds, but believe what the fuck you want to believe. Like I said, it's over between us. You can have the house; I'll find me something else." He turned to walk away.

I ran up behind him and grabbed his shirt. "You can't fucking do that. Me and my kids need you," I busted out crying.

"Man, chill out. I've been telling you that I am tired of arguing and going through this old hood-like love. I'm in the streets and when I come home I don't need a homie. I need a woman who has my back, one I can sit and talk with. You never listen; all you give a fuck about is the money. You remember when I told you that I wanted to go back to school and learn a trade?

You laughed in my face and asked me who was I gon' be with working nine to five. That was the motherfucking day I realized that you was only a money-hungry bitch and you didn't give a fuck that I was throwing rocks at the penitentiary."

I raised my hand and slapped the shit out of him. He quickly grabbed my arm and shoved me to the side. "Ay, B, keep yo' hands off me. I swear, I don't want to but I will beat your motherfucking ass." He took step toward me.

"You can try it if you want to. You know damn well you ain't man enough to try me like that. Boy, you must not love your motherfucking life. I got niggas lined up waiting for me to say the word," I spat with venom.

"Bitch, fuck you and them niggas. I bet you not one of them fuck niggas will ever say shit to me. Man, I ain't going to keep going through this shit with you." He turned around and walked quickly through the front door.

I fell on my knees and started bawling. I popped all that shit, but I loved him. "I love you," I yelled out. I was hoping he would turn back around and tell me that he was sorry. I waited a few minutes but nothing happened. With tears flowing and snot running out my nose, I sat on the carpet by the door. I was feeling so weak. I felt a sharp pain, like my soul had been torn apart. I wondered, *did he just leave me to go see her, whoever the hell she is?*

My thoughts were interrupted with the ringing of a cell phone. I quickly got up and walked to the living room. His iPhone 6 was on the coffee table and, boy, was it going off. I couldn't resist so I picked it up. The 404 number that was calling lit up the screen with the title Babe. I answered it but I was too late; the person had already hung up.

"No. Damn you, Ant!" I yelled out as I tossed his phone on the couch. I quickly picked it back up and started browsing. I didn't know what I was going to find but I knew it wasn't going to be good. I grabbed a piece of paper and I wrote down every female's number or any number that looked suspect to me. I knew some of them were friends but, fuck it, everybody was a suspect at the moment. I saw messages, but none was from this "Babe." I took one last glance and threw the phone down.

I poured a glass of wine, turned the lights off, and walked upstairs. I was on a mission to find out who this bitch was who my nigga was referring to as Babe. I hoped that bitch was ready for some drama, because if I couldn't have him, then no one was going to have him.

I drank the wine, which triggered my emotions. I started crying again. I grabbed my phone and started dialing numbers one by one.

CHAPTER TWELVE

Tiana

Micah stormed through the door with anger plastered across his face. I had never seen him so angry before and it kind of scared me. He sat at the edge of the bed fuming with anger.

"Do you want to talk about it?"

"Nah, ma, it's my ol' dumbass baby mama. Her ass was out there fighting and shit while my fucking kids are at her mama house. I swear, T, I just want to choke that bitch for real. I'm tired, yo."

"Calm down, baby. I know you mad but I can't support you putting your hand on no female. I already told you, you need to take her to court to get your kids. The judge will see that you are the fit parent."

"Ma, I'm a street nigga. I 'ont fuck with no fucking system. What the fuck I look like going up in their court? Sometimes I just want to off the bitch so I can have my motherfucking kids."

I couldn't believe he was talking like that. It made me shiver inside 'cause I was carrying his seed and, one day, I may have been the one he was angry with.

"Ma, don't look at me like that. I love you. I would never think about doing anything to you or my seed. You just don't understand the kind of shit this bitch puts me through. I've been good to her, and she ain't had to work or provide a dollar. I bust my ass in them streets to provide for them. My niggas called me a fool and laughed at me, 'cause they said I was wifing a whore. Ain't none of that matter. I really loved her, T," he cried.

I felt so bad because he was hurting behind a chick who just so happened to be my best friend. I was hurting for her too; or was I? Earlier when I saw her, she was bragging about fucking some other dude. Honestly I didn't give a fuck. My only concern was me, my man, and my baby.

My sadness quickly turned to anger. He needed to wipe those damn tears. I was like his niggas. He was a fool for taking a whore out of the strip club, taking her home, and trying to wife her. Shit, that was a dumbass move on his part especially when he had babies with her. As sad as it sounds, he was stuck with her for the rest of his life. Truth was, I wasn't worried about her. I didn't know who she was fucking and, now that I did know, it was too late in the game. Just like her little bastards needed a daddy, the one I was carrying needed a daddy too. I ain't have no problem with him playing Daddy, but I damn sure had a problem with him fucking her. I knew he had no idea that we were close, because he had never seen us together nor had I talked about her to him.

I leaned over and hugged him. "Babe, listen, it's all gonna work itself out. Just give her a little time and she'll come around." I wanted to pat myself on the back for that fucking speech. It was over with them, because he was now my man and my unborn child's father.

We finally found a house in Stone Mountain. It was a nice area and even though my child hadn't been born yet, I checked out their school system. I loved our new house. It was the three bedrooms with two and a half baths and a pool in the backyard that really got me. Now I could sit back there and study. I had no idea how Micah paid for it, but I did know his mama signed the papers.

I walked into the room that I planned on turning into the baby's room. I smiled at the thought of decorating this room. I was so caught up in my thoughts that I didn't hear when Micah snuck up behind me. He gently moved my hair out of the way and kissed my neck passionately. I shivered inside as he made love to my neck. I wanted him so bad, so instead of saying anything I just turned around and started kissing him back. I pushed him on the wall and started stripping off his shirt then I unbuttoned his pants and got on my knees. I placed his dick in my mouth and started to deep throat it. I took in as much as my mouth could hold, then I sucked it like a pro. In my mind, I knew I had to keep him happy if I wanted him to stay home. I heard his groans as I sucked passionately. He grabbed my head and forced it toward his dick. I almost choked but I didn't let up any. I felt his veins getting bigger so I repositioned my mouth.

"Aargh, babyyyyyyyyyyyyy," he yelled as he exploded in my mouth. I made sure every bit went straight down my throat. I then used my tongue to lick his limp dick clean. I stood up as he grabbed and hugged me close.

"Babe, I love you and I promise that I'm going to make you the happiest woman alive. You and my little nigga." He rubbed my stomach.

"Little nigga? Who the hell told you it's going to a boy?" I jokingly said and poked him in the chest.

"I'm just saying, ma, it'd be nice to have a little junior running around here," he said as he kissed me.

"I want a daughter, plain and simple."

"Well, we'll see."

"Anyway, let's go unpack this stuff. Ugh, I wish I had a home decorator. I swear I'm not in the mood," I whined.

"Well, you can relax. I will unload everything."

"You are the sweetest, you know that?"

"Nah, but you can show me soon as I'm finished unloading the stuff."

"Boy, go ahead with your nasty self." I pushed him and walked off.

As I sat on the steps, I felt guilty, like I was deceiving him. I wanted to tell him about Ayana and me but I didn't know how to come out and say it. Things were so good between us and I wasn't sure how he was going to act once he found out that she was my childhood best friend.

I also thought about Ayana. I used to love her like my sister, but we had grown apart. She wasn't the same sweet girl I grew up with. I felt in my heart that I didn't owe her shit. I mean, if the shoe were on the other foot, what would she have done? I couldn't speak for her, but the way

I saw it he was up for grabs and I sure as hell wasn't going to let him go just because of her. I was not cold, but the only person I needed to be loyal to was the baby inside of me and my damn self.

CHAPTER THIRTEEN

Ayana

I'd never been a dumb bitch and I damn sure wasn't about to start now. I knew that nigga didn't just get up and want to leave his family. Especially his daughters; they were his fucking life and he made sure everybody knew that.

I needed to find out more about what college bitch he was fucking around with. I remembered Tiana saying she was going to investigate. A week had passed and I hadn't heard anything from her. I dialed her number and her phone rang until the voice mail came on. I hung up and called back and this time she answered.

"Hey, chick. What's going on?" she answered with a slight attitude.

"Damn, what's wrong with you? Don't tell me that nigga pissing you off already."

"Nah, I'm just tired. What's going on though?"

"I just wanted to know if you found out anything about Ant and the bitch he fucking with."

"Nah, I ain't had time to really find out anything. I asked a few of my girlfriends, but they didn't know either."

"Oh, okay, well, that's all I needed to know. Get some rest. I gotta go."

I hung up the phone before her ass could respond. I didn't know what was going on with that bitch, but I swear I didn't like her motherfucking attitude. *I have a feeling I'ma have to check that ass soon. Real soon.*

Niggas always underestimate a bitch but, see, a hurt bitch is a dangerous one. I dialed Tahj's number because I was curious about what he was talking about the other day. Fuck that, I was ready for whatever.

"Hey, love, I thought I would never hear from you again. I was in my feelings for real. I thought you took the dick and threw me to the side." He chuckled.

"Nah, I just been dealing with some personal shit lately. Ole' boy talking about he moving out and shit."

"Shit, let that pussy nigga go. You 'ont really need that nigga around. I already told you that."

"Yeah, I'm done for real. You said the other day that you wanted to holla at me about something?"

"Yeah, yeah. Shit, I need you to let me know where that nigga and his boys keep that work. Me and my niggas wanna run up in there."

I took a long pause. So that's what this nigga wanted. He wanted me to help him set up my baby daddy.

"Listen, I got ten stacks for you if you help me pull this off."

The mention of money got me wet instantly. Then I also remembered how cold Ant had been to me lately. I smiled before I spoke. "I know there's a house out in Stone Mountain. It's off Hairston; matter of fact, it's on Redan. I've only been there twice to pick Ant up."

"Oh, shit, love, that's the one I'm talking 'bout. Shoot me the address."

"Hold up, nigga. I ain't no fool. Run my money first before I give you that address. Shit, your fuck was good, but not that motherfucking good."

"Damn, love, you harsh as hell. I like that though; that's the kind of attitude that makes my dick hard."

"Nah, I ain't harsh. I'm just not no fool. Bring me my money tonight and we can talk. Text me when you're ready and I'll tell you where to meet me."

"A'ight, I got you, love. See you soon."

I hung the phone up. I was excited. Shit, I could go shopping tomorrow with that ten stacks, stock up on some new shoes and purses. Ant ass was going to have a rude awakening when he found out his spot got hit. *Oh, well, that's his motherfucking problem. He will soon find out that he done crossed the wrong bitch!*

I decided to drop the kids off at Mama's. I knew lately she'd been fussing about watching them, but I was stuttin' her. Shit, she should've been happy to have my damn babies around her half-drunk ass.

I knocked on her door, waited about five minutes, and no one came. I started banging harder; I knew her ass was in there because her car was parked in her parking space.

"Who the hell knocking my door like that?" she hollered.

"Ma, open the door." I was past annoyed with her ass.

"Well, hello. You need to call before you pop up over here. I could've had company over here."

"Ma, cut it out. Don't nobody want your ass except Daddy."

"Hey, babies, give your nana some love." She turned her attention to the kids.

I walked in and put their bags down. She turned to me and spoke, "What's all this here? They ain't staying."

"Come on, Mama, I have a date tonight."

"A date? It's about time you started looking for another man."

"Yes, Mama, we all know how much you dislike Ant."

"Dislike? I don't dislike him. I just always thought he was too good for you. You just like yo' mama: you like a variety of 'you know what.' It takes a special kind of man to deal with you and that fella didn't seem to fit it."

I wanted to choke her ass for talking like that. I was nothing like her; she was a drunk who liked to fuck for a can of beer. I would never sell my pussy for beer. She had me all the way fucked up.

"When was the last time you seen that child you used to have here with you? What's her name again?"

"Tiana, the daughter you wished you had," I replied sarcastically.

"Child, hush. You've always been jealous of me and her relationship. I sure hope you've outgrown that foolishness," she scolded.

I wanted to entertain that bullshit, but I didn't want to upset her, 'cause when she got upset, she started drinking. "A'ight, Ma, I got to go. All their food and stuff is in their bags."

"A'ight. You better be on time to pick them up. If not I'll be calling the people."

I kissed my kids and ran out the door. I loved that woman, but sometimes she just didn't know how to keep her mouth shut. She was the same woman who taught me that if you didn't have anything good to say not to say anything at all. I shook my head and walked off to my car.

My mind raced back to when I was growing up. My life was fine up until the point when Tiana moved in with us. My mother treated that bitch better than she did her own flesh and blood. I used to sit back and watch the shenanigans take place. To this day I harbored ill feelings toward that bitch 'cause she came into my life and tried to take it over.

I got home in no time, took a shower, and got dressed. I had no idea what time Tahj was going to hit me so I wanted to be ready. *This nigga better not be playing and he better have my money.*

As soon as I got out of the shower, my phone was ringing. It's funny how niggas are always late, but be on time when it involves fucking or something beneficial to them. "Hello. You ain't playing huh?"

"Nah, love. I'm dead serious. Where you wanna meet at?"

"Let's meet at the Red Roof Inn on Panola, right off the exit."

"Bet."

"I'll see you in a little while and, Tahj, please have my money."

"Love, I got you."

I didn't know if I believed him, so I looked in the drawer and pulled out my little friend. I didn't really trust this nigga 100 percent. I just prayed that he was planning to do nothing stupid. God knows that I had to come home to my kids. How the fuck would that look, me up in the hotel with my baby daddy's rival?

I put on a pair of Aeropostale shorts and a T-shirt. I also put a hat on my head to hide/disguise my looks. I didn't want to risk anyone seeing me with this nigga. I grabbed my keys and sprinted out the door.

I was nervous, but I was determined to get this money. I swallowed my fear and drove into the hotel parking lot. I got a room, then texted him the room number. I lay on the bed patiently waiting. I put my little friend under the pillow that I was lying on. I wished I had something to drink to calm my nerves. My stomach felt kind of queasy. I thought about leaving and going home.

That thought was useless now since I heard banging on the door. I jumped up and looked through the peephole. I wanted to make sure he was by himself.

"Hey, love, you look gorgeous as usual." He smiled at me.

"Thanks. You don't look too bad yourself," I said as I locked the door behind us. "So, do you have my money? I need to see it and count it before I open my mouth."

"Damn, love, you aggressive as fuck. That shit turns me the fuck on. We gon' talk business, but first let me tap that ass really quick."

Lord knows I wasn't tryin'a fuck. I just wanted to get this money and get out of here. "Damn, babe, I thought you was just gon' give me the money and get the info. I ain't in the mood to fuck," I whined.

"Bitch, I said I wanna tap that ass." He stood up and pointed a gun at me.

I blinked twice. I couldn't believe that he went from sweet to this cold, detached person. "Damn, babe, chill out. I was just saying that I—"

"Bitch, shut up. Now take off your fucking clothes and run that pussy," he demanded.

I thought about grabbing my little friend from under the pillow, but I wasn't sure I would make it. "Tahj, don't do this," I cried.

"Bitch, shut up! I know that bitch nigga had something to do with you acting like you want to fuck wit' a nigga. See, I know the motherfucking game, so I came over and gave you the dick. Ha-ha, I would've loved to see that nigga's face if he had walked in when I was laying this dick down."

I started to cry. I had no idea this nigga was grimy like that. I'd always heard Ant talk shit about him, but on the real I thought he was jealous. Now here I was staring up at a gun. Thoughts of my kids flooded my mind and my heart started to ache. Tears filled my eyes as I realized this nigga was serious as a heart attack.

"Now, bitch, I'ma say this one more time. Take your fuckin' drawers off."

"I can't. Please don't do this." I stuttered as I begged him.

Blap! Blap! Blap! He slapped me a few times across my face. My face instantly started burning. I quickly unbuttoned my shorts and pulled my drawers down. I closed my eyes as I felt his hard, dry dick enter me. I wasn't wet, so that made it hurt like hell. He was like a deranged beast as he ripped through my walls.

"Noooooo," I screamed hoping that someone might hear me and come to my rescue. That wish was useless because that nigga had his way with me until he busted.

"Bitch, you better not open your fucking mouth and tell anyone about this shit. If you do, I'ma kill you, your mama, your baby daddy, and your motherfucking little bastards. You got it?" he warned in a cold, calculated tone.

I didn't say a word. I kept my eyes closed and just kept crying.

"Cut all that crying out. Just the other day you was Miss Big and Mighty. You wanted to get fucked; now you sitting up here hollering like you 'ont love this dick. Bitch, cut it out; and oh, yeah, run that address."

"Man, you just fucking raped me and now you want me to help you set my baby daddy up?"

"Bitch, I ain't rape you. You got a fucking room and you gave me the pussy. And you can cut out the 'poor little Ayana' act. You was willing to set that nigga up for ten grand; that's why we're here in the first place, remember?"

I continued to cry as I pleaded to God. I just wanted to leave. I wanted to go home to my babies.

"Bitch, run the motherfucking address." He walked over to me and grabbed my neck. I couldn't breathe as his big, manly hands held me tight. I gasped for air as he tightened his grip. "Now, bitch, you ready to talk?"

I couldn't speak, but I shook my head yes. I realized that this dude wasn't playing any games and I needed to get out of this alive.

Before I could muster up the nerve to tell him, he raised his hand and slapped me so hard that I fell off the bed. "Bitch, I told your ass I ain't playing. Now give me the fucking address before I blow your fucking head off," he growled.

"It's 1525 Redan Road," I stuttered, still holding my face.

"This better be the right fucking address. If not, I'll be hollering at your boy and let him know how good yo' pussy is. Now go clean yourself up, ho," he said and spit directly in my face.

I used my hand to wipe the spit off my face. Tears started flowing. I felt degraded and low. The truth was I wished I hadn't put myself in this situation. I watched as he dialed a number on his phone.

"Yo, the bitch gave me the address. Meet me on Redan in twenty."

Pop! Pop! Shots rang out! I felt a stinging sensation in my chest followed by pain. I looked down and saw blood spilling out of my chest. I mustered up enough strength to drag myself to my feet. I grabbed my chest as the pain hit me. Everything around me started to go dark. The only things I could think of were my babies. "God, please protect my babies," I barely mumbled.

CHAPTER FOURTEEN

Tiana

It was late at night and we were lying in bed relaxing. I kind of loved the idea of my man living with me, even though I was suspicious because he only stayed at the house certain nights. I was ready to check that nigga, but I decided not to because I knew that he was about to give up the streets. I was able to convince him that the streets didn't love anybody and if he wanted to be with me, he was gon' have to get a job. I swore I didn't want to lose my child's father to the streets or to prison.

His phone was on the nightstand and it kept buzzing. He lay there staring at the television as if he couldn't hear the annoying sound.

"Get the phone. Who is that calling you like that?" I said in an annoyed tone.

"Ma, I 'ont know," he said nonchalantly. The ringing didn't ease up, until he angrily snatched the phone up. "Hello," he yelled into the phone.

"Say what?" He sat up in the bed. "I'm on my way, yo." He hung the phone up and jumped out of the bed.

"What's wrong, babe?"

"That was my nigga. My baby mama got shot and is at Grady Hospital," he said and he grabbed his pants, slid into them, and grabbed his shirt, and his keys, and ran out the door.

"Micah," I screamed, but he was down the stairs and out the door already.

I sat back down on the bed shocked that my fucking friend had gotten shot. The first thought that crossed my mind was the kids. Were they all right? I didn't know who to call to find out what the hell was going on. I continued to pace my bedroom as I dialed Micah's number, but it just rang out. I cut the TV on to see if it was being reported on the news but nothing was on at the moment. I swear, I knew that messing with Micah was wrong, but I damn sure didn't wish death on her.

Later that night, Micah called me from the hospital. He was furious!

"What's going on, Micah? I tried to call you, but your phone kept ringing out."

"Ma, this fuck nigga shot my baby mama and now she lying up in the hospital fighting for her life. Word to my mother, he better pray she pulls through, 'cause if she don't I'ma cause havoc on this whole fucking city."

"Baby, calm down. This ain't the way to handle it. Do you know who did it and why?"

"Ay, ma, no disrespect, but this is the mother of my children. Fuck why he did it. All I know is this bitch nigga done violated her and I have to touch him," he yelled.

I ain't gon' lie, I was all in my fucking feelings. I knew this wasn't the time to be feeling jealous and shit, but I was. Just a few days ago, he was hollering about how annoying her ass was; now he was acting like he was all in love with the bitch. *Yeah, nigga, I feel fucking disrespected.* I just didn't say it out loud, but I was pissed the fuck off.

"A'ight, I'ma hit you later." He hung the phone up.

Was I being selfish? I didn't think so. I was hoping she made it out alive and well, but I didn't think my man/baby's father should have been getting himself all worked up over a piece of pussy he claimed he didn't want anymore.

That night I lay in bed feeling lonely and missing him. I tried calling him, but the phone kept going to voice mail. I was fuming with anger and resentment. How could he leave me and his baby alone and go out in the streets playing Captain Save a Ho? I just hoped this bitch didn't get my man in any kind of shit that could cost him his freedom or possibly his life. "God, please protect my baby out in them streets," I whispered before I dozed off.

I was tired of sitting around waiting to hear what happened. I needed to know that she was going to be all right. I knew that it would look crazy if I didn't show my face. The last thing I needed was for people to start suspecting anything. I got dressed and decided to stop by her mother's house. I was pretty sure she still lived in the same house that we used to stay in when I was younger.

I parked and walked to the door. I rang the doorbell and waited.

"Hello? Oh, child, it's you. Long time no see."

"Yes. I've been meaning to come by and see you."

"Well, I guess you heard what happen to Ayana. Some coward ass done tried to take my baby from me. My one and only child." She busted out crying.

I stepped in and hugged her tight. I hated to see her in so much pain. She was a second mother. Shit, fuck second; she was the only person I could really call Mother. Even though she stayed drunk, she kept a roof over our heads. For that alone, I'd forever be grateful to her.

After a few minutes, she managed to get the crying under control.

"So what really happen and how is she doing?" I quizzed her.

"Well, the doctors say she gon' pull through, but she was lucky that the hotel people found her. A few minutes later and she would've been dead," she said as she trembled while I held her tight.

"What? Hotel? What the hell happened and who would want to hurt her? I just saw her the other day. She didn't mention that she had a problem with anybody. And where were the kids?"

"Luckily, I had the kids so they were not in harm's way."

"So do they know who did it?"

"Yes, she said some boy's name, but you know I don't know them young people's names. I told my daughter a long time ago to leave that damn thug alone, the baby daddy, that is. If you ask me, I believe he the reason why my daughter is lying up in that hospital fighting for her life.

I told the detectives that they need to look into him and his cronies."

At that moment I let her loose. I was irritated as fuck when she mentioned that police shit. *What the fuck my man has to do with this shit and why would she set the police on him?* See I felt bad and all that she was up in the hospital, but I knew damn well that he didn't have anything to do with it.

"Well, if you don't mind, I'm going to go see her."

"You know that's yo' sister so I'm sure she'll be more than happy to see you."

"Well, I will see you then. By the way, where are the kids?"

"The kids are here with me. Their daddy is at the hospital with her so that's why I'm here. They keep asking for their mama, but I can't bring myself to tell them that their mama is in the hospital. It's really sad, you know."

"Yes, it is. I got to go see her." I gave her a hug and jetted out the door.

I jumped in my car and pulled off. I swore I hoped Micah didn't get himself into no bullshit. What the hell was she doing at the hotel and who was this dude who shot her? I knew there was only one way that I would get these answers and that was to go to the source itself.

CHAPTER FIFTEEN

Ayana

Two weeks later

Can you believe it, this bum-ass nigga tried to take my life? I was either one lucky bitch or somebody up above was watching over me. I woke up to see myself hooked up to all sorts of wires and machines. My man was sitting in the chair across from my bed.

"Hey, babe," I mumbled.

"Hey, you. You're awake!" He walked closer to my bed.

"Where are my children?" I panicked.

"They at home with your mama."

"I thought I was going to die, baby," I mumbled as tears welled up in my eyes. My mind flashed back to the day that I got shot. I remembered how that dude raped me as I screamed.

"Ay, ma, I'm happy you're doing better. All I need to know is what the fuck happened? What the fuck were you doing at that hotel?" He rushed me with questions.

"Baby, calm down. I'm trying to remember everything, but I only remember when I got shot." I started to cry. I knew him all too well.

"Man, calm down. Who is the nigga who did this shit to you?"

I paused. I wanted to tell him, but how could I set my mouth to tell him that it was the nigga I was fucking? I couldn't. There was no way I could let him know any of this. He was already acting funny toward me. I just knew if I told him this shit, he would snap.

"It was Tahj. He did this shit to me," I busted out, bawling.

"What? What the fuck you talking 'bout? Which Tahj, the nigga I was beefing with? I know that pussy nigga didn't kidnap and shoot you," he yelled out.

Before I could respond two detectives walked into my room. I swear, they were the last people I wanted to see. I had an episode with them earlier. I sensed that they didn't believe my story.

"Miss Beasly, we were wondering if you remember anything else. Something so we can find the thugs who did this to you," the white detective said with a smirk on her face.

"I—"

"She already told y'all she don't remember. She is the victim here, so why I got a feeling y'all treating her like she is the motherfucker who did this shit?" Ant opened up his mouth and cut me off.

"And you are?" the middle-aged detective asked Ant.

"Why? Y'all should be out there finding the niggas who did this to her instead of worrying about my name," he mouthed off.

"Give me your name and your ID," one detective said.

"For what? I ain't did shit, man."

"Give me your ID."

"Man, for what?"

"Boy, just give them the damn ID!" I used the little bit of strength that I had to utter.

He gave me a fucked-up look, then reached into his pocket and pulled out his wallet, handing it to the officer. I watched as they went through his wallet and took out his driver's license. I hoped this fool didn't come up in here knowing he had a warrant.

I guessed he was straight because they didn't lock his ass up.

"I guess you the baby daddy. So let me ask you, you know anything about who shot Miss Beasly?"

"Nah, I 'ont know and, if I did, I wouldn't be tellin' y'all motherfuckers," he spat.

"Calm down. I'm up in here sick and you up here showing your ass." I couldn't believe that this nigga was behaving like that. He needed to shut the fuck up so the fucking detectives could leave. I had a feeling they wasn't buying my story and I needed to distant myself from them and their investigation fast.

"Well, Detective Robinson and myself are about to leave. Here's my card. If you remember anything about the shooting, please don't hesitate to give us a call. We'll definitely be in touch." He turned to walk away.

He turned around, then spoke. "Be careful of the company you keep," he said as he stared Ant down.

After they walked out, I was ready to give Ant a piece of mind, but my energy wasn't there. The pain was kicking my ass, so I pressed my morphine button. I was ready to fall asleep and get rid of this pain.

"Yo, I'm about to bounce. I will be up here first thing in the morning, and I'm going to bring the kids with me."

"All right. Ant, I love you. I'm happy God saved my life and we can finally be a family. I think we should get married as soon as I get out of here."

I looked at his face to catch a glimpse of excitement, but instead all I saw was a man with displeasure written all over his face.

"Why you looking like that? You don't want us to be a family?" I asked confused.

"Ma, you need to get some rest. I will be up here tomorrow wit' the kids." He kissed me on the forehead.

I wasn't feeling his response, but the morphine had kicked in and my eyes wouldn't stay open. I laid my head on the pillow and dozed off.

CHAPTER SIXTEEN

Tiana

I didn't see Micah last night but he called and told me that he wasn't coming home because he had some business to handle. Ever since Ayana got shot, he hadn't been the same. When he was home, he was always sleeping, maybe because of my pregnancy. What bothered me was as soon as he got up, he was out the door.

I got dressed in a sweat suit from Aeropostale. These days there wasn't much that I could fit into. I would be happy when this baby came so I could get back to some sort of normalcy. I grabbed my car keys and walked down the stairs. I walked out the door and into the brisk air. I was happy that the nausea kind of calmed; now I was able to hold down a little bit of food.

I pulled into the Grady Hospital parking lot and parked. I hoped this girl wasn't on no bull-shit today. Shit, this experience should have humbled her and forced her to take a look at her life. She loved to be in the limelight and fuck niggas with long paper. Shit, all that shady shit that she used to do, might've caught up with her.

I walked to the front desk and gave them my name, and the clerk asked for my ID. I already knew that when a person got shot, they usually had some kind of security. I peeped into the adjacent door; she looked like she was asleep. I turned to walk away, but decided not to. I needed to see how she was doing. After all we grew up like sisters.

"Hey," I said as I walked up to her bed.

"Hey, sis. It's about time you showed your face." She gave me a big smile.

"Yeah, I know I should've come before, but this pregnancy along with my classes are kicking my butt."

"How is my godbaby doing? Did you find out what you're having? And where is this baby daddy at? I need to meet him."

"Well, the baby is doing fine, and no, we have no idea as of yet. And you haven't met the mister yet because you are in here and he's always busy," I lied.

"Oh, okay. So you hear about what happen to me?"

"Nah. I stopped by your mama's house and she was saying something about some dude. I couldn't understand. Who the fuck would want to hurt you? Did you see who did it?"

She lay there, staring at the ceiling, then she spoke. "You know you my best friend and you know I trust you right?" She stared into my eyes.

"What's going on with you? You're scaring me."

"What I'm about to tell you, you can't tell nobody at all. Promise me," she demanded.

"Damn, chill out, bitch. I got you." I was feeling annoyed.

"Ease up this pillow underneath me."

I fixed the pillow and sat on the edge of her bed. She started to tell me what happened between her and dude, how he raped her then shot her. What shocked me the most was when she mentioned how she was about to set her baby daddy up. I wanted to reach over and grab that bitch's throat, but I kept my cool. "Really? Wow, so how do you know dude?"

"Girl, him and Ant was beefing. I was so mad when he told me he wanted out of the relationship, so I called dude up and had him come over the house. I fucked him that first night in the bed me and Ant share. Girl, I never thought in a hundred years that dude would flip like that. I ain't gon' lie, I thought dude really fucked with me."

"So did you tell your baby daddy all of this?"

"Bitch, what the fuck you smoking? I told him dude shot me, but I told him that I don't know why. I can't tell him because I don't want to lose him. I swear if he ever finds out, he will leave me and probably file for custody. I can't risk that."

I sat there trying to find the right words to say to her, but I was speechless. I couldn't believe this bitch was that cruel. I just sat there staring at her.

"I 'ont know, T. I think he fucking with some other bitch. He acts funny now. Yesterday, I mentioned marriage to him and the nigga looked like he was sick. I swear whoever this bitch is she is fucking with the wrong nigga. Ain't no way my baby daddy is gon' leave a bad bitch like me for an old 'around the way' bitch," she bragged.

"How you know that she is an 'around the way' bitch? I mean what if the nigga wants to leave? Me personally, I ain't tryin'a hold on to no nigga who don't want to be with me. There are too many dicks out here to be doing all of this over one nigga."

"Damn, bitch, you defending him like you the one he fucking. I put in time behind this nigga. I gave him two little girls. I gave up my fucking life to play house to him and our children. This shit ain't going down like that. I swear it's not."

I heard the hatred in her crackled voice. I couldn't believe any of what she was saying. This bitch should have been happy she didn't die, but instead of thanking God, her evil ass was plotting on how to keep a grip on this nigga.

"Listen, how you feeling? Did they tell you when you're gonna leave up out of here?" I changed the subject fast because I couldn't take any more of this craziness.

"Yeah, the doctors say I should be able to go home to my man and kids next week. I can't wait. I hope he ain't got no bitch up in my shit. That nigga playing with the fire I tell you."

"All right, boo, if I don't come back up here then I will see you when you come home." I got up and grabbed my purse.

"Love you, chick. I promise after you have my nephew, we gonna chill more often. I sure miss your ass."

I nodded, gave her a hug, and walked away. I breathed a sigh of relief. Being around her ass made me feel like I was suffocating. I was still in disbelief as I walked down the hallway. I had no idea what I was about to do about all this information that I had.

I tried calling Micah, but his phone went directly to voice mail. I wondered where the fuck he was at. I needed to talk to him. My loyalty was to my man, not to her. We grew up together, but that was years ago. That bitch had changed and obviously we were not as close as before. I dialed his phone one more time, but there was still no answer.

"Where are you? You need to call me ASAP when you get this message." I hung the phone up.

I got into my car and pulled off. I was starting to feel ill. Not from being pregnant, but from all the fuckery that was going on. He was out there trying to get revenge on a nigga he thought had done him wrong, but in reality, that bitch played him like a fool.

I had to figure out a way to break the news to him, about Ayana being my friend and all the shit she had done. I wished he'd hurry up and call me back. Maybe he was at home sleeping.

I pulled up at the house, only to be disappointed. His car wasn't there and he hadn't called me back. I walked into the house feeling some kind of way. I didn't ask to be involved in none of this shit. I thought I found the perfect man, but here I was caught up in a love triangle that might get deadly.

I took a shower, made some tea, and got in bed. My mind couldn't rest because I hadn't talked to him since yesterday. I picked up the phone and dialed him again; still no response. I threw the phone on the bed and lay down with tears in my eyes.

I got up early, because I couldn't sleep. I looked around and Micah wasn't lying on his side. I grabbed my phone because I remembered that he told me if anything happened to him to call his mother. I'd never met the lady, but desperate times called for desperate measures.

I dialed his mother's number and waited for a response. The phone rang out so I hung up. But before I could put down the phone, it started to ring. Without hesitation I picked it up.

"Hello?"

"I guess you're the girlfriend. Well, Ant is in the hospital. He got in a shootout with some other boys—"

Before she could finish her sentence, I cut her off. "Is he all right?" I swear my heart almost jumped out of my chest.

"Well, the bullet grazed his arm, but he's gon' live. I am waiting for him to come out of the hospital right now."

"Oh, okay. Do you need me to come get him?"

"No, but you can meet me at the house. I think it's about time that I meet my daughter-in-law. You're the one he talks about all the time. I'm glad he decided to finally leave that other girl alone. That heffa ain't good for nothing but lying on her damn back. Sorry about my rant. I will text you my address. Meet us there in about twenty-five minutes."

Lord, I didn't know if I was ready to meet her. I'd heard so many stories about her and I wasn't sure now was the right time. Shit, it was too late. I already had a date to meet my mother-in-law. My mind quickly went back to Micah. What the fuck was he doing? He out there shooting at niggas over a bitch, while I was carrying his seed. I swore when I saw him I was going to dig into that ass. I didn't want no damn thug who was out running the fucking streets and I damn sure wasn't going to no jail to visit him either.

I pulled up at the address she gave me. I noticed his Charger parked in the driveway. I parked behind it and walked to the door. I rang the doorbell and waited.

"Hey, honey, come on in," a tall, athletic-look-ing woman greeted me at the door.

"Hello, I'm Tiana. You must be his mom."

"Yup, that's me, the one and only." She smiled and gave me a hug.

She then closed the door and I followed her inside. I immediately locked eyes with Micah. He hung his head down when I walked toward him.

"Hey, babe," he greeted me.

"Don't 'hey, babe' me. Do you know I haven't heard from you in over twenty-four hours and now I hear you almost got killed?" Then I decided to drop the matter for now because his mother was standing here. I just met the woman and I didn't want to be disrespectful to her.

We ended up eating breakfast. His mom threw down in the kitchen. You should've seen the plate the woman made me; it was like she was feeding a couple of people. I knew I was pregnant, but I damn sure wasn't starving. I managed to eat a little of the potatoes. I wasn't hungry because I was too pissed. I just wanted to get out of here.

"Are you up to driving or you want me to drive you home?"

"Yeah, that's a better idea."

I watched as he locked up his car and got into my car. Before I could pull off his mother walked out of the house and approached my door.

"Don't you be no stranger now. You can come by anytime you want and keep me informed about the baby. I want to get my grandbaby some things."

"Thank you and I won't be a stranger." I laughed.

"You better not. You 'ont seem crazy like that other one."

"Ma, we got to go."

"A'ight, baby, and don't forget what I told you. You need to stay out these damn streets. It could've been your body I was at the morgue identifying this morning. I already buried one child and I swear my heart can't take no more pain," she warned.

I felt everything she was saying. I did not want to lose him to these streets especially since we had a baby on the way. I swear my feelings toward Ayana went from liking to straight despising the bitch. I did not like the shit she was doing to my man and I had to sit back, not saying a word.

"Yo, what the hell you think you out here doing?" I lashed out.

"Yo, ma, lower your voice. I told you that fuck nigga raped and shot my baby moms and I ain't having that shit. I ain't stopping until I body that fuck nigga."

"How you know for sure that's what happened?"

"What you mean? I went to go see her and she told me everything that popped off."

"Really, so you gon' take the words of one person and fuck up your life? We have a fucking baby on the way. You need to think about that."

"Yo, T, I know it's hard for you to accept that I'm willing to risk my life and freedom behind my kids' mother. Shawty, please understand, me and her might not be together but she is the mother of my kids. I have to do this for my kids and, if you really rock with me, you need to understand where I'm coming from and get out your feelings. This ain't the time to get jealous."

I sat there listening to this nigga talk this crazy shit, then I spoke. "You think I'm jealous? You should know me better than that. There ain't a bitch walking this earth who can make me feel jealous. I am just saying that you got kids and you are out there willing to risk it all."

Tears were pouring down my face. I was hurting because I knew he didn't know this bitch got him into all this mess. I was ready to reveal her devious ways so he could see her for what she really was: a piece of shit.

CHAPTER SEVENTEEN

Ayana

Two weeks later I was discharged from the hospital. I was happy that Ant was there to pick me up. I had a good feeling things were going to be fine between us. I did feel a little bad when he got shot. Though he didn't say anything, but I knew it was behind me. I was hoping that he had killed dude because I had no idea what dude might be saying. I hoped he kept his mouth shut.

I was happy to be at home with the children at first, but Ant was barely at home. I started feeling like things were still fucked up. I needed to get my strength back. I just couldn't stand losing him.

My phone started ringing. I looked at my caller ID and noticed it was my bitch Lori. I was happy to hear from her because she was like the neighborhood newspaper. Whatever was going on, she'd know about it. "Hey, boo."

"Hey, bitch. So you home and didn't call me?"

"Girl, I'm just trying to adjust to life again; plus, this pain is kicking my ass. They gave me Percocet, but that shit be having me high as hell."

"I'm just happy you a'ight."

"Yeah, me too. So what's going on out in the streets?" I inquired.

"Shit, same old, same old. Bitch, where Ant at?"

"Why? What's going on?"

"Bitch, you better not say nothing, but I was over my brother's house a few days ago and I saw him getting in the car with a pregnant chick. I couldn't really see her face, but she kind of light skinned."

"Really? You sure it's not his sister?"

"Bitch, stop playing. His sister is blacker than me and no, this bitch had a big stomach. I saw his mama out there talkin' to the chick; then she went back into the house and they drove off leaving his car at his mama's house."

I sat up in the bed. What the fuck was this I was hearing? Who the fuck was this bitch Lori was talking about? And she was pregnant? "Listen, are you sure? I can't figure out who that could possibly be. He only has the one sister," I said puzzled.

"Bitch, I 'ont know who the hell she is, but I know I seen him with a bitch and her ass is pregnant."

"Well, I ain't gon' say shit 'cause you told me. I swear I hope this nigga ain't fucking around on me."

"Bitch, cut it out. You know how them dope boys are. You ain't the only bitch he fucking. You better be grateful he wifing your ass. Play your position and shut the hell up before you run his ass off. See, I know Mari be fucking them bitches, but I 'ont trip. I fuck him, suck his dick good, and keep him fed. I am not gon' lose my nigga behind these bitches."

I was irritated. I wasn't tryin'a hear none of this shit she was preaching right now. Fuck that. I didn't want to share my baby daddy. I wanted to be the only one he was fucking and eating out.

"Well, I gotta run. I just wanted to see how you was doing and let you know this little piece of info."

"A'ight, boo. I 'ppreciate you."

Tears rolled down my face. This nigga was with a bitch who was pregnant and it wasn't family, I knew that for sure. I bet his mama had something to do with that shit. The bitch never liked me from day one. She thought her son was too good for me because I used to dance at the club. Shit, that bitch should have been happy I fucked with her son.

I was fed up. It was time for me to get to the bottom of this shit. For way too long, I'd been hearing rumors of him fucking around. I tried to ignore it, but this shit had gotten out of hand. I hoped he ain't had no fucking baby on the way. I swore if he did then his ass was gonna feel it.

Ant played the position of the perfect father and man. He would help me around the house and he made sure the girls were taken care of. I sat on the sofa watching him play patty cake with the girls. I smiled as I looked at my perfect little family. He saw me smiling and quickly turned his head away.

"Girls, go to y'all room for a second. Mommy needs to talk to Daddy for a second."

"But, Mommy—"

"Go on, little girl," I snapped.

"Damn, calm down. They were just chilling with their daddy."

"Daddy? Well, let me ask you a question. What bitch you know who's pregnant?"

"Damn, what you talkin' 'bout? I 'ont know no pregnant bitch. Where is this coming from?"

"You fucking tell me. Somebody saw your ass with a bitch coming out of your mother's house the other day. So again, I'm asking, do you got a bastard on the way?"

"Yo, B, I 'ont know where you be getting your info from, but I only got two kids. You need to stop listening to them old dumbass bitches who can't keep a man of their own."

As I sat there staring into his eyes, I could tell his ass was lying. In that instant I saw him for the piece of shit that he really was. "You know what, Ant, I don't fucking believe you. Whatever is in the fucking dark will come out in the light. I swear, if you lying, I will take my fucking kids and your dirty ass will never see them again. I promise you that."

"You promise what? A, stop playing with me. If you ever take my kids, I will track you down and I will hurt you, B." He stared me in the eyes.

I didn't flinch one bit. I was hurting, but I didn't let him see that. I put on my "I don't give a fuck" face and sat there with my arms crossed. "Don't you fucking threaten me. Like I fucking said, if you lying, it's not going down that easy."

"Yo, I'm about to bounce." He got up off the sofa.

"So we talking and you just gon' up and leave like that? Really, it's like you 'ont give a fuck about me or my fucking kids. What the fuck is happening to you?"

"Man, I'm not gon' sit here and listen to your crazy rants. And let's get this straight: I will never say fuck my kids. I will never leave them and if anybody, yes, anybody stands in the way, I will kill them without thinking about it."

"Ant, you gon' do me like this? I just got raped and shot. I fucking need you. I fucking love you." I wept. I saw nothing else was working so I had to put on my best performance to convince this dude that I really wanted to be with him.

"Yo, B, cut all that crying out and clean yourself up. You shouldn't let the girls see you like that." He stormed out the door.

I jumped up and looked out the window. I saw him sitting on the hood of his car talking on the phone. I was irate. Here I was grieving and hurting and he just walked out like I didn't mean shit to him. I wiped my face just as a brilliant idea popped in my head. I walked up the stairs, as fast as I could, and gathered the girls, my keys, and my purse. I peeped through the window; he was still outside. I stood by the door waiting until he got in his car. I waited for him to pull off then I went outside and quickly got in my car. I knew I shouldn't be driving, but fuck that. I needed to see where his ass was off to in such a hurry.

"Mommy, where we going?" Diamond asked.

"We're just taking a little ride, baby."

I pulled off and sped up a little until I saw him sitting at the stoplight. I was careful not to get too close, so I allowed a car to get in between my car and his. I had no idea where he was off to. All I knew was he wasn't going far because he didn't get on the expressway. I followed closely, taking every turn he took. He pulled up at a house on Abbey Ridge in Stone Mountain. I pulled up across the street, hoping he wouldn't turn around. I watched as he opened the door with a key and went inside. So my nigga just walked into a house that I had no idea about. I wanted to run up the driveway and knock on the door, but I glanced back at my children and notice that I couldn't act a fool out here right now. I sat out there in the car waiting to see if he was going to come back out, but he didn't.

"Mommy, I'm hungry. I'm hungry," Diamond whined.

I made a mental note of the address and the house. I started the car and pulled off. I cut the music up to drown out the bickering voices of my kids and so they couldn't hear the weeping sounds of my cry.

"Mommy, it's too loud," Diamond screamed.

"Shut up already," I yelled back.

I was a nervous wreck. I wish I had a Percocet on me to pop. I drove home, crying the whole way. I got them into the house, bathed them, and got them ready for bed.

I crawled in my bed alone as I let the tears flow freely. I grabbed my phone and dialed Ant's number. His phone rang until his voice mail picked up. I sat there pressing redial about twenty times but there was still no answer. I threw the phone on the floor and cried out. I opened my drawer and pulled out my bottle of Percocet. I needed something to ease the pain I was feeling right now. I popped two pills instead of one. I couldn't believe this nigga.

My cell ringing interrupted my thoughts. I got up and grabbed it up off the floor. "Hello," I said angrily without even looking at the caller ID.

"Yo, something happen? I see you called me over fifteen times."

"Where are you? I was in so much pain. I couldn't move."

"I'm all the way in Clayton County. Can't you call your mama?"

"You just got there?" I quizzed him.

"Yeah. I came straight out here after I left the house. I got some business to handle out here."

"You're a fucking liar," I said as I hung up in his face.

I knew he was fucking lying, too, because I followed him and I knew where the fuck he was at. I cut my phone off and crawled under my covers. In the morning I had some shit to do!

I was up bright and early. I got the girls dressed and dropped them off at Mama's house. She was ready to start preaching early in the damn morning, but I wasn't having it. I was on a mission to find out what the fuck was going on. I remembered the exact street down to the house. I parked a few houses down then walked up the driveway and rang the doorbell. First thing that caught my eye was Ant's orange Charger sitting there. I swallowed hard and continued waiting at the front door. I was nervous and shaking on the inside. I didn't know what I was getting myself into, but there was no turning back.

I rang the doorbell and waited some more, but there was no answer so I pressed it without easing up.

"Who is it?" I heard a voice holler.

"It's Yana. I need to talk to the owner," I barely whispered.

The door busted open. "I'm the owner, and who the fuck are y . . ."

CHAPTER EIGHTEEN

Tiana

Trouble has a way of showing up on people's door. I heard the damn doorbell ringing early in the morning. I tried to ignore it because I wasn't expecting anyone especially early in the morning. I looked over at Micah and he was fast asleep. I guessed I had to go get the door. I grabbed my robe and wrapped it around my huge stomach. I stomped all the way down the stairs and asked who it was. I heard a voice but wasn't sure of the name. At this point it didn't matter because whoever was on the other side was going to get this severe case of tongue-lashing from me. I popped the door open.

There are no words to describe the surprise I got. "Hey, boo, what you doing here?" I tried to play it off.

"What, I can't stop by to see my sissy?"

Somehow that statement and the look on her face didn't add up. I never gave her my address or invited her to the house before. I took a deep breath and prepared myself mentally for anything. "Well, come on in."

She stepped in and I closed the door behind us.

"Are you okay? Why didn't you call me?" I tried to make conversation. This bitch was up in my shit when I didn't invite her and she had a deranged look on her face. "Ayana, what's going on with you? You know it's early; and how did you get my address?"

"Tell me, sis . . . It's okay for me to call you that right? How long have you been fucking and sucking my baby daddy?"

I almost fainted when I heard those words come out of her mouth. I froze for a second but quickly regrouped. "Uh, what are you talking about?" I looked at her.

"Bitch, cut it out. I followed Ant, my baby daddy/man to this house yesterday. Fuck yesterday; his Charger is parked in your driveway right now. So again, I ask you, bitch, how long have you been fucking and sucking my man's dick?" she asked in a real aggressive tone.

I thought about lying, but I knew the bitch had to have some sort of idea if she was here in my house. I knew now was the time to let it all out. "Ayana, I didn't know he was your baby daddy until it was too late. I only found out after I visited you that day at your house."

"You bitch! You've always wanted my life from the time me and my mama gave your homeless ass a place to live. You have always wanted to be me; now you fucking my man, bitch."

"First off, I'm not your bitch. Like I said it wasn't intentional. And as far as me wanting to be like you, that's bullshit. Bitch, you're the bottom of the fucking barrel. Why would I want to be like you? All you do is fuck and get high. Come on now, let's not go there." I was pissed the fuck off. My heart rate was rising and I wanted to jump on this bitch.

"Where is he? You are carrying his baby, too? That's why you never introduced me to the nigga you were fucking, because it's my man. Bitch, you are a lowdown piece of shit. How could you?" She lunged toward me. I raised my hands and two pieced that bitch.

God knows I didn't want to fight that bitch because I was pregnant, but fuck that. I continued punching that bitch and blocking blows. I was so caught up in guarding my stomach that I didn't hear when Micah came down the stairs.

"What the hell going on down here?" he yelled.

"You dirty bastard! Is this the bitch you've been fucking all along?"

He stood there frozen with his mouth wide open, as if he'd just seen a ghost.

"Close your damn mouth, boo. When did you start fucking my sister/bestie?"

"Man, how the fuck you got in here? You follow me or something?"

"Yes, I followed you. I knew you was lying to my face last night. Do you know this bitch and I grew up in the same house, wore the same drawers, and ate out of the same pot? This bitch always wanted to be me, so she started fucking you. Say something, you fucking bastard." She stepped in his face and slapped him.

"What I told you about putting your fucking hands on me? You should've stayed your ass at the house and stopped fucking meddling," he lashed out.

"Meddling? Nigga, I gave you four fucking years and two beautiful children and here you are with this ol' shallow-ass bitch playing house while your kids need you."

"Man, get out of here and go on home."

"Man, fuck you, this bitch, and the fucking baby she carrying. I hope that little bastard don't fucking make it. I wish all of y'all just fucking die."

I ran up on that bitch and start punching her ass again.

"What the fuck you doing? You're pregnant." He grabbed me up and pushed me into a corner.

"Yo, get out of here, for real. You can't come up in nobody shit acting crazy. You could've waited 'til I came to the house."

"Nigga, fuck you. Who the fuck you think you're checking in front of this bitch? You left your good woman at home to be with a bitch who fucked and sucked everything including her mama's man when we were growing up?"

"Bitch, you're worried about the wrong motherfucking thing. You need not worry about my pussy and who I fucked. You just mad because your man chose me!"

"Bitch, whatever. Ant don't fucking want you. We supposed to be getting married and everything. I am his woman and the mother of his children. All you are is some easy pussy. Niggas don't respect your kind. Come on, baby, let's go home. We can work through this shit." She gave me an evil look and grabbed Micah's arm.

"No, stop! Get off me. I'm not going anywhere with you. I asked you to leave because I didn't want to do this in front of anybody. But you are pushing it. I am not with you. I told you it was over. I am with Tiana now and she's having my seed."

I watched as the smile she had a minute ago disappeared off her face. That bitch looked like she was constipated and need to take a quick shit.

"Boy, quit playing. You 'ont want this hood bugger bitch who has been run through by e'ery-damn-body. Boy, let's go home to our babies." She grabbed his arm.

"Nah, B, I'm for real. I ain't know y'all was related and shit, but the fact is I'm in love with her. She is my woman and I don't want to be with you anymore."

"Are you fucking serious? I know you mad right now, but you can't be serious. You bitch, how could you do this to me? I promise on my mama, I am going to pay you back in full, bitch," she said storming out the door.

I walked over to the door and locked it. I was scared to turn around and face him. I knew he had all sorts of questions, which I knew I had to answer.

"Your sister? Did you know she was my baby mama?" he asked with an attitude.

I stayed quiet for a few minutes, then I spoke, carefully choosing my words. "Micah, I swear to you, I did not know who you were until the other day when I put two and two together. By then, it was too late and I didn't know how to tell you. I didn't want to lose you."

"You think it's so fucking easy to lose me? I fucking love you, but I didn't want to have kids by two sisters. That's some bullshit. She never mentioned that she had a sister and neither did you."

"That's because we're not blood sisters. It's a long story. My mother's boyfriend tried to rape me when I was younger, so I ran to her house. I ended up staying for good with her and her mother. I thought we were close. So no, we're not blood sisters."

He let a deep sigh of relief. "Man, this shit is crazy." He rubbed his hands over his face. Baby boy looked stressed out, like the world was coming down on his shoulders.

The sound of glass breaking caught us both off guard. We both ran to the door. I opened it and saw that bitch smiling at me as she pulled off. We both looked at each other and stepped outside, and that's when we saw what that sound was. All his windows on his car were shattered. I couldn't believe this bitch.

"I'm about to call the motherfuckin' police." I turned to go back into the house.

"Nah, ma, don't even do that. I'll deal with her myself. I can't put my kids through no more drama."

"Listen, if you keep giving her ass passes, she's gonna make your life hell. You need to get this shit under control before it gets worse." I stormed off into the house.

I was so mad that I felt my blood boiling. I tried to count backward to cool down my temper. I rubbed my stomach as I thought about my baby. I felt a few kicks and then a sharp pain ripped through my stomach.

"Aargh, Aargh," I screamed out as I stumbled to the couch.

"T, you a'ight?" He ran to my side.

"I don't know. I am hot and I'm feeling dizzy."

"Hold on." He ran out of the living room. He came back in with a glass of ice water. I gulped the water down without taking a breath. I waited a few minutes but I still felt like I was going to pass out.

"I'm taking you to the hospital. Come on." He pulled me up gently off the couch.

I hated hospitals, but I knew I needed to go so I could get my baby checked out. The last few days had been very stressful and now all this shit that happened this morning.

We got into my car and he drove off. I laid my head back and just let my mind wander off. I couldn't believe the shit that went down this morning. That bitch was dead-ass wrong to come up in my shit behaving like that. Ayana knew that the old me would've trampled her ass. *She better be thankful that I'm pregnant and don't want to cause harm to my baby. I bet she would get satisfaction out of me losing my baby.*

"You a'ight over there?" he inquired.

"Yes, just feeling a little queasy that's all."

He put his hand on top of mine and rubbed it. "Babe, I love you and I ain't goin' nowhere. I just want you to know that!"

I didn't respond. I just smiled at him. I believed he loved me, but this was a hell of a love triangle that we were involved in. I knew how evil she could get and I knew shit was about to get ugly.

CHAPTER NINETEEN

Ayana

I'd met a lot of grimy bitches before, but I knew how to deal with them. What I didn't know how to deal with was a bitch who pretended like she fucked with me. I done fed this hungry bitch, let her wear my fucking clothes down to my drawers, and this was how she repaid me. After I busted out all his windows, I jumped in my car and pulled off.

Driving fast through the subdivision, tears started to flow as it finally hit me that my nigga was having a baby with another bitch. Not just a regular bitch, but one I knew. My heart felt like it had been ripped out of my body and there was a big hole. This shit wasn't going to end like this, mark my words; the game was just beginning. I hoped all the players were ready for the drama that was about to unfold.

I pulled up at Mama's house. God knows I didn't want to hear her damn mouth. I just wanted to grab my fucking kids and head on home. If only it was that easy.

I rang the doorbell and she answered with an irritated look on her face. "You really need to find you a babysitter to watch these children. I am sick and tired of you running over here dropping them off," she vented.

"Damn, Mama, you act like you got shit to do. The way I fucking see it, you should be happy to watch them; after all, you were too fucking drunk to watch my ass when I was growing up," I lashed out.

"Excuse me, you better watch your mouth up in my house. You lay down and made them, so you better put on your big girl's panties, you and that bastard. Shit, I was the one who kept them while you were in the hospital. So before you turn your disrespectful ass to tell me what I didn't do, look around. I am the only person you have."

"Where are my damn kids? Diamond and Dominique, come on. Let's go home," I yelled toward the back room. "You know what, you never liked me anyway. You always picked that bitch Tiana over your own flesh and blood. You know what, I'm dead to you."

"I've loved you from the day I felt you growing inside of me. It is you who grew up rotten and spoiled, thinking e'erything should be your way. Hell, Tiana was more appreciative of the little things I did for her, but not you. You always fussed and carried on, whenever you didn't get your way. I'm not shocked that boy didn't stick around; your damn mouth done ran him off."

"I hate you, bitch! You will never see me or my children any-fucking-more," I said as I took a step closer to her face.

I grabbed my kids' stuff from the couch and dragged them out of the house. This bitch was another one I was done with. I didn't need no fucking mother anyway.

By the time I got home I was exhausted to the point where I wanted to just fall out. These fucking kids didn't make it any easier. They kept crying and asking for their daddy. I needed a fucking cigarette so I grabbed one out of my purse and smoked it. That didn't help so I went in the cupboard and took out a bottle of gin he had. I didn't bother to grab a cup; I took it straight to the head. Going down my throat, the strong, fiery sensation stung my throat. I wanted to scream out, but I didn't flinch. I continued drinking until the bottle was empty.

I staggered upstairs to my bedroom, grabbed my bottle of Percocet, and took out a few and swallowed them with bathroom water. I looked in the mirror at my reflection. I was hurt and broken. *I'm a bad bitch, my pussy is tight, and it stays wet. My head game is mean, so why would this nigga choose a boring-ass bitch over me?* This was the question that I kept racking my brain about.

I scooted down on the floor by the tub and cried my heart out, tears of pain, deep pain. "God, please let Ant come back home to his family. I need him. God, I swear if you let him, I will be the best woman to him. I promise, God," I said as I bawled my heart out.

CHAPTER TWENTY

Tiana

I was told by the doctors that I was dehydrated. The doctor also ordered an ultrasound to check on my baby. After the ultrasound, the nurse wheeled me downstairs and hooked me up to an IV. I instantly felt my energy starting to come back. I made a mental note to myself to do better. I was only four months away and I couldn't risk anything happening. The nurse asked me if I wanted to know the sex of the baby, but I told her no. Even though I knew Micah wanted to know, I urged him to let us wait until the day when I give birth. I wanted a girl, and he wanted a boy so I thought it was best to not know. Either way, I was going to love my baby.

I turned to my side and saw that he was asleep in the chair. I felt a slight bit of anger toward him. I mean, he should've settled that shit he had going on with Ayana before he even tried to holler at me. I told his ass I wasn't the kind of woman who messed with a nigga who had a bitch. I felt betrayed because, the way she was talking, it's like he was still sort of playing house with her ass. I swore I would leave his behind if he didn't get this straightened out. *Ain't no motherfucking way I'ma play any nigga's side bitch or even the main bitch who knows that he got a side bitch.*

After a few hours, they finally discharged me from the hospital. I was happy that I didn't have to spend the night. Ever since I was a little child I hated the hospital.

The ride home was kind of quiet. I felt like he was as deep in his thoughts as I was in mine. I was trying to come up with the right way to let him know that Ayana had set up the whole thing with dude. I wanted to just blurt it out, but after the way he accused me this morning of being jealous, I had to do it differently.

"I need to talk to you," I said in a low tone.

"Whaddup, talk to me," he said as he continued staring straight ahead.

"Listen, this is serious and I need you to know this has nothing to do with jealousy."

"Come on, ma, stop beating 'round the bush already."

"Well, since it's all out in the open that Ayana and I know each other, I have to tell you that she was trying to set you up with dude who shot her."

"What the fuck you mean, B? You 'ont know what you talkin' 'bout. She is nagging and getting on my last motherfucking nerves at times, but one thing I do know is shawty is loyal as fuck. She wouldn't do no shit like that."

"Really? Do you really know her, or do you just know the image she tries to portray? I know you don't know this, but I went to go see her in the hospital, and she told me everything that went down. How she fucked dude in y'all bed, and she called dude up one night when y'all was beefing and they agreed to meet up at the hotel. I guess the shit backfired, 'cause dude ended up taking the pussy then he shot her. Have you ever wondered how the hell she got to the hotel? Her car was parked outside of the hotel, so when did dude kidnap her?"

"Man, I hope you ain't making this shit up 'cause you mad. I heard some rumors the other day that dude was bragging that he was fucking my bitch. I laughed that shit off, 'cause I know shawty would never fuck wit' a nigga she knew I was beefing wit'. Now you sitting here telling me this bullshit," he said through clenched teeth.

He banged his hand on the steering wheel, and then yelled, "Fuck!" I saw the anger displayed on his face as he started doing eighty miles per hour down the highway that was only sixty-five miles per hour. I grabbed on to my seat as I stared out the window.

"So how long you know this shit and didn't say anything to me about it? Damn, you supposed to be my bitch, my ride or die, my everything and you knew this shit and kept quiet. I could've lost my fucking life a few weeks back behind this bitch!"

"First off, lower your fucking voice. Don't you get a fucking attitude because that bitch betrayed you. True enough, I should've told you when I found out but I didn't know how to even bring that to you when you had no idea that you was fucking with two friends. But you need to man up and take responsibility; you are the one who chose her and got yourself into this mess. I learned a long time ago you can't turn no ho into a housewife so quit throwing the blame around. You chose a ho to wife."

I knew I was a bit harsh, but he needed to hear it. I wasn't into sparing niggas' feelings especially when my feelings were crushed and nobody gave a fuck about mine.

CHAPTER TWENTY-ONE

Ayana

I was feeling really down, so my homegirl came through to see me. She brought some good weed and a bottle of vodka. It was exactly what the doctor ordered to fix my broken heart.

"Bitch, so tell me what happened when you went over the bitch house."

"Bitch, I was shocked as fuck when I saw it was the bitch I call my sissy. This bitch been fucking my nigga all along and my dumb ass didn't know it."

"Are you fucking serious? I hope you dragged that bitch. If it were me, I would've given her an ass whipping that she'd remember for the rest of her fucked-up life," she said. "So what the fuck that nigga say?" She looked at me.

"Girl, you ain't gon' believe this shit. This bum-ass nigga gon' tell me to leave because he's with her now. You should've seen my face when that bum said that." I took a long pull off the blunt and passed it to her.

"You better than me, 'cause I would've whupped that bitch so bad and his ass would've got beat down too. Mari know damn well he can't play them kind of games with my ass." She shook her head.

"Bitch, I swear, I'ma fix that nigga's ass real good. I just need a little break to clear my head. That ho gon' wish she never crossed me," I warned.

"I 'ont blame you. That's your man; don't let no bitch step in and take your man from you."

I remained quiet and took a sip of my liquor. They had no idea what I was capable of. *But soon, and I mean soon, they'll find out that Ayana is not to be fucked with.*

I quickly snapped back to reality when I heard my door opening. Only one person had a key so I knew it was him. I couldn't believe that after all that went down, he had the nerve to come up in here. I knew he couldn't stay away from me and this good pussy. I got up and walked out into the hallway. "Hey, babe," I greeted him with a big, broad smile.

"Yo, who in here?"

"Why, it's only Lori."

"Yo, B, you need to go," he said in an angry tone.

"What kind of shit you on? You can't just come up in here and put my motherfucking bitch out," I screamed. I was livid at this nigga's behavior.

"Bitch, shut up! Nah, B, you heard what I said. You need to get the hell on before I throw you out."

"Nigga, I 'ont know who the fuck you talkin' to like that, but I ain't this bitch. Girl, let me get outta here before I hurt this nigga's feelings."

"Like I said, bitch, get out."

"Yo, you are so fucking disrespectful. I don't disrespect your fucking friends, so please don't disrespect mines." I locked the door behind Lori.

"Bitch, shut the fuck up." He grabbed me by my hair.

"Let me go. What the hell are you doing?"

"Sit down." He shoved me onto the couch.

"Boy, what the fuck is wrong wit' you? Don't come in here putting your fucking hands on me." I was fuming with anger.

"Yo, I'ma ask you this one time and one time only. What the fuck happened the day you got shot? Bitch, you better think wisely before you speak." He pulled a gun out of his waistband.

"I told you what happened numerous times. So what's up with all this questioning?" I was annoyed as hell.

"Bitch, was you fucking ol' boy? And how the fuck you end up at the hotel? See, at first I didn't question all that, 'cause I trusted you. But, bitch, I know you was fucking him, even in the bed I shared with you. You a dirty bitch for real," he yelled.

Tears rolled down my face, but there was no way I was going to sit there and listen to him talk to me like I was a piece of shit. "Really, you over here talkin' 'bout loyalty? You been left; that is my fucking bed. The minute you started screwing that ho, you gave all them rights up. I am a grown-ass woman so if I want to fuck another nigga, I can."

Blap! Blap! Blap! He slapped me across my face back to back. I grabbed my face and leapt toward him. "Bitch, I dare you to jump out there." He looked at me with the coldest evil look I'd ever seen in my life.

"Daddy, Daddy, Daddy," the girls ran in and said in unison.

I looked at him then back at my girls. "I swear on my girls, you will never get to see them again. You chose that bitch and her fucking bastard she's about to have. We good over here, I promise you that."

He walked toward me again but my daughter yelled, "Daddy, please don't hurt Mommy."

He pulled back, but mouthed, "Fuck you, bitch."

"Now get your ass out of my shit before I call the police on you." I folded my arms and stared him down.

"Come here, babies." He stooped down to their level hugging and kissing them.

I turned my fucking head because I knew that shit wasn't sincere. How could it be? He left us to start a whole new family with that two-faced bitch. My daughters were his first children, but now he done moved out and replaced them. *He better get ready, 'cause come Monday morning my ass gon' be the first one at the child support office. I'll be damned if that bitch and her child is gon' take food out of my kids' and my mouths.*

That bastard then got up, and walked past me and through the door. I ran to the living room and grabbed my phone off the coffee table and dialed 911.

"Hello, 911 operator. How may I help you?"

"Hello, hello, I need the police at 2654 Rock Chapel Road." I started crying.

"Ma'am, can you tell me what the problem is?"

"My baby's father just beat me up bad, real bad," I cried.

"Can you give me his name? And is he still on the property?"

"His name is Anthony Micah Brown. Oh, no, he ran out the door. I'm not sure if he's outside. I'm so scared. Please send me some help please," I bawled into the phone.

"Ma'am, make sure the door is locked. Paramedics and the police are on the way."

I didn't even respond. I quickly hung up the phone and ran upstairs. I knew this was going to hurt, but this pain was no match for the pain I was feeling inside. I took my head and banged into my bathroom wall until blood started spilling. I banged my forehead a few times, until the pain became unbearable. I then got up and grabbed a towel to stop the flow of blood. I looked in the mirror and was very pleased. I then went downstairs where the girls were watching TV. "Come here, y'all. You see what Daddy did to Mommy?" I removed the towel so they could get a good look at their daddy's handiwork.

My youngest daughter started yelling, "Daddy hurt Mommy bad. Mommy bleeding."

"Mommy, I don't like Daddy, 'cause he hurt my mommy." She too started crying. The crying from my babies triggered my tears. I sat on the couch and held them close as all three of us mourned.

Boom! Boom! Boom! I heard loud banging on the door.

"Mommy, someone is banging on the door." Diamond grabbed my arm closer to her.

"It's the police. No need to be scared. Remember if they ask you any questions, just let them know what Daddy did to Mommy, okay?"

"Okay, Mommy."

I got up and removed the towel so the blood could run freely and then I opened the door.

"Ma'am, you call 911 because you're injured?"

"Yes," I said as I "fainted" in the ambulance worker's arms. I was careful not to go down too hard just in case that fool didn't catch me. I closed my eyes and slowed my breathing down.

"Get a stretcher," the female yelled.

"I got a pulse," someone else hollered.

A few minutes later, I started to slowly open my eyes.

"She's coming to."

"Ma'am, can you hear me? What's your name?"

I slowly opened my eyes and looked around as if I was confused.

"The oldest girl said, 'My daddy hurt my mama.' Get her in the ambulance."

During the ride to the hospital, they checked my pulse and asked me questions about what happened. I told them everything they needed to know and then I gave them that bastard's name along with that bitch's address.

"Ma'am, is there anyone we can we call to come get your daughters?"

"Yes, you can call my mama." I gave them her phone number. I knew we weren't talking, but that bitch needed to come get these kids.

I watched as the officer wrote down the information that I was giving him. Ant's ass was going to regret ever playing his fucking games with me.

I closed my eyes as I daydreamed about them picking up that bitch-ass nigga. I could see the look on that bitch's face when her man was dragged off to jail. The DeKalb County court system did not play that bullshit. Domestic violence was a very serious charge.

CHAPTER TWENTY-TWO

Tiana

Micah stormed in the house earlier huffing and puffing. I was scared because of the look he had on his face. I'd seen him angry before, but nothing like this. What scared me the most was when he took his shirt off and I saw the gun tucked in his waistband.

"What's going on with you?"

"Yo, I might be going to jail tonight."

"What the fuck happened?" I sat up in the bed.

"Ma, I hit that bitch."

"Why would you do that? I mean I know you mad because of the shit I told you earlier, but you know better than that. You a man; you don't put your hands on no woman."

"Ma, fuck all that. That bitch was popping off at the mouth. Anyways, if I get locked up, I want you to hit my man Lo up and he will bring you some money for my bond and lawyer."

"You think she called the police on you?"

"Shit, that bitch tried to set me up to get robbed so I wouldn't put it past that bitch."

No sooner than the words left his mouth, I heard a loud bang on the door. I knew it was the police. I just looked at him.

"Yo, put this gun in a hiding place and tell them this your shit. They can't just come up in here without a search warrant. Yo, ma, you know I love you and I will be right back home. Call the number I gave you and get on it ASAP. I'll more than likely have a bond." He grabbed my face and kissed me passionately.

"I can tell them you were here with me all day."

"Nah, hell no, I don't want you to get involved in any of this. You have our seed to worry about. Now go answer the door."

Tears filled my eyes as I walked to the door. This was the kind of shit I was trying to escape.

"Hello, may I help you?"

"Yes, ma'am, we're here to talk to Anthony Brown. Is he here?"

I thought about lying but his car was parked out front and I didn't need them coming in. Especially with the illegal gun being in the house. I was a ride or die to a certain extent, but going to jail for a nigga wasn't included in me riding. "Yes, he's here. Let me get him."

I slightly closed the door and yelled, "Micah, the police are here to see you." He was right behind the door. I was just playing it off. He stepped out in the open.

"You Anthony Brown? Step out here for me. We need to talk to you about an incident."

As soon as he stepped out, one of the officers stepped closer and grabbed his arm, put it behind his back, and pushed him up against the wall.

"What the hell you doing that for?" I asked in a loud tone.

"Ma'am, please step back," he warned.

"Babe, go back into the house and do what I told you to do."

"Anthony Brown, you're under arrest for the assault on Ayana Beasly. You have the right to remain silent."

I didn't wait. I went inside and slammed the door. I went over to the window and peeped out as they dragged him off to the police car that was waiting by the curb. It was so hard to see them dragging my man off as if he was a hardened criminal. I wanted to break down as I stood in the window still staring into space as they drove off. I saw a few people standing outside so I closed the curtains and wiped my tears. It then hit me that I should be calling his homeboy.

***

I called the jail to find out what he was charged with. The clerk at DeKalb County Jail informed me that he was charged with battery and was given a $20,000 bond. I felt a sigh of relief when I learned he had a bond. His homeboy already had a bondsman on the way to get him out.

I was feeling drained. I cried so much that the tears would not come out anymore. I took a hot shower to soothe the pain of my aching body. I had my eyes closed while the water beat down on my body. I felt a sharp pain followed by more sharp pains. I clutched my stomach and cut the water off. Then I grabbed my towel and wrapped it around me. I could barely walk because of the pressure between my legs.

I grabbed my cell phone and thought about calling 911 but quickly decided against it. I grabbed a pair of sweatpants and a white tee and put them on. I grabbed my keys and made my way down the stairs. I used all my energy to get to the car. I got in and sped off. The nearest hospital to me was DeKalb Medical on Hillandale. I didn't like that hospital, but I didn't have a choice. *I hope my baby is all right,* was the only thought in my head.

I sped all the way to the hospital. I pulled up by the entrance and hopped out. As soon as I stood up, I felt a gush of water coming down my legs. "Help me, my water just broke," I yelled out.

The guard rushed over to me and picked me up. "Get some doctors out here. She's in labor."

An hour later, my baby boy, Anthony Micah Brown Jr., entered this fucked-up-ass world. I was so angry that his daddy wasn't with me to experience the joy that I felt. I had to say it was the best feeling when I looked into my li'l man's eyes. It was love at first sight and to know he was conceived in love made it even more special. I wiped away a tear as I held him close to my heart. I made a vow to protect him by any means necessary and that meant to make sure that his daddy was always around him.

CHAPTER TWENTY-THREE

Ayana

Ant, the man I fell in love with and gave two beautiful girls to, had turned into a selfish bastard. If I had any hope of us getting back together, it was totally gone after he got arrested. I was determined to destroy him and that bitch and I didn't care how it happened.

I called the jail and found out that Ant was out. This kind of fucked my nerves up because I didn't know if he was going to come to the house. I got up early because I had some things to do, including getting a bigger gun.

I searched my phone and found the number I was looking for. I hadn't spoken to Daquan in years, but I knew he was still around. He was that nigga you need to talk to if you need anything, and I mean anything.

"Hello, Daquan?" I asked.

"Who wants to know?" he asked with an attitude.

"Boy, it's me, Ayana." I laughed.

"Who?"

"Ayana. So you gon' play like you 'ont remember me?"

"Oh, damn, Ayana. It's been a minute. What's good wit'cha, girl?"

"Nada. I need to holla at you 'bout something. You know."

"Oh, word. Well, in that case, you know I'm always available; plus, I'll get to see your sexy ass," he joked.

"I'm at home. You can come through today."

"You in the same spot over on Rock Chapel?"

"Yes, I am. Just hit my phone when you coming."

"A'ight." He hung up the phone.

I guessed he wasn't playing no games because an hour later he was calling my phone to let me know he was on his way to the house. I immediately jumped into the shower. I bathed, got out, then got dressed. I put on my little sundress without underwear. I looked in the mirror and saw my fat pussy print showing. I smiled at myself in the mirror. *What nigga in his right mind would leave all this pussy to go chase another bitch?* I thought as I used my hand and patted my pussy.

I heard the girls in their room playing. I sure wished I didn't cuss Mama out because I could've taken them over there. I didn't give a fuck though as long as they kept their little asses in their room. Their daddy should've kept his ass at home; then Mama wouldn't be bringing no other nigga in the house.

I heard the doorbell ringing so I sashayed down the stairs. I opened it and let his fine ass in. That nigga looked and smelled like new money. He was iced out from head to toe and, when he smiled, he showed his mouthful of gold. His appearance immediately gave me a tingling sensation between my legs.

"Whaddup, shawty, how you been?"

"I've been good," I flirted with him.

"Shit you look good. You still fucking with your baby daddy? Last time we talked, you was tryin'a settle down and shit. How that work out for you?"

"Nah, me and that nigga broke up awhile back."

"Oh, okay, I hear you. So what kind of business you tryin'a discuss?" He kept looking at my breasts.

"Damn, you see something you like?"

"Hell yeah, all that." He pointed at my body.

"A man who knows what he wants. I like that," I said seductively.

Before you knew it we were on the couch bumping and grinding and tonguing down one another. This was my first time having sex after that nigga raped me and I thought it was going to be painful, but to my surprise I enjoyed it. He dug into every inch of my pussy and I ground on his dick, almost breaking it off. Every nigga I fucked I was always determined to show that I was a bad bitch, and he wasn't no different. I felt his dick getting harder, so I knew he was about to cum. I threw my ass up in the air as he gave my pussy the business.

"Aargh, aargh, aargh," he yelled out as he nutted all up in my pussy. I was shocked that this nigga took that chance even though he had a girl. I quickly took my mind off that bitch. Shit, a bitch took my baby daddy, fucked him, and got pregnant by him without giving a damn about my feelings.

I watched as he walked out of the bathroom. "Yo, you on birth control right?"

"Sure am," I lied. These niggas were backward as fuck. You were supposed to find out if a bitch was on birth control before you nutted all up in her, not afterward.

"So what is it you want to discuss?"

"I need a gun, a bigger gun."

"I thought you had one." He looked at me.

"That's only a .22. I need something bigger, maybe a nine or .360."

"Damn, who you tryin'a kill?" he joked.

"Nobody. It's getting dangerous out in these streets and I need to protect me and the girls. My greatest fear is somebody running up in here and harming them." I sounded so sincere.

"Say no more. I got you tomorrow. Yo, just be careful."

"Thank you. How much is it?"

"Shit, nothing, if you let me come over and beat the pussy up on the regular. Girl, you got some fire."

"You got some good dick too though. That's a deal." I smiled at him.

"A'ight, I'm out. We'll link tomorrow."

I locked the door behind him. Shit, it wasn't that bad; at least the nigga had some damn money. If he thought he was going to be coming up in here fucking for free, he needed to reconsider that shit. Now that this bum wasn't lacing my pockets anymore, some other fool needed to step up to the plate.

I washed off and got the girls dressed. I was on my way to the DeKalb County DFACS office. *This nigga wanna play, I'm going to show his ass how I do it. Let's see how he feels when he gets this child support summons. I don't give a fuck if he can't pay. Matter fact, his bitch can step up to the plate and help take care of his children.*

CHAPTER TWENTY-FOUR

Tiana

The first day Micah came to visit me in the hospital, we both went to the NICU and it was a sight to see. I watched as his face lit up as he stared at his little man in the incubator.

"Man, I am so sorry I wasn't here to see you enter this world, but Daddy promises from this day on that I will always be here, li'l man." Tears welled up in his eyes as he stood beside me. This was my first time witnessing a softer side of a thug.

"Nurse, can his dad hold him for a second?"

"Sure, as long as he washes his hands." She smiled at Micah.

I was so happy that I wasn't the only one who felt the kind of love I felt the first time I held my baby boy. I knew then that father and son were forming a bond that couldn't be broken!

I was discharged from the hospital after four days, but my baby had to stay. He was only three pounds, five ounces and he had to stay in the incubator in the NICU until he could suck a bottle on his own. Leaving him was the hardest thing, but I took time off from school so I could be my baby's side every day. Micah and I got to the hospital early every morning and spent all day there. It was good that I had him to lean on because this was hard for me.

One day on our way home from the hospital I decided to ask Micah a question. I knew that we were dealing with so much at one time, but something was bugging me and I needed to know the answer. "Babe, did you really beat that girl up like that?"

"Hell nah, ma. I think that bitch did that to herself. When I left, she wasn't bleeding or anything."

I believed him because I could tell he was hurting behind that shit. "I can't believe she's so vindictive that she would actually pin a fucking charge on you. I swear, when I feel better I'ma beat her ass."

"Nah, don't even do that. You see she's a rat and she'll call the police on you too."

"To be honest, I don't give a fuck right now. This bitch violated us when she got you locked up."

"Babe, listen; we have our little man to worry about. I'm already in the system, but you aren't and little man needs to have his mommy caring and giving him all the love he deserves. My lawyer saying we gon' beat that charge. Ma, I got this. Let your man handle this." He put his arm around me.

"You right. I'm just so damn mad."

Truth was, I wasn't trying to hear that shit. I didn't give a fuck if that bitch and I grew up together. She was my fucking enemy right now. I got it, she was mad that I took her dick, but bitch took it too far when she got my man locked up.

"Babe, I need to ask you something. I know that we haven't been together that long, but I'm checking for you hard. You are the mother of my son and the woman I want to spend the rest of my life with. I want to make you Mrs. Brown. Will you let us make it official?" He got down on his knee and in his hand he held one of the biggest rocks that I'd ever laid eyes on outside of television.

I sat there staring at him, or more so the ring.

"Is that a yes, no, or maybe so?" He poked me.

"Are you sure this is what you want to do? I mean, we got a lot going on right now."

"I'm dead ass. I want to make you mine forever. I'm done wit' these streets. I want to be the best husband and father to our child."

I was confused. I wanted to say yes, but something kept reminding of all the shit we were going through. I was about to say no when a little voice in my head said, *bitch, you better stop tripping and cuff that nigga.*

"Yes, I will marry you."

He slid the ring on my finger. I couldn't take off my eyes off of it. I grabbed him and hugged him tight. I didn't care what happened or who tried to break us up; he was my man and I was his queen. I wasn't going anywhere!

"Well, now you have a wedding to plan. You know I got to show off and let the world know you my wife!"

"Really?" I busted out laughing. I ain't gon' lie, I was smiling all over. My life hadn't been easy, and most of my life people treated me like shit, but here I was with my own little family. I looked up to the roof and whispered, "Thank you," to the Man above. Finally, I was happy.

The next morning, I got up and made breakfast for my future husband. I was still floating on cloud nine. I was happy to see it wasn't a dream because this big-ass rock was still on my finger. We sat at the table eating and laughing while talking about the wedding.

"What about your family? You mentioned your mom a few times, but I never hear you talking about your dad."

"I don't have any family. As for a dad, I never met the sperm donor and, as for a mother, that bitch chose her man over me so that's the reason why I don't talk about her ass often. Ain't nothing good to say."

"I'm sorry, ma, that you had such a rough childhood. Well, you have a family now: my family."

"Thanks."

His question about my family kind of blew my mood. Every once in a while my mind wandered about the bitch who birthed me. I hadn't seen her or heard from her in years and frankly I didn't want to. The last I heard that bum she was with had raped a young girl and got sent to prison. I swore on everything that bitch was dead to me. What woman would choose dick over her seed? I guessed a lonely bitch would. She was the reason why I chose to study psychology, so I could counsel abused children. I vowed to never treat my children the way she treated me.

"Babe, you all right? I didn't mean to upset you."

"Nah, I'm good. I just don't want to hear about no family. You and my son are my family now."

"And you know I got you right? I promise you from this day on you ain't got to worry 'bout shit ever. You and my little man good, you hear me?"

The ringing sound of my phone caught my attention. I grabbed my phone off the table. I looked at the caller ID. It read Private.

"Hello."

No response.

"Hello, who is this?" I said in a high-pitched tone.

There was still no response, just heavy breathing followed by laughing. I could tell it was a female voice.

"Listen, whoever this is, you need to get the fuck off my phone and go find something to do with your life." I hung the phone up without waiting for a response.

"Who is it?"

"I don't know, 'cause the dumb ho didn't say anything. She just kept breathing hard and laughing."

"Really? I hope it ain't Ayana doing that stupid shit."

I didn't respond. I just sat there thinking, *this bitch is really trying it. I don't know how much of this shit I can take.* "I know it's her stupid ass. I ain't never had nobody calling my phone before all this shit popped off. I'm telling you this: this your kids' mother, but that bitch doesn't mean shit to me and I am sick of this shit already," I yelled and walked off.

He grabbed my arm. "Damn, you going off on me like I'm the one doing this shit. I told you that bitch was childish and that's why I ain't wanna fuck with her anymore."

"I understand everything you're saying. But I fucking blame you. You should've made sure you and that ho was totally over before you started fucking me. I told you from day one I don't do drama well and I also don't do bitches with drama. The truth is I fucking love you, but I love me more and I am not gonna live my life going through this shit wit' your dumbass baby mama. All you niggas need to think first before y'all stick your dicks up into these dumbass bitches because this shit is the outcome."

I snatched my arm away and walked up the stairs. I loved this man, but I was not prepared to deal with this dumbass bitch.

CHAPTER TWENTY-FIVE

Ayana

These fucking nights were getting hard without Ant. I was so angry that this nigga chose that dumbass bitch over me. He hadn't even come around to check on the girls and when I called his phone it kept going to voice mail. I lay in the bed twisting and turning. I couldn't sleep so many thoughts of hurting him and his bitch invaded my mind.

I can't wait 'til he gets those child support papers and gets served with my restraining order I took out against him. He can't come within fifty yards of me and the girls.

I got up and took my Percocet out of the drawer. I went downstairs and poured me a huge cup of Cîroc. I downed around three Percocet. Within minutes I started to feel the effects of the pills mixed with the liquor.

I walked into my living room and cut on my stereo. I already had my favorite K. Michelle CD in. "These Niggas Ain't Loyal" was the first song on the CD.

I sang right along with her. I was mad and the alcohol made me even angrier. I picked up my phone to call his mama. I swore this bitch had to know about this bullshit.

"Hello," I said when she answered.

"Yes? How my grandbabies doing?"

"My kids are fine, but I ain't call to update you about my kids. I want to know how long have you known your son was screwing my sister?"

"Excuse me, have you been drinking? Don't you ever call my phone and ask me no dumbass question like that. My son is a grown-ass man and is very capable of choosing who he wants to be with. You need to stop worrying about who he is screwing and worry about taking care of them babies. And, just so you know, I know my son ain't hit you like you said. I raised my boys better than that, but I tell you what: if my baby get any time behind your ass, I'ma be there to whup that ass."

"You know what, bitch, it's women like you who's raising these dumbass niggas. I know your dumb ass never liked me, but I didn't give a fuck about that. My thing is you wasn't woman enough to tell me; instead, you pretended with your phony ass. My fucking kids don't need you or your fucking family."

"I am not even upset with you. You're the definition of a scorned woman. Let me give you a little bit of advice before I hang this phone up on your dumb ass—"

I hung the phone up before that bitch could get out the rest of her sentence. Who the fuck did this bitch think she was? Tears continued flowing as I realized that everybody knew what this nigga was doing and they all laughed in my face.

I blocked my number and called that bitch Tiana. If I couldn't have a bit of peace, there was no way her ass was going to be enjoying anything, especially not my man. I sat on the phone while the bitch kept on saying, "Hello." She eventually cussed some shit that I wasn't trying to hear. She knew what it was hitting for. I wasn't going anywhere anytime soon. I made up my mind. I was going to fight for my man, no matter how much it may have cost me.

I cried all night as I kept dialing his number, but it kept going to voice mail. Then I tried the bitch's number again but it was also turned off. I couldn't imagine him kissing her the way he used to kiss me, sliding up in her the way he used to slide up in me. The more I thought about it, the more my heart hurt. *This pain is getting to be too much,* I thought before my tired ass finally dozed off.

The next day ol' boy came through for me. He brought me a .360. I showed him how grateful I was by sucking him off in his car. Even though I liked him, he wasn't Ant, and that's who my heart belonged to. I swallowed his cum, wiped my mouth off, got the bag he gave me, and exited the vehicle. I wasn't feeling any better and didn't want to be around anybody for real.

I couldn't eat and I definitely couldn't sleep. The hatred in me just kept building up. All I did for the next few days was drink and pop pills. I felt bad that all I kept feeding the kids were noodles and cereal. I wasn't in the mood to cook shit. I remembered when I didn't want no fucking kids. All I wanted was to travel around the world. It wasn't until I met this bum that the idea of kids popped in my mind. *Now look at this shit; he don't even want the fucking kids I gave him. I had them for him, to keep his ass around with that money. Now I'm stuck with all this fucking aggravation of raising these fucking kids by myself.*

CHAPTER TWENTY-SIX

Tiana

A month later

Today was a great day for us. Our baby boy, who we nicknamed Baby Micah, was released from the hospital. My family was now complete. Just watching the way Micah interacted with his son made me aware that I made the right choice when I chose him to become my child's father.

That's why I knew he was going through turmoil because he couldn't see his daughters. About a week ago, we were outside sitting on the porch when a sheriff walked up and handed him a paper. When he opened it, he noticed it was a temporary restraining order against him. He was not allowed to go anywhere near his daughters.

As he sat there playing with our son, I saw a tear drop from his eye. "You a'ight, babe?" I quizzed him.

"Nah, man, I ain't good. I'm hurting, B. I want to see my daughters. Since the day they were born, I made sure that I was there. I'm their fucking daddy and they are my everything. This bitch is really trying it. On the real, I want to hurt her really bad."

"Babe, listen, hurting her is not going to solve anything. You need to deal wit' her through the courts. Take her to court so you can get visitation. I'm not telling you to get full custody, but if that bitch playing, I say go for it."

I hated that he was hurting and there was nothing I could do to ease his pain. That bitch was selfish and wasn't thinking about her children, only about her fucking feelings.

I got dressed and left the house. Micah and Baby Micah were spending a daddy and son day together. I told him I was going to the mall at Stonecrest, but I lied. I was on a mission that I couldn't let him know about. I knew I was out of pocket for this one, but I'd be damned if I was going to sit back and do nothing.

I pulled up at Ayana's address and dashed up the driveway. I sat on the doorbell without easing up.

That bitch popped the door open with an attitude look on her face. "What the fuck would you want with me?"

"I want to talk to you."

"Talk to me? Bitch, you funny. We ain't got shit to talk about. Now get the fuck off my property before I call the police on your ass." She tried to slam the door in my face.

I used my foot to block it and pushed the door open wider.

"Bitch, you can't get just come up in my shit."

"Like I said, we need to talk. First off, what the fuck is wrong with you? It's stinking like hell up in here. This place is a hot fucking mess." I took a quick glance toward the kitchen. I could see dishes piled up, garbage on the floor, and leftover food all over the place. I was so disgusted that she was living like this. "Where are the kids at? I hope they are not here in this mess."

"Ha-ha, you're a funny bitch! Now you're worried about my children? Were you worried when you was fucking their daddy and taking him away from them, 'Auntie'?"

"I already told you already that it wasn't my intention and I did not know that he was your man. Now that I know, I see things differently.

I don't want to fight with you at all. We are supposed to be better than that; you are my sissy."

Clap! Clap! "Standing fucking ovation. Bitch, you need a fucking sisters of honor medal award for that fucking speech."

"You know what? I came here in peace, but I see you're not trying to work it out."

"Work it out? I see you had the little bastard so now you're his baby mama. What is there to work out? Can you bring my kids' daddy back home where he belongs?"

"Yes, you can have him. I don't want him anymore after I found out he was your children's father. I swear we're not together anymore."

Her face lit up as she looked at me. "You lying, bitch."

"You know me better than anyone else and you know I don't like to lie. We are done. I still can't believe you ain't cut his ass when he beat you up like that. I put him out the day he got bonded out."

"Since y'all broke up, I know I can tell you. That nigga didn't do shit to me. I banged my head into the wall until I drew blood. I swear that shit hurt, but it was well worth it. I can't wait for our court date, but if he comes back home, I'll drop the charges against him. See, sis, this nigga don't know who really fucking with."

You were lying? So you telling me your psychotic ass banged your own head into the wall?
"So he didn't hit you?" I asked.

"Bitch, no. You know damn well if a nigga hit me like that, I would be trying to cut his face up. I ain't playing that shit."

I stood there. I was shocked this bitch was standing here bragging like that. I was boiling on the inside, but I couldn't let it show. "Damn! You a bad bitch. I swear."

"Yeah, but don't tell anybody. I'm sorry it didn't work out between y'all. I'm sure there's a good man out there for you, boo. I just really need him in me and my children lives."

"Well, you got him. Well, I got to run. You will see me soon."

"Come here give your sissy a hug."

"Sure." I cringed as I hugged her because she smelled like the garbage truck. I assumed that she hadn't bathed in a while.

I was happy to be out of that fucking apartment and back into fresh air. I took a long sigh as I walked to my car. I got in, locked my door, and pulled off. I saw her peeping through the window. When I was well past her house, I pulled out the mini recorder that I had under my shirt.

Gotcha! That bitch thinks she is the smartest, but in reality she is just another dumb ho.

CHAPTER TWENTY-SEVEN

Ayana

At first I was pissed off that Tiana came to my house, but I soon got over it after she informed me that she was no longer with my baby daddy. I was dancing on the inside, but I was careful not to let her see the joy I was feeling on the inside.

I wanted to knock myself in the head because I was so caught up in the moment that I told that bitch what I did. It wasn't until after she left that I realized that I fucked up. *Anyways that bitch better keep her mouth shut.* That bitch really thought that I fucked with her; hell no. I was just being myself by being fake to that ho. *Oh, well, now that Ant done left her ass . . .*

Yes, I knew she didn't leave him, with her weak ass. I knew it was only a matter of time before Ant was going to come to his senses and come home to me and the girls.

CHAPTER TWENTY-EIGHT

Tiana

I Googled the number for the Georgia Division of Family and Children Services. I wasn't familiar with how the system worked, but I needed someone to get over to the apartment and check on the children. I knew they were not my kids and maybe I was overstepping my boundaries, but those were Micah's children and, after I saw the condition that house was in, I couldn't sit back and not report this shit.

The lady who took the report was very nice and listened attentively as I gave her details of why I thought the kids were neglected.

"Ma' am, I really do appreciate you contacting us and we will look into these allegations immediately."

"Thank you. At the end of the day I'm not trying to get anyone in trouble. I just want the kids to be safe."

"Thank you. I wish more people would do the same to protect our children."

"You're welcome. Have a good day."

"Babe, who was that you were talking to you?" Micah startled me.

"Oh, that was one of the counselors at school. She was just going over my leave of absence with me." I smiled. "Speaking of school, are you gonna go before you get dropped from the course?"

"Babe, I ain't gon' even lie to you. I ain't focused on that right now. My life is fucked up, I'm looking at time, and I can't see my fucking kids. I need to grind harder so I can have more money so you and little man can live comfortably if I go to prison."

"Don't you talk like that! You're going to beat it, you hear me? You need to do a leave of absence for a month or two, but don't just give up on getting your degree."

"I wish I could be as positive as you are, but this shit doesn't look good. This is the mother-fucking South and they love to lock niggas up without proof."

"What if I tell you I got proof?" I looked at him, not caring if he got mad about it. Shit, he should have been happy that I was smart enough to get him his "get out of jail" ticket.

"What you talkin' 'bout?"

"I don't want you to be mad at me, but a few days ago I went to go see Ayana."

"What the fuck you do that for? I thought I told you to stay away from that bitch. I 'ont want her to keep feeding you no lies."

I got up and opened my drawer. I took out the recording and threw it on his lap.

"What's this?" He looked puzzled.

"Just cut it on."

I sat back on the bed as he listened to the voices of me and his baby mama. This tape was even clearer than I thought.

"What the fuck? How you get her to tell you all this shit?"

"I knew that you didn't do that shit to her; plus, I was mad that she was playing games with you, especially using the kids as a pawn."

"Damn, babe, I'ma call my lawyer and tell him about this. This shit should clear my name. Ma, you just made my day."

"You know I love me some you. I just hope it helps because I can't lose you."

"Shit, I can't stand to be away from you and little man for a day much less years. Y'all my life for real."

He started kissing on me and boy was my body reacting. We hadn't had sex since I gave birth to my li'l man and that was almost two months ago. I'd been to my six-week visit and my doctor gave me the okay. I started kissing him back. He didn't waste any time. He pulled my drawers down and start playing in my pussy. My pussy was wet and he dug his fingers deep down then licked his finger.

"Just go ahead and taste it. I know you miss me, daddy," I teased.

"Say no more, baby girl." He flipped me onto my stomach and positioned me on my knees. He started licking me from the back. The touch of his cold tongue sent chills up my spine. I wanted to fuck but he had me pinned down. I couldn't move at all.

"Ohh, ohh," I moaned and groaned. My body shivered as I busted in his mouth.

He didn't move; instead, he licked up all my sweet juice. He turned me around and started kissing my breasts slowly. I felt his hard dick throbbing between my legs. I wanted him so bad, I felt like I was losing my mind. Then he slid all the way up in me then he paused for a quick second. I ground on his dick until he started grinding back. He held me close and slowly fucked me. It wasn't rushed and our souls were definitely in cahoots.

"Baby, you need to pull out."

"Damn this pussy too good. I swear I want to bust up in you."

"Well, don't. We just had a baby; plus, I don't want no more kids right now. I got to finish school."

"Babe, I'm about to busttttttttttttt," he yelled out as he jumped up off me and came all over my stomach.

I lay there trying to catch my breath. A bitch was getting old because I was breathing all heavy. He wasn't no better because his ass looked like he couldn't move.

"Let's take a shower before the baby wakes up."

"Yeah, 'cause you know he is almost up."

We got in the shower and instead of washing up, he got behind me and started rubbing his soft dick on my ass. In no time he was rock hard again. He slid up in me and started fucking me real hard. I threw my ass back on him, as he threw that dick on me. After we were finished, we washed each other and got out.

Worn out from fucking. I lotioned up and got dressed in my pajamas. It was safe to say that nigga rocked my ass to sleep.

***

I didn't see the need for a big wedding. I didn't have any family to invite. His family and a few of my friends from school were the only ones I knew. I didn't have anyone to walk me down the aisle, because my sperm donor was unknown.

Micah's mother was happy to assist me with planning the wedding. I wanted to wait until his case was over, but he didn't want to wait. I think in his mind he was scared that I would leave him if he went away for a long time. I wasn't tripping because he was really my soul mate and I wasn't going no-damn-where.

I found a cute Maggie Sottero wedding dress online, so I ordered it. I also found a pair of heels. I planned on killing it on my big day; after all, I was marrying one of the hottest niggas in DeKalb County. I knew bitches were going to be screenshotting pics and there was no way I was going to be caught slipping.

CHAPTER TWENTY-NINE

Ayana

A day went by, then two days, then three and Ant didn't call or try to come by. By the fifth day I kind of realized that he wasn't coming back. I was running out of options. The only hope that I had was I knew his behind was going to jail for beating me up.

I tried to call his cell phone but it was disconnected. His bitch ass done changed his number on me. I was about to call Tiana and ask for his number; the bitch said we were cool, so I wanted to see how cool we really were. The interruption of the doorbell prompted me to put the phone down and answer the door. On my way to the door, I said a quick prayer. "God, please let this be Ant."

I took a quick glance through the peephole and saw two women dressed in suits. I swore these Jehovah's Witness people were about to get cussed out.

"Yes? How many times I'ma tell y'all, I don't want y'all knocking on my door," I yelled.

"Excuse me, Miss Beasly?"

"Yes? And who are you? How do you know my name?"

"My name is Miss Warren and I'm with the office of Child Protective Services."

"And what is it you want with me?" I stared this bitch down.

"Someone filed a complaint about child abuse and neglect of your two daughters. Can we come in?"

"Complaint? Ain't shit wrong with my children so, lady, you can go on back where you came from."

"We need to come inside and look around to make sure the children are not being abused or neglected."

"And what's going to happen if I don't let y'all in?"

"I will call the DeKalb County Police Department and have the children removed from the home until our investigation is completed. It's in your best interest to let us inside."

I moved out of the doorway and motioned for them to come on in. I knew it didn't look good but I hadn't gotten around to washing the dishes or cleaning up yet.

"Where are the children?"

"They are in their rooms, right across the hall."

"Ma'am, it's best if you stay out here."

I watched as they both walked into the girls' room. I walked back into the living room and lit a cigarette. I was shaking so damn hard, it felt like I was convulsing. I took a few drags. I was trying to calm my nerves. Twenty minutes later they emerged from the room.

"Miss Beasly, we need to ask you some questions. Do you work?"

"No. What does that have to do with anything?"

"Do you receive any kind of assistance from the children's father or the government?"

"No, that bastard doesn't help. Matter of fact, I just put his ass on child support."

I watched as one woman walked away while she talked on her cell phone. I tried to eavesdrop, but I couldn't make out what she was saying. I swore I had a bad feeling about these two bitches.

"Ma'am, it's in the children's best interest to remove them from the home while we investigate these allegations."

"What the hell you just say? Remove them from what home? Lady, you bugging out," I shouted.

By the time I said that, I heard a loud bang on my front door. I looked at them bitches, back at my kids' room, then to the front door. I had that queasy feeling that shit was about to go down.

"That's the police at the door. They are here to assist us with the removal of the children."

The short bitch walked over to the door and opened the door. "The kids are in the back room. This is the mother."

"Ma'am, please stand back."

"You can't take my babies." I dashed to the back room, but the female cop snatched me up.

"Please calm down. You don't want your girls to see you get arrested."

"Noooooo, please don't take my babies from me. Please I'm begging y'alllllll," I screamed.

"Ma'am, please get yourself together. I don't want to cuff you."

"I don't care. I just want to die. Please don't take my girls from their mama."

I saw the male officer leading my babies out of the room and out the door. I tried to get loose from this bitch but her grip on me was too tight. My heart was minced into pieces as they walked away. The fucked-up part was my kids didn't say a fucking word to me. I was their mother and they didn't even drop a tear. That alone was piercing my soul.

"Ma'am, your kids will be put into state custody. Within forty-eight hours a petition will be filed and a court hearing will follow to decide if your children should be returned to you. It is very important that you attend all of these hearings, and follow the service plan ordered by the court."

"Bitch, fuck you! You a female; how can y'all do this to me? I am their mother," I screamed as the bitch walked out and the officer let me go.

I collapsed on the living room floor and started bawling. *How did this happen? Who did this shit to me? God, I swear I'm a good mother. My girls are all I have.* I felt so weak, like all the energy had been sucked out of my body. I knew Ant did this shit. What kind of man would do this to his children and their mama? I knew: a fucking monster.

CHAPTER THIRTY

Tiana

My big day was coming and I was more than ready. Things were kind of looking up for us. Micah gave the tape to his lawyer and we were just waiting to see if the DA was going to drop the charges. I was sure they were, but he wasn't.

I was grateful because his mother was there with me planning every step of the way. Me and this lady had grown so close that I even start calling her Ma. It was easier for me to look forward to this day, even though the bitch who birthed me wasn't going to be there.

The wedding was taking place at the Ashton Gardens all-inclusive wedding venue in Atlanta. The minute I laid eyes on that place, I knew that's where I wanted our wedding to take place. I hit up my homegirl Ebonee Oliver, from Events by Ebonee, to help us plan the wedding. I told her from the jump I didn't want a big wedding, just a small event. She jumped on it and, before I knew it, everything was well put together. She gave me a discount, which also helped, because I had no idea things were that expensive. Micah didn't care about spending; he just kept telling me I should let him worry about money. That's one of the things I loved about him: he was in control and always made sure his son and I were well taken care of.

It seemed like every time we tried to be happy something always stood in the way. So, after I called social services on Ayana, I thought they was going to go over there and investigate and at least give the bitch a warning. Wrong! Micah stormed in the house yesterday, yelling about how the state got his babies. I was just as shocked as him, because I didn't expect them to do that. The kids had a father, so if the mama was incompetent, their next choice should've been their daddy.

I ain't gon' lie, that shit hurt me when I saw him collapse on the ground hollering. I knew how much he loved those girls, and I knew he was hurting deeply.

"Baby, I'm sorry. Is there anything I can do to help you? You know I'm willing and ready." I rubbed his back.

"Ma, I 'ont know what the fuck to do. How the fuck they just gon' take my motherfucking kids? And the fucked-up part is that bitch got a restraining order against me so I can't call to see what the fuck goin' on with my kids. I want fucking answers. Who the fuck called these people and why?"

I knew then I couldn't let him know that I was the one who called. I couldn't risk him hating me. I vowed to keep my mouth shut and to act like I was just as shocked.

CHAPTER THIRTY-ONE

Ayana

A bitch must've done some fucked-up shit in life for all this to be happening to me. A few years ago I had it all: the man, the kids, and lots of money. Fast forward to today and that nigga done left me, and the fucking state took my motherfucking children behind some bogus allegation. Yes, it was bogus because even though I ain't clean up the house in a while, I made sure the kids ate. They weren't suffering like those motherfuckers claimed. I was broke as hell, I only had a few hundred dollars in my account, and I couldn't afford a good lawyer.

I still couldn't believe that Ant left me and his kids like that. I thought that after he heard about what happened to his girls, he would've at least come home so we could both fight for the girls. I now knew that nigga never loved me because, if he did, he wouldn't have been able to just up and say fuck us.

"Hey, Mama," I said as she opened her door.

"Hey. I see you got out your feelings."

"Yeah. I'm just going through a rough time." I busted out crying.

"What the hell wrong wit' you and where are the girls?"

"The state took them, Mama."

"The state? What yo' ass done did now?"

"See, you always jump to conclusions. I ain't did shit. Some dumbass bitch or nigga done made a bogus report that the kids are living in a dirty house and are not taken care of."

"Hmm, seems like you done piss somebody off. By the way, did you know that child getting married on Saturday?"

"What child you talking about? And why would I care? I got my own fucking problems."

"I'm talking 'bout Tiana. Y'all still tight right? I saw her mama the other day when I went to the food stamp office and she told me how hurt she feel because she didn't get an invite."

I looked at her to see if she was drunk. She had a habit of making up shit when she'd been drinking. "You joking right?"

"No. I thought you would be one of the bridesmaids, you two was so close. I heard she marrying some big timer with money."

I stood there in a trance. I saw her mouth moving, but I could no longer make sense of what she was saying to me.

"Did you hear what I said?"

"Uh, what?"

"Never mind. So what you gon' do about the kids? It's a shame that you let them people take them precious babies from you."

I was going to respond to her but I changed my mind. "I gotta go." I turned around and walked out of the house.

I jumped into my car and grabbed my cigarettes, quickly lighting up one. I started to shake so bad as I thought about what that drunk bitch just said. *This can't be true! And if it is, who is Tiana marrying? I need to find out.*

I called up Lori. I knew she would know because she was fucking one of Ant's boys. "Hello."

"Hey, girl, what's up?

"I have a quick question."

"What's up?"

"Did you hear anything 'bout Ant getting married on Saturday?"

"You know I don't want to get into this, but yes. I heard Mari and them talking about the wedding and they're going to a bachelor party Friday night. I called yo' ass the other night, but you ain't pick up."

"Do you know who he marrying?"

"I heard it's the girl who had his son. Girl, I was shocked 'cause I thought y'all was gon' work it out."

"I thought so too. I got to go." I hung up on that bitch. What kind of friend was she, she heard this shit and didn't tell me?

Tiana's bitch ass played me. That bitch stood in my house and lied to me. That ho deserved a medal for that performance she gave.

CHAPTER THIRTY-TWO

Tiana

Love is a beautiful thing especially if you are sharing it with the right person. I never thought this day would come, when I would be walking down the aisle and tying the knot with the sexiest man alive. We done had some rough times, and there were times when I thought we weren't going to make it, but our love for each other kept us grounded.

"You know, I am so proud of you and I am proud to call you my daughter-in-law. I never thought my son would grow up and finally find the right woman for him. Welcome to our family. You are now one of us," his mother said to me as she hugged me.

I tried my best not to shed a tear because my face was beat and my makeup was flawless. "Thank you. I love your son with everything in me and I promise to be the best wife, friend, and life partner."

"Well, let me get out here. I hear the music playing. It's almost that time."

"I will be out in a few." We hugged again before she exited the dressing room.

Savage Garden's song "I Knew I Loved You" blasted through the speakers. I sang along and rocked my head to the music. The minute I heard that song a year ago, I knew if I ever got married it would be the perfect song. I smiled in the mirror as I admired my reflection. I turned around ready to go sashay down the aisle and into the arms of my future husband.

I took two steps forward but stopped dead in my tracks.

"Going somewhere, bestie?" Ayana stood in front of me with a gun pointed to my head.

"I'm pretty sure you already know where I'm going. If you didn't then you wouldn't be here."

"You lying, conniving bitch! You thought you was going to take my man and just live happily ever after. No, bitch, wrong! Anthony, or Micah as you know him, is mine."

Pop! Pop!

I felt a sharp pain in my chest as I fell to the ground. I grabbed my chest and felt something wet and sticky. I raised my hand and noticed blood. I tried to yell, but blood was spewing out of my mouth and the words didn't come out because my tongue felt stiff and heavy. I was in so much pain, and the room started to spin as I started losing consciousness. I heard Micah's voice yelling something, as he knelt over me.

"Baby, please hold on. I got you, baby girl, I got you. Please, God, I can't lose her."

CHAPTER THIRTY-THREE

Ayana

See, bitches think shit is a game, until you pop off on them, showing them this is not the motherfucking movies. This was real life. I was not playing any games when it came down to my baby daddy. I loved that nigga's dirty drawers, and there's was no way I was goin' let a bitch walk in and snatch him up.

It didn't make a difference that the bitch who took my man was none other than the old stupid-ass bitch I clothed and fed. I provided a roof over her head and let that broke bitch sleep in my bed. See, Tiana thought that she was untouchable, but she was wrong. The minute she decided to start fucking with my nigga, she crossed the fucking line.

I was determined to end this bitch's life today. See, this bitch was so caught up in herself that she didn't notice that I was following her the minute she left her house. I watched as she pulled up to the Ashton Gardens venue. Jealousy spewed through my veins; this was my man and I should have been the one walking up those stairs. I shook that feeling off quickly. It was what it was.

I waited a few minutes, then I snuck in. Everyone was too busy laughing and talking; they didn't notice when little ol' me walked past them. I glanced at the front where everyone was sitting. I didn't see her. My sixth sense kicked in and I thought the dressing room may be the place she was at.

I was about to walk in when I heard voices. I recognized them right away; it was Tiana, and Anthony's bitch-ass mother. Seeing that two-faced bitch warmed up with Anthony's ho only angered me more. I hid behind the curtains and waited for her to leave.

I stood there for a minute watching as she glowed. She thought she was getting ready to marry my man, but I had other news for her. You should've seen that bitch's face when I pointed the gun at her. I almost busted out laughing at how pathetic this bitch looked.

Without wasting any more time, I fired two shots at her. I watched as she fell. I paused for a second, but quickly turned around and ran out. I spotted a door on the side. I pushed it, and was happy it was not locked. There was an alley directly behind the building. I quickly disappeared down there without bringing any kind of attention to myself.

I finally made it to my car, and jumped in. I was trembling, but I was determined not to get caught. I slowly pulled off to the next street. I heard police cars' sirens coming toward me. I panicked, and I slowed down.

They sped past me. I let out a long sigh and pulled off. I needed to get this gun up off me, so I started thinking of a good place that I could get rid of it. That's when it popped in my head: Chattahoochee River was only about twenty or twenty-five minutes away from me.

I jumped on I-20 West and made my way to dump this gun. I parked and looked around, to see if any nosey motherfucker was looking. The coast was clear, so I got the gun from up under my seat. I grabbed an old shirt that I had on the back seat. I wiped it down carefully; then, I wrapped it in the old shirt, got out of my car, and walked to the edge of the river and threw it as hard as I could. I then walked calmly back to my car and pulled off.

CHAPTER THIRTY-FOUR

Tiana

I was losing lots of blood and, to be honest, a bitch was scared I wasn't gonna make it. I whispered a prayer to God as I barely squeezed Micah's hand.

"Hurry the fuck up," he yelled to the EMT workers.

I wanted to tell him to calm down, but I was too weak and I couldn't get the words out. I closed my eyes as they rushed me into the ambulance.

"Do you know what happened here?" I heard a policeman asked Micah.

"Yo, my girl is fighting for her life and you think I'm worried about answering your fucking questions? Get out of my way."

"You need to calm down now, sir. I understand this is a difficult time, but this is a criminal investigation and I need to gather information.

Officer Bell, please seal off the area and don't allow anyone to leave the premises."

"Man, fuck all that, just make sure y'all save my baby's life."

The entire ride to the hospital I kept praying with everything in me. I refused to die when I had a baby to take care of. There was no way I was going out without a fight.

The ambulance sped down the highway as Micah held on to my hand and kept talking to me. I was in too much pain to pay full attention to everything he was saying. I did make out: "God, I swear whoever did this shit to her goin' pay," he said in between his sobs.

I wanted to hold him, to comfort him, but fuck that. I was fighting for my life and couldn't focus on no nigga.

CHAPTER THIRTY-FIVE

Ayana

I made my way back to the east side, and that's when it hit me: I couldn't go home. I was scared. If the police were looking for me, that's the first place they would go. I knew I shot her ass, but I wasn't sure she was dead. I knew if she made it, her old police ass would snitch on me. I was getting agitated, because I didn't come up with an escape plan.

I couldn't think straight. I needed a fucking drink for real, something to calm my nerves. I grabbed my pack of cigarettes, and I snatched one out of the box. I drove to Mama's house even though I didn't want to deal with this bitch; but, shit, I didn't have anyone else to turn to.

I rang the doorbell and nervously waited, all while looking around. I wasn't sure if the police had been here.

"What the hell you ringing down my damn bell like that for?" She swung the door open.

I pushed her out of the way and walked inside. I wasn't in the mood to deal with this bitch.

"Well, excuse me; you must think this is our shit. Nah, this my house and I would love for you to call before you pop up over here. Shit, I could've had company. Plus, the last time I saw your ass, you cussed me out like a dog."

"Isn't your old ass tired of fucking?" I asked sarcastically.

"Watch yo' damn mouth," she scolded, still holding the door wide open.

"Did the police come here? And shut the damn door," I yelled.

"Why would the police come here?" She looked at me. "What kind of trouble have you managed to get yourself in?" She stepped closer to me.

"Don't you look at me like that. Just answer my damn question: did the police come here, bitch?"

"Ain't nobody come here, but I tell you what: if you know yo' ass in trouble, you need to leave up out my shit. I 'ont need no police snooping 'round here."

"Man, shut up already. You ain't say all that shit when yo' ass was bouncing checks left to right. Who help yo' ass pay off that shit? Yes, that was me. So get off your fucking high horse. I need a place to crash for a few days."

I walked away from her. This bitch had my nerves on the edge. I walked in the kitchen and started searching the cabinets. I saw a bottle of Paul Masson. I didn't like that cheap shit, but it would do for now. I put the bottle to my head and drank. The cheap liquor stung my throat as I swallowed. I leaned against the counter as the liquor hit my body. I put the bottle back and walked into her back room. I was tired and distraught; I just wanted to lie down. As soon as my head hit the bed, I heard her hollering.

"Ayana, come here," I heard Mama holler.

What the fuck her drunk ass wants now? I thought as I got up off the mattress that was on the floor. I didn't have to ask why she was calling me; as soon as I entered the living room, my eyes landed on the breaking news on the television.

"There was a shooting at the Ashton Gardens all-inclusive wedding venue in Atlanta. There was a wedding taking place at the time of the shooting and the bride was shot by an unknown assailant. The victim was identified as college student Tiana Caldwell. She is listed in critical but stable condition and now being treated at Grady Memorial Hospital."

I stood in a trance with my mouth wide open! *The bitch is still alive,* I thought as I stared at the television screen. *How can that be? I shot her at point-blank range.*

"Isn't that our Tiana? Who the hell would do such a terrible thing on her wedding day? I wonder if her mama heard about this."

"No, Mother, correction: that is your Tiana. I don't fuck with that snake-ass bitch," I said before I walked away.

"Jealousy is gonna kill you, little girl," she hollered behind me.

I didn't respond. I walked back into the room and flopped down on the dingy-ass mattress. Tears started to flow heavily. I was so angry at myself for not making sure that bitch was dead. I couldn't believe I left her breathing. Now my freedom was in jeopardy.

I thought about running, but where the fuck was I going to run to? I didn't even have enough money to buy food. The other day I tried using the card that Ant and I shared and the account was closed. That nigga took everything from me. This angered me. I started crying harder.

I meant to kill Anthony's prize bitch, but instead the bitch was still breathing. I couldn't take it. I held my chest as a sharp pain hit me. I fell onto the bed and just broke down.

CHAPTER THIRTY-SIX

Tiana

Six weeks later

I was finally being discharged from the hospital. I was too ready to go. I sat on the bed waiting for Micah to pick me up. I was ready to hold my little man, and tell him how much I loved him and missed him. I also wanted some real food. I was sick of this mush the hospital served. I was looking forward to just starting over with my life.

I couldn't believe I still couldn't remember what the hell happened that day. I was shot in my arm and my chest, but I bumped my head when I fell to the ground. That caused my temporary memory loss. I did hope the doctors were right because I needed to remember what the hell happened to me and soon.

I heard the door to my hospital room door open. "It's about time you show your face. You know I hate waiting," I complained.

"Good morning, Miss Caldwell," the overzealous Detective Robinson said as he walked into the room with a dumbass look plastered across his face.

"What do you want again? I told you over and over I don't remember what happened at all."

"Well, I know, but the doctor also said your memory loss is temporary, so I am just checking to see if anything popped up since the last time we spoke."

I was about to respond, but Micah walked in as soon as I opened my mouth.

"Damn, this guy is everywhere. Do you know him?" the detective asked sarcastically.

"Yes, this is my fiancé, Micah."

I knew he was trying to be an asshole.

"Really? Last time I saw him he was at this same hospital with another woman who was also shot. I am starting to think he's the one the shooter, or shooters, are after," he said sarcastically.

"Detective Mr. Fuck Nigga, I think it's time you leave the room."

"Miss Caldwell, you seem like a smart young lady. I suggest you get rid of this guy right here. I promise you, he is bad news and you don't need to get caught up in his illegal activities. Here's my card. Call me as soon as you remember anything." He placed the card on the table, shot Micah a dirty look, then walked out the door.

I looked at Micah. I noticed his dark skin tone was now a dark red and his nose was flaring up. "Yo, I have no idea what that dude problem is. He got it out for me."

"Hmmm," was all I managed to say. This was definitely not the life I wanted. I never got myself caught up in no kind of bullshit. I was pissed the fuck off, and didn't feel like pretending like shit was sweet.

The entire ride to the house was spent in silence. He had the music on, and Plies's voice blasted through the speakers. As much as I loved Plies's music, I was in no mood to hear any music. All kind of thoughts ran through my head. Especially what the detective said earlier. I knew Micah told me that he left that old life alone, but I couldn't help but wonder if he was telling the truth. I also wondered if his old ways had anything to do with me getting shot. Tears welled up in my eyes. "Micah, can I ask you a question?"

"Yeah, whaddup?"

"Why is this detective after you like that? If you left the streets, like you claim, why is he so determined to bring you down?" I looked at him with every bit of seriousness I could muster up.

"Man, come on with all that," he said with an attitude.

"Don't be catching a damn attitude with me! Just answer the question," I barked back. I may have been feeling sick, but I damn sure wasn't no pushover.

"Man, this fuck nigga mad 'cause he been trying for years to charge us with some bullshit. But it's like e'erytime he try he end up empty, so he make it his business to harass us. I am done with them streets, yo, so don't come at me with no shit just 'cause that fuck nigga put that shit in yo' head."

"I don't know who you think you are talking to like that. But I suggest you tone that shit down. I ain't one of them bitches out in them streets. I'm just fucking asking because it seem like it's personal with him," I snapped on his ass.

"All this fucking attitude you giving me is for what? My only concern is to find out who the fuck shot you. All that extra shit is in the motherfucking way. That's what your ass should be worried about also. Not about some irrelevant-ass nigga."

This nigga done lost his mind, I thought as I turned my head toward the window. He was behaving like I wasn't concerned with who the fuck shot me. Shit, I'd been racking my damn brain to remember. But each time I ended up drawing a blank.

We got home and I waited for him to park. I was happy to be home after being gone for so long. I couldn't wait to jump in the shower so I could wash the hospital scent off of me.

"Let me help you." He walked to my side of the car and opened the door.

"I got it," I said with an attitude.

He threw his hand up in the air and walked to the other side. I took my time to get out of the car. I was feeling a little dizzy and weak. I used my little strength, walked to the door, and pushed it because it was half open. I wondered why the door was open, but before I could ask him, I got my answer. "Surprise," a bunch of people yelled.

I noticed it was his mother and his family. They had a WELCOME HOME banner posted on the wall. I smiled and greeted everyone, even though I would have preferred that no one was here.

I instantly spotted my little man across the room. Before I could move his mother walked toward me. "Here go a seat. Sit down, baby," she demanded, holding my baby in one hand. I sat on the chair and she handed him to me. I held him tight in my arms, like it was the first time. Tears started to flow. I missed him so much: his smell, and that smile that he gave me.

"He miss his mama," Miss Debra whispered in my ear.

"Thank you so much for taking care of my little man. I missed him so much." I smiled at her.

"Child, it's my pleasure. My grandbaby and his nana had a ball. I wouldn't trade these moments for anything."

As I listened to her talk about her grandson, the bitch who gave me life ran across my mind. I wondered where her ass was at. Did she know her only child almost died and, if she did, did she care?

Baby Micah started crying, which interrupted my thoughts. "Hey, li'l man, do you know yo' mama loves you with everything in me?" I kissed him on his forehead and put him close to my bosom and rocked him.

We ate, laughed, and talked for another two hours. By 3:00 p.m., everybody was gone. His mother was the last one to walk out the door; she's stayed behind to clean up the kitchen.

"Just know I am a phone call away. Call me if you need anything. I know you are my son's fiancée, but you are also my daughter." She hugged me and walked out.

"Thank you. I appreciate you."

After she was gone, I got up and walked slowly up the stairs. My baby was fast asleep; I guessed he was worn out from all the partying that took place.

I needed a hot bubble bath to ease my mind. As soon as I got into my room, I heard Micah enter the house. I was about to get into the shower when he walked into the room. I was still irritated with him, so I kept my distance.

I grabbed my clothes and walked into the bathroom. The water pounded on my sore body, but it didn't hurt. Instead I welcomed the warmness. I closed my eyes and washed from head to toe. I blocked everything out of my mind and, for those few minutes, I had no thoughts. I enjoyed the simple things such as bathing.

I dried off and oiled my body down with Africa's Best Herbal Oil. The fragrance from the oil soothed me in a way I can't explain. I got dressed and walked out of the bathroom. Micah sat on the edge of the bed with his head down. I tried to walk past him, but before I could do so, he grabbed my arm.

"Let go of me." I tried to snatch my arm away from him.

"Nah, B, sit your ass down and listen to me," he demanded.

I looked at him, and peeped the seriousness written across his face. I sat on the bed, unwillingly, but I knew there was no way he was gonna allow me to move.

He sat beside me and took my hand into his. "I know you're angry with me and I can't blame you. But, B, I want you to know that I didn't lie to you. I gave these streets up for you, ma. I know what that detective is trying to do, but I need you to believe me. I'm your man and I need you to trust me." He stared in my eyes.

I didn't really know what to believe. I didn't feel like fighting and I couldn't accuse him until I had proof. I reached over and hugged him and busted out crying. All I wanted was to be happy. I was tired of rainy days.

He held me tight while he rubbed my hair. No words were needed. There was complete silence as I cleansed my soul.

He finally let me go and leaned me back on the bed. He then slipped up under my nightgown. He slid my underwear off and dug his face into my pussy. My body trembled as his tongue made a connection with my clit. I remembered how much I missed him making love to me. He sucked my pussy like it was his last supper. I held his head down as my legs trembled and I came into his mouth.

I wanted to fuck him, but he didn't want to. "Nah, B, let's just hold each other tonight."

I was kind of in my feelings when he refused to give me the dick, but I understood. I went into my son's room and stood there staring at him in the crib. I was happy that God saw it fit to spare my life. I loved him since the day he was conceived. My heart started to hurt as the thoughts of me getting shot sank my heart. I wiped the tears and bent down to kiss him. "Mommy loves you, baby boy," I said as I pulled the covers over him.

CHAPTER THIRTY-SEVEN

Ayana

After hiding at my mama's house for days, I was starting to get bored. The bitch was also plucking my nerves. She kept asking for fucking money to buy alcohol like I was the fucking bank.

"Ma, what the hell I look like, the bank? Every day you got your damn hands out," I snapped.

"You lying up in my shit without paying rent. Shit, you ain't going to disrespect me in my shit. Ayana, I swear, I didn't raise you like this. I may not be the world's greatest mother, but I damn sure wasn't the worse. But it's like you have this resentment toward me."

"Bitch, please, you can keep that performance for a bitch who gives two fucks about what you saying. Yo' ass should be happy to help me out. Remember when I used to help you out when I was younger? When you was too fucking drunk to get up and do anything? I was the bitch who got up and cleaned up, made sure you ate. Now you want to act all high and mighty. I'm going to get out of your shit, but don't you ever fucking call me for anything. You hear me?" I looked at her, shook my head, and walked away. I thought about knocking that bitch's head off, but instead I walked out the door, slamming it behind me.

"Ayana," that bitch started to say, but I didn't want to hear nothing from that bitch.

I got into my car and immediately broke down. How could my own mother treat me like this? I knew this bitch never liked me since I was young. She chose Tiana's ass over me and this was the reason why I hated her so much.

I rested my head on the steering wheel as tears flowed down my face. I was angry and hurt that Anthony dogged me out. I missed my damn kids. A few months ago I had it all, but how did all this happen? How did I lose everything in the blink of an eye, all because of this one bitch? I should have killed her ass. I sat out there for a good ten minutes before I took a glance back at Mama's house. There was no way I'd ever go back there. I didn't give a fuck if that bitch was dead. It was over and done with for me. I had nobody to rely on in this world but me, and I was going to make it work.

***

I was up bright and early. Today was the hearing for me to get my girls back and, as much as I hated their daddy, I knew I needed my girls. They were the only ones who gave a fuck about me. Plus, I needed them back so I could put Anthony's ass on child support. This nigga thought he was goin' to take care of this bitch and her motherfucking child and not worry about me and mine. He had this game all the way fucked up, because as soon as I got my girls back his ass was going to come up off major paper. I knew he had some money saved up and I wanted half of everything for me and my girls.

I got dressed in a cute dress. I put my hair up in a bun. I was trying to look my best even though I was tired and I felt like shit.

I walked into the juvenile courtroom. Water gathered in my mouth as I walked toward the front. I didn't have a lawyer; it was just me. I noticed the bitch who took my babies; she was seated on the right side flipping through papers. My first instinct was to run up on this bitch, but I quickly dismissed that idea.

"All rise. The Honorable Judge Graham is presiding. Your Honor, this is a removal hearing. The State of Georgia versus Ayana Beasly."

"Thank you. Please be seated," Judge Graham said.

"Your Honor, I am Attorney Steward, representing the Department of Human Services for the State of Georgia. The defendant's children were removed from the home because someone filed a complaint with DFACS. When the workers arrived at the home, they witnessed deplorable conditions the children were living in. The kids were then removed from the home and put into the custody of the state. We ask that the children remain with the state until the mother can prove they are safe with her. We will also be looking at the other parent or family members that can provide care for the children."

"Miss Beasly, talk to me. What is going on with your living situation?"

I took a deep breath. "Your Honor, I'm a single mother and even though I don't have no help, I do the best I can for my children. Your Honor, the workers came to the house right when I was getting ready to clean up the house, and they assumed that was how my children were living."

"Well, Miss Beasly, the welfare of the children is very important and we can't allow them to live in deplorable conditions. Do you have an attorney?"

"No, Your Honor."

"The court will appoint an attorney if you can't afford one. Also an attorney will be assigned to the children. You will need to follow the orders of the court and the Department of Human Services. From one mother to another, you need to step your game up and do what you need to do, so you can get your children back. Where is the father of the children?"

I wanted to say, "Chasing pussy," but I didn't. "Your Honor, he is not involved in his kids' lives."

"Well, you will need to provide his name and contact information if you have it. Do you understand me?"

"Yes, Your Honor."

"Well, I am setting a date for the next hearing for September tenth, at ten a.m. This will give the state enough time to investigate these allegations filed against you. At that time I will consider releasing to the children to you if there is no proof against you, and only if you cooperate fully with the workers and do what you're supposed to do. Court is adjourned."

I sank down in the chair. The words of this bitch echoed in my head. I hadn't seen my children since the day they took them and now this bitch was telling me I had to prove some shit to them. Who the fuck did these bitches think they were? I carried these fucking children for nine fucking months. I took care of them.

I felt so sick inside. I barely managed to grab my purse and walk out of the courtroom in a daze. I walked hurriedly to my car and got in. I banged my head against the steering wheel as I let out my frustration. "God, I can't live without my kids. I need them. I need Ant to come back home. Please, God, I'm begging you," I cried.

After wallowing into self-pity, I finally pulled off.

I opened the door to my apartment. I looked around to see if anyone has been there, but there was no sign of anyone. The smell of rotten food hit my nose. I glanced over at the kitchen and noticed the pile of dishes. I threw my purse on the ground and walked into the kitchen. I grabbed the bottle of gin I had in the kitchen. There was no need to look for a glass. I put the bottle to my head. I needed it bad.

CHAPTER THIRTY-EIGHT

Tiana

Adjusting back to life was kind of hard. The pain was unbearable at times. I would pretend like everything was fine in the daytime. But at night I would suffer silently. Also I was scared, because I had no idea who shot me and I believed they might come back if they were aware that I made it. Micah also was acting paranoid. He stayed armed and he often displayed his frustration, because he had no idea who shot me.

"Babe, listen, I wish we could move on from all of this," I said as he lay in the bed with his back turned to me.

"What you talkin' 'bout?"

"I see how distant you've become ever since I came home. I mean, you barely talk to me and you walk around here high and armed. I mean, you have a little boy who needs his daddy to play with him. You also have a woman who is lonely and needs her man. I'm hurting too, especially because I can't remember shit."

He sat up in the bed, then turned around to face me. His eyes were bloodshot. "I'm yo' motherfucking man, and I couldn't protect you. How the fuck you think this shit makes me feel? A fucking coward shot you while I was in the same building. I got niggas in the streets putting a bounty up. I need to know which one of the fuck niggas violated you like this. And when I find out, I'm going to torture that motherfucker, the bitch who gave birth to him, down to the fucking babies related to him," he spoke through clenched teeth, with his fist balled up.

This coldness and his words sent chills up my spine. "Micah, I don't want to lose you. I need to know as bad as you do, but it's not going to help anything if you get locked up or dead," I tried to comfort him.

"Nah, fuck that, ma. These country niggas done violated you and that means death to everyone and all involved." He got up and stormed out of the room.

I laid my head back on the pillow. If only I could remember who the fuck did this to me, then most of our stress would be over.

***

I was determined to marry Micah even after everything that went down. At first I was angry, but I quickly came to my senses. Ain't nobody perfect and, truth was, I didn't want a perfect man. I wanted a man who loved me and respected me. I had no doubt he loved me and I wasn't gonna waste another minute.

"Babe, do you want us to go to the courthouse and get married?" I quizzed him as we sat at the table eating breakfast.

"Why would we do that? Shit all we got to do is set a new date. Everybody still got their outfit and shit. All you need to do is buy you another gown."

Oh, shit, I forgot. I got shot in my gown. "You're right. Well, let's set it for two weeks from now. I will hit up the chick from Events By Ebonee and get her to make us new plans. I might have to throw her a few extra dollars since it's so sudden."

"It don't matter what it is. Money ain't an issue. Lemme know if you need me to do anything."

I smiled at him; my baby was a gangsta with a touch of softness. "I got it, babe. Also I want to go back to school next semester. We need to find a good daycare for Baby Micah."

"Oh, shit now! We need to do a background check and everything. The way these mother-fuckers be hurting these kids and shit. I'm telling you, T, I will fuck up a nigga or a bitch when it comes down to my seed."

"Who you telling? I 'ont like drama, but I swear I will beat a bitch ass quick. Is it safe to say Baby Micah has some crazy parents?" I busted out laughing.

"Call it what you want! I'm dead-ass serious."

We continued eating breakfast. Then he helped me clean the kitchen up. We were alone because his mama had the baby. I definitely welcomed the little bit of free time alone with my man. Micah got quiet, and stared out in space.

"Hey, boo, let me ask you a question. You think Ayana had anything with you getting shot? I mean this shit happened right after she lost the kids." He looked up at me.

I sat there quiet for a few minutes, letting his words sink in. "To be honest with you, I suspect her ass, but I know Ayana. She talks all that shit, but I don't think she would be that bold to run up in a place where people were who may recognize her. So I quickly dismiss it."

"Just thinking. None of this shit don't add up! You're not in the streets and you don't have any enemies. If a nigga were after me, I'm always in the streets. They wouldn't wait to do something to you. You ain't got no beef so it's strange, that's all."

I agreed with what he was saying. I wasn't in the streets. I mean, a few bitches didn't like me, but it wasn't nothing major. They knew I didn't address lower-level bitches so they stayed their distance. I thought whoever shot me had a connection to Micah. I didn't say anything though because he was already too riled up and I didn't want to throw gas on fire!

I twisted and turned all night! I was feeling anxious and nervous. Months ago, I was ready to marry my man and tragedy struck. I just hoped this time nothing crazy happened. Micah and I both decided to have security posted at the two entrances. I also chose a different location. Even though I didn't remember what went down, I still didn't want to go back there. I was afraid that I may have a panic attack.

We found a great spot to have the wedding: Vecoma at the Yellow River, out in Snellville. The first day I saw that venue, I knew it was perfect. The weather was great so their outside setup was perfect for the ceremony and then their air-conditioned hall was definitely what we needed.

I ordered another wedding dress from the same company, but a different style. I didn't want anything that would remind me of that horrible day. I got my hair pinned up and my girl Ken, from Ken Hall, did my makeup. I was already beautiful, but after she was done, I was hottttt.

Before I left the house, I closed my room door and got on my knees. I asked God to protect me, to keep me away from my enemies. Tears flowed as I had a personal talk with God. I wiped my tears and got up.

I felt refreshed and ready! Most of my life was filled with pain and struggles. Today was a new day for me. I was ready to start a brand new life, one that was filled with happiness and love. "No more pain," I mumbled as I took one last glance at myself in the mirror.

I exited the limo and walked toward the entrance. Micah's mom was beside me. I looked over at this woman; she was everything I needed in a mother. She took my hand and squeezed it. I thought she sensed my nervousness.

The music was blasting! It seemed like déjà vu, only this time I decided not to go in the fitting room. I was a little paranoid because I had no idea who was out to get me.

I greeted a lot of people in the hallway. Most of them I really didn't know; they were Micah's guests. "You ready?" his mom asked me.

"Yes, I'm ready." I swallowed hard and walked slowly down the aisle. I could see Micah far ahead. I smiled as I got closer. In front of me was the world's sexiest man. He looked fine in some street clothes, but he was sexy as hell in that tux. That haircut and his deep dimples complemented his dark ivory complexion. He stared deep into my eyes as I reached the altar and took my position beside him.

The ceremony was well on its way. Before you knew it, we were man and wife. I proudly tongued my man down in front of everyone. My anxiety level was low, because everything happened without incident.

The rest of the evening was spent dancing, eating, and just having a great time. I was happy as I danced the night away with my love. I would occasionally sneak off to pop a kiss on my baby's cheek. Micah walked off to go rap with his boy. My feet were hurting from standing so long in those six-inch heels. I had a pair of flats tucked off in the corner. I decided it was time to change out; no need to try to be cute then end up with corns on my toes. I finished switching shoes when I noticed a brown-skinned chick in a tight red gown approaching me. I had never met her so I assumed she was either a relative of his or a close family friend. As she got closer, I noticed her smile turn to an evil grin. I stared at her, because I did not know her and wasn't sure what she wanted.

"Well, well, well! So you the bitch he decided to settle down with." This two-dollar ho caught me off guard.

"And who might you be, bitch? Let me guess: one of the bitches he done fucked and you can't get over the fact that he decided to settle down with li'l ol' me? Bitch, I advise you to run along and find you another bitch to play with! 'Cause I guarantee this is not what you want," I spat as I took a step closer to this stupid bitch!

"Ha-ha." She clapped. "That was cute, but don't you feel special 'cause he put a ring on it. Trust me, he will be back up in this pussy." She patted her front.

I lunged toward that bitch, but someone walked up behind me and grabbed my hand. "No need to do that, ma. Yo, what the fuck you doing up in my wife's face like this?" It was Micah.

"We were having a friendly girls' chat. I was letting her know how much you love eating my pussy."

"Yo, B, you talking recklessly right now! Get the fuck outta here before I throw yo' ass out. Don't you ever get in my wife's face like this again. Bitch, I said get the fuck out." He grabbed her arm and pulled her toward the door.

I let out a long sigh. The nerve of this bitch.

Micah's mother walked up to me. "Listen, baby, don't you ever come off your throne to address these lower-level bitches. You are now a wife, so wear your crown proudly. There are gonna be bitches who gonna tell you your man fucking them, but what is the point of them telling you after the fact? I know, they tell you so you can get mad and leave him so they can get him. Don't fall for the foolery. My son loves you."

I stood there taking in everything she was saying. It threw me off how blunt she was. However, I got the message she was conveying to me.

"Come on, let's party. I am pretty sure my son dealt with the little leech."

We both walked on to the dancing floor. I tried to dance, but my mind raced back to what that bitch told me. I was so caught up in my thoughts that I didn't notice when Micah walked up on me. "Let me get this dance, beautiful." My man held me tight as we danced slowly to Sade's mellow tune, "No Ordinary Love."

I threw the bouquet and some chick caught it. We then said our good-byes and ran to the limo; we were going to get dressed so we could catch a Delta flight to Jamaica. I'd never been there before so I was looking forward to this mini vacation.

Micah's mother and my baby accompanied us to the airport. I was kind of sad leaving him behind, but I knew he was in good hands. I kissed him, and his daddy hugged him; then we were out.

If I do say so myself, Jamaica is a beautiful island. This was my first time there, and from the minute we stepped off the plane, it was pure enjoyment. We stayed at the Sandals Negril Beach Resort and Spa. After checking into our room, we took a shower and changed into more comfortable outfits. We then went to the area where the restaurant was located. We had dinner, drank wine, and then went swimming in the pool.

After a long day, we retreated to our hotel room, where we made love. I mean we tore that hotel room up. Micah picked me up in the air and ate my pussy until I had multiple orgasms. I had never felt anything like this before. I mean, I'd been with this man, but hell, tonight he acted savagely as he devoured my pussy. After he put me down, I dropped to my knees. I slowly licked the tip of his dick to get a response out of him. After his dick became rock hard, I took all his manhood into my mouth. I sucked his dick so damn good; I was proud of myself. My goal was to show my man that I was a beast in the bed. He was no longer the nigga I was fucking or just my baby daddy. This fine specimen of a man was my husband.

"Aarghhhhhh," he growled as he busted into my mouth. I opened my mouth wide to catch every drop of my husband's cum. I licked up every drop, using my tongue to wipe his dick down.

He then got up and spun me around on my stomach. He slid up beneath me and started rubbing his dick against my pussy tongue. I was already wet, and my pussy welcomed his soft dick. Seconds later, his dick was hard again.

"Awee," I groaned as he entered me. He slowly fucked me as I bit down on the pillow.

Micah had a way of teasing me. I threw my ass back on his dick as he held me tight. Baby boy dug deep into my soul and touched all the spots that sent me into multiple orgasms. I held tight to the pillow and took in every inch of his manhood.

When we were finished, I jumped in the shower while he rolled him a blunt of that good ol' Jamaican ganja. I smiled as I soaped up my body. I felt good; honestly, I was in a great place in my life. My health was getting better, even though my memory of the shooting was still gone. I figured maybe it was a good thing that I didn't know.

I got out of the shower and dried off. I could smell the strong scent of weed coming from the room. I walked into the room and dropped the towel. I grabbed my lotion and bent down and started to lotion my body in a seductive way.

"So that's how you gonna play, right?"

"Who, me? What are you talking about, babe?" I giggled.

"Keep playing, and watch me unleash this beast on you," he joked.

I just smiled at him and went about my business. In no time, I was dressed in my little bootie shorts and tank top. After he took his shower, we took a long walk along the path of our hotel. He put his arm around me, and we walked in silence.

I was used to Georgia's weather, but Jamaica was super hot. I was ready to hit the beach. Our second day was spent swimming and relaxing on the beach. This was definitely the kind of life I could get used to fast!

We ended the night with a quiet dinner of oxtails, rice and peas, with cabbage on the side. I also ordered Red Stripe beer and Micah ordered a Guinness. We sat in the dimly lit area in silence, taking in the sweet reggae melodies. I wished this moment would last, but the reality was it wouldn't. However, it was a break from everything that was going on in our lives. This was the first time he didn't bring up who shot me, and I welcomed it because it was like he was obsessed or something.

We boarded our flight back to Georgia. Even though I enjoyed myself, I was happy to be going home. I missed my baby and was looking forward to holding him and just kissing all over him. Two hours later, our plane landed at Hartsfield-Jackson Airport in College Park. I was happy we made it safely.

Micah's mother was there to pick us up, along with my sugar pooh. I was anxious to clear customs so I could get to my little man!

"Babe, grab my bags for me," I said to Micah before I dashed off to my baby. Without saying hello, I snatched my baby out of Miss Debra's hands. No words were needed. I held him close and kissed him all over. He seemed to be missing his mama also, because he slobbered all over my face.

"Hey, Miss Debra," I managed to say in between kisses.

"Hey, child. You acting like you been gone for years." She chuckled.

"I swear, it feels like it," I joked back.

"Hey, Mama." Micah walked over with the bags in his hands.

"Hey, baby." She reached over and kissed him on the cheeks. "Let's get out of here," she said.

I held my baby tight as we walked out of the airport and into the brisk Georgia air.

CHAPTER THIRTY-NINE

Ayana

I heard a loud banging on the door. My heart instantly sank; I figured the police finally caught up to me. I thought about going through the back window, but fuck I was all the way up on the third floor.

Bang! Bang! Bang!

I was irritated as fuck. Who the hell was banging on my door like that? I got up and stormed to the door. I popped the door open; whoever it was was going to get cussed the fuck out. I was caught off guard. "What the fuck you want, Ant?" I said to the bitch-ass nigga who had the balls to pop up at my damn house.

Without responding, he pushed inside my house, almost knocking me to the ground. He then shoved me and slammed the door. "Yo, where were you the day Tiana got shot?"

"What, nigga? You funny as hell. Don't tell me you came over here to quiz me about my whereabouts?"

"Answer the fucking question, A. Did you shoot Tiana?"

Something in my head was screaming to tell that nigga yes, but I couldn't. He looked spaced out, like he was high off something serious. "Boy, no, I ain't shot your bitch, 'cause if I did, trust me, I would've killed her ass." I nervously grinned.

"I swear, bitch, something is telling me you had something to do with it. But I promise you, on my seeds, I will kill you if I find out you had anything to do with it."

He tried walking off. I tried grabbing his shirt. "Bitch, let go of me."

I pulled his arm. "Really, Ant, this how you goin' to treat me? I can't believe you, nigga. I'm your baby mother. I love you," I pleaded.

"Bitch, I just told you get the fuck off me! I wouldn't look at you if you were the last bitch on earth. I can't believe I stuck my dick in your rotten pussy ass," he said, then took a step toward me and spit in my face.

"Fuck you! Fuck you. You just spit on me, you sorry-ass nigga." I lunged toward him, but I missed and fell on the ground. He looked at me with disgust and stormed out the door, leaving my door open. "Fuck you, Ant," I screamed out, not giving a fuck who heard.

I didn't even try to move. Instead I cried until I couldn't cry anymore. I loved him; how could he treat me like this? This bitch had his ass wide open. He was over here talking shit. *He better be happy I didn't kill that bitch.*

I woke up the next morning realizing I was still on the cold floor. I stumbled up and walked into the kitchen; my back was touching my stomach. I opened the refrigerator to grab something to eat. I grabbed the only thing that was available: the jug of milk. I put it to my mouth, but the stench of rotten milk hit my nose. I threw the jug back in the fridge and shut it. I wanted to cry because I just can't catch a break. I walked to my room and got into my bed.

I must've dozed off, because a loud bang startled me. I pulled the cover over my head and try to go back to sleep, but the knocking persisted.

I got up out of the bed and walked to the door. I was nervous and my palms were sweaty. I looked through the peephole and noticed the sheriff standing in front of my door. That was strange because the police should've been here, not the sheriff's department. I was pretty sure it was a mistake. I opened the door. "May I help you?"

"Yes, ma'am, we are here to evict you from the apartment."

"Evict me? What the hell you mean, evict me?"

"Here are your removal papers. We are ordered to remove all your possessions from the apartment."

As I stared down on the paper he handed me, it finally hit me. I hadn't paid my rent in months; and I remembered a few months ago there was citation for me to go to court. *Fuck. I missed my court date.*

"Can't y'all come back another time? I mean, I will pay the rent." I looked at them with pleading eyes.

"I'm afraid we can't do that, ma'am. Please step out of the building," he said as he stepped toward me. I started to cry. This couldn't be happening to me, not right now.

"I need to grab my personal belongings." I turned around and went back in. The sheriff was on my heels.

I grabbed my purse and car keys. I walked out the door as they started to move my things out onto the lawn. I got in my car and watched as they threw all my belongings out. I started to cry as I lit up a cigarette.

Knock! Knock!

The banging on my car window startled me. I quickly noticed it was my nosey-ass neighbor Sharon. This bitch knew damn well I didn't fuck with her. She was the neighborhood gossip bitch.

I wound my window down. "What do you want, lady?" I asked with an attitude.

"Girl, relax. I see they throwing you out of there." She smirked.

"And? Why is that your business?"

"Damn, bitch. I was only tryin'a help your ass. You know I got an extra bedroom. You always welcome to stay with me, long as you help out with the bills."

I looked at that bitch like she was a creature from a different planet. "Nah, I'm good. I wish you'd get yo' nosey ass out of my face."

"Fuck you, bitch! I bet yo' high and mighty ass ain't feeling so high and mighty now." She giggled as she walked away.

I looked in my mirror; I noticed there was a group of nosey bitches gathered around. I had a few dollars. I knew I needed a U-Haul truck to take my stuff to a storage facility. There was no way I was going to lose my designer purses and shoes Ant bought me.

I quickly dried my tears and scrolled through my phone. I needed to find someone to help me.

I got the perfect name. I dialed his number. I knew he would be happy to help me, if the price was right.

After he packed my stuff into the U-Haul, he pulled off and I followed him.

CHAPTER FORTY

Ayana

This was what homelessness felt like? I got me a room at the Red Roof Inn on Candler Road. It wasn't the best area, but it was what I could afford. I had to figure out a way to make money fast.

After speaking with my bitch Lori and letting her know all the shit that happened, she told me to come stay with her! I was a little reluctant at first, because even though she was my nigga, I loved having my own shit.

I parked in the driveway and grabbed my purse. I then popped the trunk. I had to grab the bags that contained some of my belongings.

"Bitch, it is about time you bring yo' ass," she popped the door open and said.

"While you running yo' mouth, how about you come help a bitch carry these bags?"

"Uh-huh! You just like the damn bag lady dragging all these plastic bags around," she joked.

After we took the bags in the house and into the spare bedroom she had, I returned to the living room and flopped down on the couch. "Before you start asking a million and one questions, light that damn blunt up and pour me a glass of something strong."

"Damn, bitch, do you need anything else?" she quizzed me.

"Nah, that's all I need for now," I joked.

She rolled a fat blunt up and poured me a glass of Hennessy Pure White. I picked the glass up and took a big gulp. I started to cough. Lori scooted closer and started knocking my back. "Damn, ho, calm yo' greedy ass down."

"Shit, I needed this. This past week I've been through hell and back," I said as I thought back on all the shit that happened.

"Girl, you better than me. I would've gone off on them motherfucking people about my damn kids. You push them kids out of your pussy; they can't just walk in and take them. By the way did you ever find out who the hell call CPS on you?"

"Hell nah, but it's two bitches who would do such shit. Micah's ol' stanking-ass mama or that bitch Tiana. I swear I should've killed that bitch whe . . ." *Fuck I'm tripping. I didn't mean to say that shit out loud.*

"What you mean, you should've killed her? Wait. Was that you who shot that bitch?" She stared in my eyes.

I wanted to lie, but I knew this bitch wasn't gonna let it go. "Bitch, I swear; you can't tell anybody what I'm about to tell you." I looked her dead in the eyes!

"Girl, bye, you know you my motherfucking nigga. Plus I would never tell no shit that's gonna get you in no shit."

I continued staring at her. I needed this bitch to know how serious I was!

"If you goin' to act like you 'ont trust me, I really don't need to know then," she complained.

"Bitch, shut up already." I started to tell her everything about the shooting. I watched as she sat quietly taking in everything that I was spitting to her. I really hoped she'd rock with me the way she said she would, because this shit was serious and it could land me in prison for life.

"Damn, bitch. I swear you got more guts than me. I wouldn't be able to pull it off."

"Don't say what you wouldn't do until you get put in the situation. I gave this nigga the best years of my life and gave him two beautiful girls and this is how he repays me? And to try to leave me and marry a bitch I call my sister? I ain't goin' to lie; they will never have a 'happily ever after.' Not over my dead body."

"Trust, hon, I feel your pain. I know how much you stack behind him. He wrong for that shit. He could've handled it like a real nigga. And the bitch definitely a grimy bitch, not after all you say you did for her. She is ungrateful as fuck. I probably would've done the same thing if I were in your shoes. Well, I just thought of something. Did this bitch see your face when you shot her? Because you do know she ain't dead right?" She looked at me with her face balled up.

"I know, bitch. That's why I've been feeling so damn nervous. I thought the police might be looking for me or something, but I haven't heard anything."

"Well, you need to lay low until you figure out what you goin' to do. You know Mari be here and I can't bring no heat to him. Don't tell nobody you staying here and shit."

"I mean, I can go if it's going to be an issue," I said with an attitude.

"Bitch, get out your feelings! I just don't want to bring no heat to my man. You know he be having that work with him. That's my meal ticket and I can't lose that."

"I understand. I just need a week or two to figure out what I want to do."

"Well, first you need to drink the rest of the liquor and then you need to wipe them damn tears. Fuck crying; that bitch ain't said shit yet, so she might be shook and, nine times out of ten, that scary bitch ain't goin' to say shit. You need to clean yourself up and get back to the old you. You got a motherfucking pussy, so you need to use it to get whatever the fuck you want. The Ayana I know ain't no weak bitch."

I needed to hear those words, 'cause lately I was feeling defeated! Her strong words along with the weed and alcohol definitely gave me the boost I needed.

I got my hair done, and cleaned myself up good. I was definitely in a better mood these days! I called Daquan and we decided to do lunch. I made sure I washed my pussy good and shaved. I was sure that he going want to fuck and I wanted to fuck too. I lotioned down then put on my sexy Victoria's Secret panty and bra set. I sprayed my body with perfume. I then grabbed my purse and headed out of the room.

"Damn, bitch, where the hell you going, looking like you about to catch?" Lori busted out laughing.

"That is correct! I'm trying to catch something big. See you later," I joked, and winked at her as I walked out of the door.

He was already parked at the Red Lobster on Candler when I get there. This wasn't my favorite place. This was the hood Red Lobster and I was kind of reluctant going up in there because I didn't want to bump in anyone I knew, just in case the police were looking for me. I applied some lip gloss to my lips and sashayed out of the car. He spotted me and got out of his car. He walked into the restaurant. I followed loosely behind. I thought he chose this one because it was close to where he hustled; plus, it wasn't close to places his bitch frequented.

"Hey, you," I greeted him.

"Whaddup yo." He gave me a hug and squeezed my ass.

"Yes, may I help you?"

"I need seating for two," he said to the waitress.

"Follow me, sir and ma'am."

After we were seated, he sat across from me smiling. "What's good, shawty? You still at the hotel?"

"Nah, I'm staying with my homegirl over there in Stone Mountain."

"Oh, okay. Cool."

We ate our food in complete silence. He kept rubbing my leg underneath the table. I smiled at him as I took a drink of the Moscato that I ordered. "What's going on with you?" I finally asked with a devilish grin.

"You already know what's good with me! I'm tryin' a get some that good good up off you."

"Sounds interesting, but you do know that pussy ain't free these days," I said bluntly.

"Ma, you already know money ain't no thang. Let's get out of here," he demanded.

"Ohhh, fuck me, daddy," I screamed as his big dick tore my pussy up. I braced myself as he sank every inch of his manhood inside of me.

"Take this dick, bitch! Take it," he said as he punished my pussy. I ain't goin' to lie; I was enjoying every bit of his brutal punishment. It'd been a minute; shit, he was the last one I fucked and I was loving it.

"Arghhhhhh. Shit I'm about to cum. Shit this pussy so fucking good, I'm about to cum." He grabbed me closer.

"Ohhhh, ohhhhh," I groaned and dug into his back as he exploded inside of me.

I lay there trying to recuperate from the best fuck I'd ever had in my life. He lay on top of me until he finally got up.

"Damn, ma, no shit you got that fire pussy. I need this on the regular."

I sat up and stared at him. "Well, you know, we can definitely make it happen. As long as the price is right." I winked at him.

"Like I said, money ain't no issue. I got you. The only thing I ask is that you don't tell your homegirl shit about me. She got a big-ass mouth; plus, I 'ont want this shit getting back to my girl."

I wanted to say, "Fuck your girl," but I didn't. I was broke and I really needed his help. So instead I smiled at him.

"Well, I'm about to bounce." He peeled off a thousand dollars from the wad of cash he pulled out of his pocket, and handed it to me.

"Thank you, *papi*." I winked at him.

"A'ight, ma, I'm out. You know my number; call me whenever you want that pussy serviced."

"I got you," I said as he walked out the door.

After he left, I got up off the bed and decided to wash up really quick. My pussy was sore and the cheap-ass soap in the hotel made it worse. I got out, and quickly got dressed. I was definitely in a better mood. I had a few dollars and I had the perfect arrangements. As long as this nigga kept paying, I would be putting this sugar pussy on him.

CHAPTER FORTY-ONE

Tiana

The honeymoon was over and life was back to regular. I was also feeling a lot better physically, so I decided to start back going to school. I ain't going to lie, it would be something to get me back on track; plus, I needed to get my career going. I was now a married woman, and lying up at home was definitely not what's up. After I met Micah, so much had changed. I was so wrapped up in our relationship and all the drama that followed that I didn't have the time to focus on what Tiana wanted!

Baby Micah was also in daycare. I sure missed my baby. The first day we dropped him off, my soft ass broke down. I sat in the car about twenty minutes trying to see if the daycare workers were going to call. They didn't so I pulled off. As the days went by, I welcomed the break that I got.

Micah opened a barber shop in Stone Mountain and so far his business was doing good. So far our marriage seemed to be doing well. He also assured me that he would start classes soon.

The pain was still nagging at me, and sometimes it became unbearable. I started to pop more and more pain medicine to help manage the pain I was feeling. I wished I had someone to talk to, but I was scared to tell Micah. I was scared that he might think that I was a junkie of some sort. So I kept it to myself and made sure no one else noticed.

"Hey, babe, I'm home," I yelled as I walked through the door.

"I'm in here," Micah yelled back.

"Mommy, Mommy," my little man yelled as he ran to me. This was one of the greatest moments every day when I came home. My little man was always excited to see me. I picked his tall ass up and kissed him.

I walked into the living room where his daddy was at. "Hey, babe." I walked over and kissed him. I noticed he wasn't his happy self. So I took a step back. "What's going on with you?"

"Man." He sighed. "A social worker called me today. They are not giving the girls back to Ayana until she takes classes and proves to them, she is capable of taking care of them. Until then, they are gonna be in state custody, living with a foster parent." I saw the tears in his eyes.

"So what are you gonna do?"

"I need my girls, T. I swear they are my life. Ever since this shit happened, I really can't sleep. I need to get my girls out of the system," he cried.

I wanted to say something, but I couldn't find the right words to say. In front of me was my husband crying for his children. I couldn't say I knew how exactly how he felt, but it was visible he was hurting bad. My heart broke even more when Baby Micah crept over to his daddy and hugged his leg. Tears welled up in my eyes. I couldn't take it anymore so I walked out and up the stairs.

Later that night after everyone was sleeping, I lay wide awake in bed. I couldn't help but feel guilty that I was the one who called CPS on Ayana. I assisted the state, which resulted in her kids getting taken, and now my husband was hurting. Tears flowed from my face; I wished I could take his pain away. At the time, I was so sure I was doing the right thing, but right now I wasn't too sure about it. I cried silently as I dozed off, thinking I had to help my husband.

I was up bright and early. I had to drop our son off at daycare before heading to class. Micah was awake when I walked down the stairs. "Good morning."

"What's good, ma? Sorry I didn't make it to the room last night."

"No, you good." I sat down beside him. "Listen, I was up all night thinking."

"Thinking? Thinking about what?"

"I know how much those girls mean to you, so why don't you step up and get custody of them?"

He looked at me like he just saw a ghost. I wondered if I just said the wrong thing.

"I'm sorry, I did—" I started to say.

"Nah, I was thinking that all along, but I didn't know how to bring it to you," he cut me off.

"Listen, Micah. Those are your children and they were here before me. If you want to get them, then go for it. When I married you, I knew that your children will forever be in your life. Plus, Baby Micah needs to know his sisters."

"I don't know what to do though. I'm a street nigga. I ain't never had to deal with no court and shit."

"Well, I am no expert, but I am going to find you a custody lawyer today. He or she will be able to steer you in the right direction."

"Damn, ma, this is the reason why I fucks with you. You don't have a selfish bone in your body. After all Ayana has done to you, you still willing to help out. I love you, woman."

The mention of that bitch's name put a bad taste in my mouth, but I didn't say a word. This wasn't the time to show my bad side. "You just said the correct word: woman. Little girls do stupid shit, but a grown woman will see the pain her man is in and will try to find solutions to help him out! We are a team, so this is a team effort."

He moved closer and wrapped his hands around me. I wasn't ready to be anyone's stepmother or play mommy to that bitch's children, but they were my husband's children and the best thing was for him getting them out of the system.

The entire time I was in class, my mind was elsewhere. I knew I said one thing to Micah, but I also knew who I was dealing with! Ayana wasn't the kind of bitch who was going to sit back and let Micah and me raise her children. I knew her all too well to know drama was on the way. I was ready though. I knew I would have to show this bitch that even though I hated drama, I never backed down from it before! If she brought it, I would be prepared to show my ass off.

I saw the teacher walk in, and I quickly dismissed the thoughts that were invading my mind. *I hope for this bitch's sake she just easy herself.*

CHAPTER FORTY-TWO

Ayana

If I thought these bitches from social services would at least give me a break, I was in for a rude awakening. They had me doing classes three hours of the day, and then I had to turn around and submit to a fucking drug test. I mean, come the fuck on. I had to do a fucking parenting class to prove to these bitches I was a good parent? I wanted to tell them to shove that shit, but the judge made it clear that was the only way I would get the girls back.

I was tired as hell. The night before, Lori and I were up in Club Obsession partying. I swear I had not partied like this since before I got with Micah. I was kind of loving this single life, because I could come and go like I wanted to without a nigga questioning me. Shit I was free to fuck whoever I wanted. Speaking of fucking niggas, last night while I was at Club Obsession,

I bumped into this nigga Keyshawn who I knew way back when I was dancing. He was a known dope boy all over the west side of Atlanta. We ended up talking and I brought him back to the house with me. I swear that nigga ate my pussy so damn good I busted over six times. I ain't goin' to lie, I missed fucking him; however, he was a known ho and he wasn't into settling down with no one woman. While he was up inside of me, he kept telling me how much he loved me and he wanted us to be together. I didn't believe that nigga, but he was talking really good and I was prepared to play the role.

I lay beside the nigga as his ass snored up a storm. I meant to get his ass up early before Lori woke up, but the nigga was knocked the hell out after I put the pussy on him. I decided to let him sleep for another hour or so. I sure planned to get a few hundred dollars up off him before he left.

I was on Facebook politicking when I heard a knock on the door. "Ayana, open the door," Lori yelled.

What the hell she wants? I thought with an attitude. "Hold on a minute," I yelled back with annoyance in my voice. I jumped up out of the bed and grabbed my T-shirt that was on the chair beside the bed. I quickly put it on, then opened the door a little, making sure she couldn't see in the room.

"Yo, you lost your damn mind! I know damn well you didn't bring this nigga Keyshawn up in here," she said in a high-pitched tone.

"Lower your voice! I didn't think you'd mind, if I kept him in the room the entire time."

"Are you fucking serious? That nigga is from the west side and you know Mari and them don't fuck with them west side niggas. You wrong as fuck. I gave you a place to stay, not make my home into your personal whorehouse."

I was getting upset with this bitch! I was pretty much aware that this was her shit. But I wasn't no little girl and I just gave that bitch $400 the other day, so technically this was my damn room for the time being.

"Really? This is how you goin' to carry it? I would never carry it like this with you." I shook my head in amazement.

"You know what, Ayana? I stepped up to help you when no one else would. Not even your own mother. I love my man and I'm not gonna jeopardize his safety over some nigga you're only fucking. Get this nigga out of my shit before I have to throw him out."

"Nah, fuck that Miss High and Mighty. I will leave with him. Don't you ever think because you got an apartment you better than me. Bitch, I just had a minor setback. But watch me; you will see when I make a comeback. You carrying me over a lame-ass nigga who's fucking everything with a pussy in Atlanta," I spat.

"Girl, bye! He might be fucking everything, but at least he didn't leave me for my best friend."

I lunged toward that bitch, but I missed.

"Babe, what's all this commotion?" her man, Mari, asked, as he stepped into the hallway in his boxers.

"Go back to lie down, boo. Ayana was just getting her things so she can leave." This bitch stared me down. She knew that he just saved her behind from getting a beat down.

I walked back into the room and slammed the door behind me! "Keyshawn, you need to get up! We got to go." I starting shaking this nigga.

"Man, what you need?" he asked groggily.

"We got to go! This ain't my shit and Lori bitch ass mad that I brought you over here. So we got to go."

"We? Where the fuck you going?"

"What you mean? I'm going with you. Last night you were telling me how you want to be with me."

"Ma, that was the alcohol talking. I ain't ready for all that. I mean, we cool and shit, but I ain't tryin'a be in no relationship and shit. I'm a street nigga."

Tears welled up in my eyes! I wasn't crying over this fuck nigga; I was mad that I believed that bullshit-ass lie.

"You know what? Fuck you, nigga. I was only trying you to see where your head was at! Now I know. Get the fuck out of my face and please lose my number," I lashed out.

I started to gather my belongings and stuff them into garbage bags. I was tired of everybody and their bullshit. I was shocked that my bitch behaved like this all because of her nigga. These bitches were all the same; they would fuck their friends over all because of a piece of dick.

I grabbed my bags and walked out the door. I went back inside twice to grab the rest of my shit. The lame-ass nigga Keyshawn finally got his ass up and walked out. He didn't say a word; he jumped into his Impala and burned tires pulling away. I slammed the door shut and walked to my car. I placed the bags into my trunk then got into my car. I looked back at the house. I was mad at this bitch; I could have beaten her ass.

I pulled out a cigarette and lit it. I took a few drags before I pulled off. *This shit got to end,* I thought as I drove down the street. I had a few hundred dollars, but I knew it wouldn't last long.

I had to get a room so I could figure out my next move fast!

I had enough money to pay for a room at the Metro Extended Stay on Memorial Drive. I dialed Daquan's number. It was time to fuck him again so I could get some more money. I hoped this time he was more generous because I needed enough money to get a lawyer so I could fight for my children. I ain't goin' to lie, I missed having them around; plus, this was the only way I was going to get child support from their no-good-ass daddy!

I got out of the shower. I was about to get dressed when I heard my phone ringing. First I ignored it, but it kept ringing. When I picked it up, I noticed it was the social worker's number. I wasn't in the mood to deal with this bitch right now. But I picked up anyway.

"Hello, Miss Warren, how can I help you?" I asked in a dry tone.

"Hello there. I have some news concerning your daughters."

"What might that be? Y'all letting them come home to their mama now?" I asked with an attitude.

"No, ma'am, at least not as yet. You need to first find a place that is suitable for you and the girls, then the court will consider giving the girls back. However, the father of the children, Mr. Brown, filed court papers. He wants to get custody of the children. A court date is set for the hearing."

"What the fuck you mean, this nigga filed for full custody of my children? So this nigga can whup my ass, abandoned his children and me, and now he filing for custody? Are you kidding me?"

"Well, as the paternal parent of the children, he has all rights to file for custody of his children. If the courts deem you unfit, they will then look at the next parent to see if he is fit to take the children. I advise you to be present at all court hearings if you do not wish to lose full custody of your children."

Without saying another word to this bitch, I hung the phone up. This bitch pretended like she was on my side, but she really wasn't. I threw the phone onto the floor and grabbed my hair and screamed, "Nooooooooooooo!"

This couldn't be happening! This nigga was trying to get custody of my children. The same children I carried for nine fucking months and pushed out of my pussy. There was no way I was gonna allow my children to be around this nigga and his bitch. I grabbed the bottle of cheap wine I had on the nightstand and I put it straight to my head. I didn't give two fucks that it was burning my chest.

"Noooo. It will never happen, Anthony," I screamed as I threw the bottle into the wall. Glass splattered everywhere; kind of how my soul was feeling! I fell to my knees crying. I couldn't believe Anthony would do me like this. This was me, the love of his life. I gave him his firstborn. I was hurting inside. "God, please help me, please, God. I can't take this anymore. I just want to die, God," I cried as my lips trembled.

CHAPTER FORTY-THREE

Tiana

The lawyer said as long as we could prove that we could provide care for the girls, he had a strong feeling that the judge would grant him full custody. I wasn't sure how I felt about the full custody part. I mean, I knew that Ayana wasn't the best mother, but I didn't think no mother should lose their children. I really hoped she would get her shit in order so she could get joint custody of the children.

We were up bright and early. I could tell Micah was nervous. It was a big day for him. I prayed for him and his children. I prayed for our marriage and the drama that was sure to come.

"You ready, boo?"

"Yup! How you feeling?"

"I'm good, ma."

I didn't believe him. I thought he was trying his best not to show his true feelings. "A'ight, come on, boy. Let's go."

Micah and Baby Micah got in the car and I pulled off. I tried to make small talk to kind of break the silence in the car.

I dropped Baby Micah off at the daycare and we proceeded to the juvenile courthouse on Memorial Drive. I searched for a parking space in the packed parking lot. I finally found one; I quickly pulled in before the car in front of me had a chance. I parked and we got out, walking toward the front of the building. I spotted the lawyer, so I touched Micah's arm and pointed toward his direction. We walked over to him, where he explained everything that we could expect today. All in all, he explained that Micah should be prepared to take the girls home today.

I watched as Micah's face lit up like a child right around Christmastime. I, on the other hand, had mixed feelings. However, I hid that shit and smiled like there were no worries.

We finished talking to the lawyer and walked off. Micah must've sensed my uneasiness, because he placed his arm around me and squeezed my shoulder.

"Well, well, well, if it ain't my baby daddy and his whore," Ayana said as she cut in front of us.

"Yo, B, this ain't the place for this shit for real," Micah said with clenched teeth.

She pointed at Micah. "Don't you dare address me." She turned her attention back to me. "Well, hello there, Miss Bitch. You have a nerve showing your face up in here. If you think you're gonna get the chance to play mommy to my fucking kids, you better think again."

"You know what, Ayana, you still pitiful as the last time I saw you. Next time you gonna address me, please address me as Mrs. Brown. Now get the fuck out of my and my husband's way before I push your ass down." I grabbed Micah's arm and we walked off.

That bitch started screaming obscenities, but we kept walking. I had hoped she would've kept her rachetness under control today, at least for today, but I guessed she didn't give a damn.

We sat beside our lawyer and waited for the judge to get on the bench. I could tell Micah was bothered by the way Ayana behaved. Shit I couldn't really say I felt for him, because he chose that ho!

CHAPTER FORTY-FOUR

Ayana

I got up early and got dressed. I made sure I was well put together. I knew Anthony's ass would be at the courthouse today. My goal was to flaunt my ass in front of him so he could see exactly what he had been missing. I hoped this nigga would wake his ass up and realize it was all a mistake and he really wanted to be with me and his girls. I ain't goin' to lie, I really missed him spoiling me and throwing money at me. I applied some Vaseline on my lips and took one last look in the mirror and walked out.

On the way to the courthouse, all sorts of thoughts invaded my mind. I hated that bitch Tiana. I knew one thing: that judge better not make the mistake of giving that nigga and his bitch my damn children.

As I walked into the courthouse I wondered where that court-appointed lawyer was at! That bitch wasn't worth shit for real. I needed to make some money so I could get me a good lawyer. When this shit was over, I planned on taking my children and moving out of this damn state. This nigga would never see my fucking kids again.

I was walking toward the courtroom door when I noticed Ant, and guess who had the nerve to be up in here? That bitch Tiana. See, this bold bitch thought she was some kind of parent to my kids. So, being the bitch I was, I stepped out in front of them. See I saw the fear in that nigga's eyes because he knew I was all about that life and his bitch wasn't. I knew better than to show out in the courthouse though. But I had to let them know this shit wasn't sweet. *They better hope that judge doesn't give my kids to them.*

I addressed both them motherfuckers, but I was thrown off when that bitch said, "Mrs. Brown."

"Anthony, you married this bitch? Are you fucking serious? You left me to be with this bum-ass bitch?" I took a step closer toward that nigga.

"Watch your mouth, B. This my wife now and I need you to stop disrespecting her."

"Fuck you and this bitch. Bitch, you are the lowest kind of ho there is. You wore my old drawers when you was young, and now you fucking and sucking the same dick that I had.

How dare you call my kids your godchildren when you're fucking over their mama? Bitch, I hate you, and I wish you and that little bastard die, you hear me?" I yelled before I stormed off.

I stormed off before I caught a case up in here. I rushed to the bathroom. My heart was beating fast and my palms were sweaty. I scooted down on the floor as I started crying. How did I not hear about this new wedding? I was furious, but an anxiety attack was taking over. I tried to calm myself down, but the pain was intense. "God, noooooo!" I screamed out.

"Are you okay, ma'am?" A white bitch walked up to me and touched me. Without responding, I shot that bitch a dirty look. She hissed at me, then stormed off.

I managed to get my anxiety level to the point where I could breathe. I got up off the ground and quickly washed my face. I used a paper towel to dry it off. I hurried out of the bathroom. I didn't want to miss court.

"Miss Beasly, I was looking for you," a bitch in a cheap-looking suit said to me as soon as I walked in the courtroom.

"Who are you?" I asked with an attitude.

"I'm your court-appointed layer. I called and left several messages for you the other day. I wanted to go over this case with you. We don't have any time right now so we will talk after court is over. Let's go sit over here." She pointed to a table.

I sat beside my lawyer as they sat on the other side beside who I believed to be their lawyer. I tried to shoot their asses dirty looks, but they didn't look my way. I still wasn't feeling good. I heard mumbling as the judge entered the court-room. I was feeling confused. I couldn't make out anything they were saying. I was becoming dizzy. My heart rate sped up and I became hot.

"Listen, can you request a recess?"

"What's the matter?"

"I . . . I don . . ."

CHAPTER FORTY-FIVE

Tiana

Talk about a drama queen. How was this ol', retarded-ass bitch gonna pass out in the midst of the judge's ruling? I knew I wasn't the only one there thinking that it was foolery. I heard a thump and when I looked over I saw her hit the ground. Micah walked over that way to see what was happening, but I couldn't bring myself to be part of this mockery. The ambulance was called and she was wheeled out of there.

"What happened?" my nosey behind asked Micah as he walked back to the table.

"Ayana fainted. I think she faking that shit."

"Oh, okay," was all I managed to say before the judge called for order.

Court was back in full swing. Her lawyer pled her case, the lawyer for the state spoke, and then our lawyer spoke. There really wasn't anyone disputing that she was an unfit parent at the moment. Our lawyer provided proof why we would be the best possible choice for the girls. The judge agreed and gave Micah full custody of the girls. However, the judge did say if Ayana found a place to live and completed her classes, she would share custody with him.

"Yes!" he yelled and grabbed me up in a bear hug.

"Congrats, babe."

"When can I get my girls?" he turned and asked the lawyer.

"Well, as soon as everything is signed. I believe the girls are here in the courthouse."

I saw the excitement on his face. *I hope this is for the best,* I thought as I scooted down into my seat. I was happy being mommy to one little boy, but now our lives would be forever changed!

The first night the girls were at the house was very awkward.

"Auntie T, I haven't seen you in a while. Where have you been?" Dominique asked.

I was hoping that they wouldn't ask too many questions because I could imagine how weird this looked to them. At one point I was their auntie and now I was here playing stepmommy to them.

Things really got bad the first morning we sat at the table to eat breakfast.

"Girls, we need to talk to y'all," Micah said.

"Do you need to do this alone?" I asked.

"Nah, you need to be here. Girls, this is Baby Micah and he is your brother."

"But how? This is Auntie's baby," Dominque blurted out.

I breathed hard. "Yes, this is Auntie's baby, but he is also your daddy's son. So he is your brother."

"I don't get it. How can you be my auntie and his mother, and he's daddy's son all at the same time?"

"Well, it is all grown-up stuff, but your Auntie Tiana and I are married now. We are a family."

I could tell she was confused. There was no easy way to explain this to her. Bottom line was, her auntie was now Daddy's wife and for now we were a family.

I spent the next few days taking them to the doctor and the dentist. It was a shame that they were behind on their shots and you could tell they hadn't been to the dentist recently. After getting their immunization records up to par, Micah took them to the school and registered them.

Finally, things were starting to be a little normal again. Micah's mother would take them on the weekend so we could get a little break. God knows I needed that because I had finals coming up and the struggle was real. I couldn't risk failing a class, because I would have to pay to take it over.

CHAPTER FORTY-SIX

Ayana

I woke up and looked around, and that's when it hit me that I fainted while I was in the courthouse. "Fuck," I blurted out.

"How are you feeling, Miss Beasly?" the nurse asked.

"How the fuck you think I'm feeling? I fainted in court, and now I don't know what happened with my kids. I need to get them," I yelled as I jumped off the hospital bed.

"Ma'am, wait for the doctor. He has to discharge you."

"No, bitch, you wait for him. I'm outta here."

I grabbed my clothes that were nearby and got dressed right in front of her. I grabbed my purse, and dashed out of the room. I made it outside, but then I realized that I didn't drive my car up here. *Fuck, as if this day could get any worse.* I dug into my purse and pulled out my cell. The battery was dying, which was not a good look since I didn't have my phone charger with me. I frantically searched through my phone contacts and pulled up Daquan's number. I knew he probably was tired of me, but I had no one else to call upon.

"Hello," he answered with a slight attitude.

"Damn, what's wrong wit'cha?"

"What's good, yo! This ain't no good time," he said dryly.

"Who is that on the phone, babe?" I heard a female voice ask.

"This a fien' tryin'a cop sump'n," he lied.

"Oh, okay," she said.

"A fien'? Are you fucking serious?"

"Yo, man, I just told you, this ain't no good time."

"Well, I'm stuck at DeKalb Medical on Hillandale and I need a ride to the hotel."

"I can't leave right now yo."

"Listen, boo, I need you to come pick me up. I would hate for your bitch to hear that I was fucking and sucking her nigga on the regular."

There was a long pause on the phone, then he spoke. "A'ight, I be there." He hung the phone up in my ear. I hated that I had to go there with him, but I had no one else to call.

I found a bench to sit on, and about thirty minutes passed before I saw his car pulling up to the entrance. I stood up and walked over to the car as soon as he stopped.

"Man, get in," he demanded. I got in, and he pulled off. "What hotel you at?"

"The Red Inn Roof on Candler Road."

There was total quietness on the ride to the hotel. I could tell he was irritated, because his face was screwed up and not once did he glance my way. He pulled into the parking lot and stopped.

"Are you coming in?"

Without responding he parked the car and we got out. I opened the door and we walked in. I decided to take a quick shower while he rolled a blunt. I knew it wouldn't be long before he got over that little attitude he had. There was no way he could stay mad at me after I gave him this tongue game and clamped this pussy down on him.

I quickly washed off and made sure my pussy smelled good. I lotioned down then walked out into the room area. He was laid back on the bed smoking his blunt.

"So, you 'ont plan on speaking to me?" I asked sarcastically.

"Shit I'm speaking now. How about you get on your knees so I can fuck you from the back?" he demanded.

I wasn't tripping. I knew that I was bound to get a couple Gs up off him. So I gladly got on all fours. He unbuttoned his pants and got behind me. He used his hands to push my head down into the mattress and pull my ass up toward him, arching my back. He slid into me, and started fucking me aggressively. In spite of the enormous amount of pain I was feeling, I still managed to throw my ass back at him. I noticed that he was fucking me harder than usual. He then stopped. I felt his hands clasped around my neck. *Oh, so he into rough sex, I see.*

That thought quickly left my mind when I felt his hands tighten around my neck. He pulled out and flipped me over on my back. I tried to remove his hands from my neck, but he was strong and he had a tight grip.

"Bitch, don't you ever threaten to tell my woman shit about what we do. Do you fucking hear me?" He squeezed tighter.

I tried to answer, but I couldn't. So I shook my head so he could know I understood him.

"Matter of fact, lose my motherfucking number," he said before he let go.

I started coughing as I raised my hand to feel my neck. I was heated as fuck. "Yo, fuck you and that bitch. If she were all that, your ass wouldn't be blowing me up like you do."

"I'm a man, so yes, if I see free pussy, I'm gonna take it. You damage goods though; ain't no nigga tryin'a wife you. I heard about that shit with you and that nigga from the west side the other day. B, your pussy is community pussy for real." He laughed.

"Get the fuck out of here. Like I said, you better hope I don't see your bitch. I bet you she'd love to know how you eat my pussy up and lick my ass."

"I ain't goin' to sit here arguing with you. But you already know I let my gun do the talking. Be careful. Your mama might find yo' ass at the bottom of the river." He opened the door and left.

I fell out crying! My neck was still hurting from the grip he placed on it. I tried to stop the tears, but the more I thought about everything, the heavier it came pouring down. I got up and ran to my purse. I dug deep, trying to find some pills. I couldn't find any, so I threw the bag over in the corner. I'd heard people talking about hitting rock bottom, but this was my first time really feeling it. My insides felt empty. Anger built up as my thoughts wandered to Ant and his bitch.

***

I was asleep when I heard a loud banging on the door. I grabbed my cell phone and noticed it was after 11:00 a.m. "Damn, I slept this long?" I said out loud. The banging grew louder, so I got up out of the bed. I peeped through the hole and realized it was the hotel clerk. That's when it hit me that my bill was due. I tried to ignore him, but he wasn't letting up.

"Yes, how may I help you?" I opened the door with an attitude.

"You have to pay today if you want to stay," he said bluntly.

"Can't I pay this evening or tomorrow?" I tried to buy more time.

"No, it was due last night. You have to get your things and leave the property if you don't have the money."

"Listen, look, you can hold my bracelet and I also have a chain I can give to you," I damn well started pleading.

"I'm sorry, I can't accept those."

I didn't know what to do. This Indian man stood in front of me with his arms folded.

"Listen, I don't have anywhere to go right now. Can we work something out, please?" I pleaded.

He looked at me like he was trying to size me up.

"Listen, I can make you feel good, daddy," I said in my sexy voice. I pulled the door back and, just like a man, he stepped inside.

"What did you have in mind?" he asked in his thick Indian accent.

I didn't waste any time. I dropped to my knees. I took out his wrinkly, pale dick and started massaging it. I swear, I didn't want to do this, but a bitch was desperate. I got it hard; then I started to lick the tip.

"Aargh," he groaned.

I then took the full length into my mouth, which wasn't much in the first place. I closed my eyes and pretended like I was making love to Ant. This made it so much easier for me to please this old fool. He moaned and groaned and wiggled. I felt his veins getting bigger. I knew he was ready to bust, so I removed my mouth. Seconds later, sperm shot out. I backed away because I didn't want that shit on me. I got up and looked at him. "So we good right? I can stay another month?"

"I want some of the pussy," this bold-ass fool said.

I looked at him. There was no way I was gonna let that little-ass dick nigga fuck me.

"Come on, I got to hurry up and get back to the front desk."

I huffed hard, then walked off to the bed. I reluctantly took my underwear off. I lay on my back. I was hoping it would be quick. I closed my eyes as he climbed on top of me. I cringed as he entered me. I wanted to literally die.

"Ohhh, damn it, this is good pussy," he mumbled as he thrust deep inside of me.

I wish he'd just hurry the fuck up, I thought as I tried not to snap on this fool.

Within minutes, he pulled out and busted all over the bed. I quickly jumped off the bed. "Okay, so we good right? I am going to stay here for another month."

"No, not good. I can do another week."

I took a step closer. "Listen to me, you ol' banana boat nigga. I said a month, do you hear me? If not, trust and believe I will call the motherfucking police and let them know you barged in here and raped me. See, nigga, I'm not in the mood to be playing."

I guessed he understood English pretty well, because he looked at me and shook his head in disgust. He mumbled something under his breath, and walked out of the room.

I ran to the shower and jumped in it. I scrubbed between my legs viciously. I was trying to erase every scent of this motherfucker off me. I felt sick to my stomach. After about twenty minutes, I was satisfied. I got out, wrapped a towel around me, then grabbed my toothbrush. I gagged as I brushed thoroughly. I then rinsed for a long time with my mouthwash.

I sat on the bed, just thinking. I needed to map out my next move. I was pretty sure that Indian motherfucker was going to let me stay for a month, but I was still broke. I had to figure out a way to make some money.

I definitely missed my bitch Lori. I still couldn't believe that shit happened between us. I hadn't talked to my other bitches either because they were closer and I had no idea what she had told them; and I damn sure wasn't in no mood to explain myself to anybody.

I got dressed, and decided to grab me a few things out of the grocery store. I couldn't tell the last time I ate a good meal; plus, I needed some soap. *If a bitch ain't got shit, I got to have soap to wash my ass.*

I decided to go to the Kroger on South Hairston. They be having fresh everything up in there, because the uppity black people and the whites shop there. I wasn't surprised to see the parking lot packed. I drove around a few times before I spotted an elderly lady pulling out. I quickly positioned myself so I could turn in as soon as she pulled out.

I locked my car and walked into the store. I headed to the snack aisle. I needed something to appease my appetite. I was looking down when I bumped into someone. "Excuse me," I said as I lifted up my head. "Miss Judith, is that you?" I asked in astonishment.

"But, wait, I know you?" she asked.

"Yes, Ayana. Your daughter Tiana and I were best friends. She came to live with my mom and me after she left your house."

She took her glasses off and stared at me from head to toe. "Yes! Yes! I remember you. It's been years; how you been doing?"

"I'm good. I know. I haven't seen you in years. I kept asking your daughter for you, but she act like she didn't where you was at."

"Hmm. That worthless child. Of course, she don't know what is going on with her own mama. I could've been dead, her ass wouldn't know that."

"Yes, I know. I used to tell her that she shouldn't be like that toward you, but you know how she is."

"So where you staying at now?"

"Well, I'm staying at the motel over on Candler Road for a little time."

"Why? You ain't got nowhere to stay?"

"Not right now. Going through some things. Your daughter did some messed-up things to me and caused me to lose everything."

I knew I had her curiosity now and that's exactly what I intended.

CHAPTER FORTY-SEVEN

Tiana

It'd been three months since the girls moved in with us. Some days were better than others. I tried my best to let them handle things pertaining to them. I made sure they were well taken care of when Micah was around. Baby Micah loved having his sisters around and they were happy they had a younger brother around.

"Hey, ma, you good? You look tired," Micah said as he walked into the room.

"Yes, just have a migraine that's all."

"You need to make an appointment! I don't like how these headaches be having you. This started happening after the shooting. Them motherfuckers need to do another MRI on you," he said in a concerned tone.

"I know, right? I don't know. I keep taking that Elavil that they prescribed. I was hoping it would do better. A girl at school says I should try drinking coffee, because it helps with migraines."

"Well, you need to get on that ASAP. I hate to see my baby hurting like that." He gave me a kiss on my cheek.

"So, husband, when are you gonna start back at school? I mean you keep on putting it off, but I think you need to get back in there."

He rubbed his head and breathed out loud. I could tell he wasn't feeling my questioning. But I didn't give a fuck. See lately I'd noticed that he was leaving early and coming in late and I'd also noticed that he had been spending a little more than usual. See I ain't no dumb bitch; his behavior was screaming to me that he was back out there in those streets.

"Damn, ma, ease up already! I told you I will. I just got a lot on my mind right now and I am not ready to jump back into school already."

"Really? I don't see what's stopping you. The shop is doing good. The kids are in school. So please explain to me what the problem is."

"Damn, T, you need to know when to chill the fuck out. What if school ain't for me? What if I don't want to go back? What's gonna happen then?" he asked angrily.

"Well, say that then. Stop sitting up in here lying and shit. I ain't no damn fool, so I suggest you stop acting like I am."

"You know what, B, sometimes you just need to shut the fuck up. Ain't nobody taking you for no fucking fool. Yo, I'm out."

I started to respond, but my head was pounding and I really didn't feel like reading him his rights. I done told his ass I wasn't interested in being no jail nigga's wife. Me or my child wasn't gonna be taking no trip to the penitentiary. And trust and believe, I meant that shit.

I was kind of suspicious that he might be fucking somebody else. I didn't have any proof, but the way he'd been behaving lately I wouldn't put nothing past him. *I swear, he better keep that shit away from me, 'cause if I ever catch him cheating it's gonna be over for good,* I thought as I dozed off.

I jumped up, looked around, and realized I was still on the couch downstairs. I was sweating and I had tears in my eyes. I'd just had the worst dream. It was very strange, because I dreamt that I was getting married. Matter of fact, I had on the most beautiful wedding dress. I was in the dressing room, then out of nowhere Ayana appeared. She had a devilish look on her face, and she had a gun pointed at me. In my dream, I was talking to her; then she shot me. I didn't remember anything after that.

I sat there scared for minute, even though I was awake. I still felt terrified. I wondered why I had that dream. I mean, I knew Ayana and I were not talking now, but what did this dream mean? I finally pulled myself together. I got up, and walked in the kitchen to get a glass of water. I felt drained, like the dream drained all my energy. I leaned on the counter, trying to regain a little bit of energy. That's when flashes of me getting shot flashed in my mind. I was terrified when Ayana aimed the gun at me and fired the gun.

The glass fell out of my hand and splattered all over the ceramic tiles, spreading splinters everywhere. I didn't care that I didn't have any shoes on my feet. I ran out of the kitchen and up the stairs. "Micah! Micah!" I yelled as I busted in the room.

To my surprise, the room was empty and the bed was still made. I glanced at the clock on the wall. It was 2:00 a.m., and my husband wasn't at home in our bed. I sat down on the bed, feeling disappointed. This was the first time since we got married he stayed out this late. This heightened my suspicions about him.

I walked back downstairs to search for my cell phone. I called his phone, but it went straight to voice mail. I tried again, but the same thing happened. I turned the lights off, and walked back up the stairs. I lay across the bed. The dream and the flashback I had had me feeling some kind of way. Ayana? Could it be true that Ayana shot me? Was I making up things because I was angry with her or because her children were here with me?

I needed answers. I needed to know if this bitch really crossed the line by trying to kill me. I thought about calling the detective who was on my case, but I quickly dismissed that idea. I needed to find out on my own, because I ain't no wicked bitch but if this bitch tried to kill me, I promised I was gonna end her life.

I waited for another hour. Then I tried Micah's number again, but there was still no response. I threw the phone beside me, grabbed a pillow, and put my head on it.

I was up bright and early. I walked downstairs to check if this nigga made it home. There he was, asleep on my couch. I walked over shaking his legs.

"Yo, what's good?"

"What's good? You didn't come home last night, and you asking me what's good? Nah, honey, I should be asking you what the hell is going on?"

"Ain't nothing going on! You was on your bullshit, so I left to go hang with the niggas and we got to drinking and smoking."

"Do you see how that sounds? You're a married man. Hanging out smoking weed and coming into the house all times of the night isn't acceptable. I already know what kind of bitches you are used to. But you already know I'm not one of them. If you feel the need to be single, you need to get a fucking divorce. Because I will not, and I repeat, will not be doing this with you. I'm a grown-ass woman and there's no way I'm gonna hang around playing childish games."

"Damn, you wake me up with all this? It's too damn early for this." He closed his eyes.

"You heard me, Anthony Micah Brown. This is not a game."

I walked out of the living room before I could go off on this nigga. In a way, I was relieved to see that he was fine. God knows these Georgia streets were cruel.

At 7:00 a.m., I woke the kids up so I could get them ready for school. This morning I was in my feelings though. I didn't make these damn children, but I had to be up with them. Their mama was off somewhere being a ho and their daddy was lying on my couch pretending like he was so damn tired.

"Auntie, are you okay? You look sad," Diamond asked.

I faked a quick smile. "Yes, sugar, Auntie doing just fine," I lied.

"Oh, okay. I love you."

"Love you too, baby girl. Now get your things and your sister's. Let's go," I yelled as I walked up the stairs. I had to finish dressing Baby Micah.

I got them into the car; then I pulled off. Even as I could hear them talking and singing in the back seat, my mind was far away. I wasn't tripping off Micah's ass. Even though I loved him, I could easily get a divorce. My mind was more on Ayana and my dream.

I dropped the kids off, then headed back home. I didn't have school until the afternoon, so I had time to wash some clothes and clean up the house a little. First I stopped by Dunkin' Donuts to grab a cup of coffee, trying to see if I could get this migraine down a little.

I parked and walked into the house. I went upstairs and turned the television on. I loved watching the news early in the morning so I could kind of catch up on what was going on in the city.

CHAPTER FORTY-EIGHT

Ayana

I ended up moving out of the hotel and into Miss Judith's house. She lived alone in a two-bedroom house. It wasn't located in the best neighborhood, but it would do just fine. It was really sad how she treated me better than my own damn mother.

I ended up telling her about the situation between her daughter and me. I wasn't too shocked that she believed everything that I was saying. I didn't know what the hell Tiana did to her, but whatever it was, it made her angry even after all these years.

"Here go some bacon and eggs," she said as I entered the kitchen.

"Thank you. I was starving, too." I sat down at the table where she was sitting.

"Lemme ask you a question."

"Whassup?"

"Are you gonna just lie down and let this bitch play mommy to your kids?"

"No, I'm not. But I need to make some money first so I can go after him and get my kids."

"Lemme tell you something, child. You better put on your big girl panties and fight for your man and your damn children. That daughter of mine is trifling; she should've never crossed that line. But that's why the old code is you never tell your girlfriends about the man you screwing."

"Yes, I learned the hard way. There's no way I could've known that Tiana would do me like this. I mean, you know how close we were."

"Well, fuck all that now! That little bitch isn't loyal to anyone; you see how she do me, and I'm her damn mama. She didn't even invite me to her damn wedding. I was hurt, because I gave her life and did e'erything for her. Hmm, enough about me, the thing is what are you gonna do about it? I mean, if you're cool with letting her take your kids and your man, then that's cool. But if you're not, I say you need to get your shit together and show her who the real head bitch is."

Finally, I had someone on my side who understood me and where I was coming from. I bit a piece of my bacon as I let what she said sink into my head. She had no idea how much of a boost she gave me just now! I wished my own mama would be this supportive. Instead, her ass was too busy drinking.

"Now that we're talking, I've always want to know what the hell happened at your house between Tiana and your boyfriend. She told me her side, but you already know she can't be trusted," I said.

"Child, that little bitch was a liar. Ain't no damn way Aubrey wanted to have sex with her. Her little ass was fast, and would try to throw her little ass on him. I blame myself because I knew she was hot in the pants, so I should've made sure she wasn't listening to us at night when we were having sex. I figured she wanted to feel what I was feeling and, when he turned down her advances, she turned around and accused him, thinking I was goin' to get rid of him, but see I wasn't no fool. I know her kind and even though I pushed her out of me, I still didn't trust her little ass."

"Oh, I see. I've always wanted to know what really happened. I should've known, because you are her mama and she did that shit to you. I wish I never brought that bitch in my life. She even have my mama fooled."

"Aubrey never fully got over her spreading these lies about him, so after years of trying to work it out he left and married some woman from Clayton County. I almost lost my sanity behind him leaving. I could never forget what that little bitch did to me. I moved and I sank into depression. I guess you can say I hit rock bottom. It was two years ago. I tried to commit suicide, and it was like God intervened, because it was my wake-up call to stop drinking and using drugs. So I checked myself into rehab and, thank God, I've been a year clean. That little bitch screwed my life up."

We ended up talking some more. I even started crying my eyes out. I ain't goin' to lie, it felt good when she got up, walked over to me, and rubbed my back. "Baby, it's gonna be all right. I'm here now. Trust me, you'll never need anyone else."

I looked at her and smiled. "Thank you. You have no idea how much this means to me."

"No thanks needed! That's what real women do; we uplift each other. Now dry them damn tears. We need to figure out how to get your man and your kids back."

I just nodded in agreement. I didn't know what her motives were for going after her daughter, but I didn't give a damn! I was just happy that I had an ally and someplace to lay my head.

***

Social services came to visit the other day at Miss Judith's house, but they didn't think the living conditions were suitable for the girls. Bullshit, this lady's house was clean. I swear these motherfuckers were not worried about giving my kids back. The bitch told me I also needed a job to take care of them. Even though I didn't want to go back to stripping, I had no choice; plus, I missed being in the spotlight and being able to spend money the way I wanted to. I remember being one of the baddest bitches to dance in the clubs so, minus the few pounds I put on, I still was one of the best to do it.

I drove over to Pin-Up. I knew the manager; he used to beg me to dance at his club. So I already knew he wouldn't say no to me.

I was happy that he gave me the job. Now I just had to get all my stuff and it was on and popping.

My first night back was better than I thought. It'd been years since I swung on a pole, but it felt like I'd never left. I slowly wound, twerked, and grabbed the crowd's attention. At the end of the night, I counted my money. I realized I made over two grand on a Thursday night. I was amped up, because the weekend was coming up and I knew the club was going to be packed.

I got dressed, gave the club their cut, and left. My body was tired, and my bed was calling my name. I need some energy drinks if I wanted to stay dancing.

I walked into the house feeling drained. I quickly snatched off my clothes, and got into my bed. I cut the phone off and threw it on the chair. I smiled to myself; here I was worried about making money. I must've forgotten that I was a beast when it came to grinding.

Even though I enjoyed staying here, my next move was to find my own shit. I couldn't wait to get my children back, and far away from that nigga. I was too tired to focus on his bitch ass right now. So I closed my eyes, trying to catch some sleep, because tonight I would be back at it again.

CHAPTER FORTY-NINE

Tiana

Micah called himself not speaking, but I didn't give a fuck. One thing I'd learned about niggas: if you give them an inch, they will take a damn yard. I'd already been through a lot with him and his bitch as it was. I refused to continue letting him think shit was sweet. Don't get me wrong, I was in love with my husband; but I wasn't going to support his foolishness.

He finally woke up off my couch and took a shower. This was the kind of way he was living now. He got dressed, grabbed his keys, and left. I guessed he thought I was going to say something, but I didn't.

I got up off the couch, and decided to mop the kitchen floor before it was time to leave for class. As soon as I walked into the kitchen, I heard my doorbell ringing. *Who the fuck is that?*

I turned back around and walked toward the front door. It was definitely too damn early for these Jehovah Witnesses people to be ringing folks' doorbells. I opened the door. I was ready to cuss them out, church folks or not. I blinked twice, swallowed hard, then spoke. "What the fuck are you doing at my house?" I stepped outside to address the bitch who gave me life.

"Well, hello to you, daughter," this bitch had the nerve to say.

My blood was boiling and my chest tightened. I flashed back to the last time I saw that bitch. It was the same day she accused me of wanting her man.

"I'm not your daughter because you damn sure ain't nobody mama. How the fuck you got my address, and what in the world would possess you to come to my house? The day I left your house I hoped to never see you again."

"You better watch your mouth, Miss Mighty. I am your damn mama, and you not gonna sit in my face and disrespect me like this."

I balled my fist up and stepped closer to her. "Try me, bitch! I'm not that helpless little girl you cussed out. I'm a grown-ass woman, so don't you think for a second I won't jump on your ass, Mama! Now get the fuck off my property before I call the police on your ass for trespassing."

"Ha-ha, you finally grew some balls. You think you can just go around and treat people like this? What you did to me, and now Ayana, is dead wrong. That girl took you in; now you done slept with her man and took her children. God damn sure don't like ugly! You gonna get what's coming to you," she spat.

"Oh, I see you've been talking to that bitch. I'm not surprised, since both of you are deadbeat parents. What do they say? 'Birds of a feather flock together.'" I turned and walked back into my house slamming my door shut.

I leaned on the closed door, giving myself a second to digest this crazy shit. I hadn't seen this bitch since I ran out of her house. Not one time did that bitch try to find her teenage daughter. I could've been raped or killed, but she didn't give a fuck; she was too busy chasing that dirty-ass dick nigga.

I got myself together; then I walked into the kitchen. I needed a strong drink. Micah had Patrón, so I poured myself a big glass. I knew I needed to be in class, but I wasn't going today thanks to this bitch. She just fucked my entire day up.

Okay, so after I calmed down, I put on my thinking cap. I wondered how the hell this bitch got my address. Not too many people knew where I stayed at. I sat there quiet, and that's when it hit me. She'd been talking to Ayana, and that bitch knew my address from the address on the custody papers. So these two bitches were in cahoots against me.

I dialed Micah's number. At first he pressed ignore, but then I called right back. He answered. "Yo."

"Listen, you need to come to the house now," I yelled.

"What's wrong? You good?"

"If I were good, I wouldn't be asking you to come to the house, would I?" I asked smartly.

"A'ight, on the way." He hung up.

I sat down, trying to keep my anger under control. That bitch Ayana couldn't come at me like a grown bitch, so she was gonna go find this bitch to come do her dirty work. At first, I couldn't remember what happened when I got shot, but for the last few days my memory was back and, each time, all I saw was Ayana standing in front of me with a gun. I knew this bitch was mad because Micah stayed with me, but would she go to the extreme of trying to kill me?

I heard the door open, and Micah walked in. "What's wrong? Why you crying?" He rushed over to me.

I fell out, and my bawling got louder.

"Yo, ma, what's good? Talk to me. Did someone do something to hurt you?"

I couldn't get the crying under control long enough to tell him what was going on. He held me tight while he rubbed my back.

"T, come on now, let a nigga know what's going on. Why the hell you crying?"

I took a few seconds to get my crying under control. Then I started to tell him about my mother showing up at the house. He sat there listening and I could tell he was also thinking.

"Ma, I know you angry and e'erything, but she your mother. Do you think you're overreacting?"

"Nah, I'm not. I was young. I needed her. Her man tried to sleep with me and when I told her, she accused me of wanting him. I didn't want him; I was a young girl, not even thinking about no man. She should've kicked his ass out. Instead, she turned her back on me and accused me of wanting him. I never got over that shit. Now that I'm grown, she gonna show her face. I don't need no damn mama now," I yelled.

"Calm down, babe. I am on your side. I just want you to look at it from a different angle."

"Micah, you will never understand. Your mother has always been in your life. So trust me, you have no idea how bad this hurts. She was dead to me, so yes, I wish she would stay that way."

"T, I know it's been rough between us lately, but I love you. You got your own family now. Maybe one day you will find it in your heart to at least talk with her. Our son gonna want to know who she is one day."

I wasn't even thinking about what he was saying. I felt like my mental state was deteriorating. These bitches were fucking with my life and I wasn't feeling that. I didn't give a fuck that that bitch gave me life. In my book that bitch was dead!

The next day, I got up and decided to go find me a bottle of Mace and I also decided to buy me a gun. I was never the type of woman who believed in violence, but this bitch took it there. Yes, I could call the police and tell them what I remembered, but I didn't want to do that.

I went to the gun shop over in Clayton County. I bought me a light blue 9 mm Glock. I also bought a Taser and Mace.

I picked up the children and headed home. I bathed them, made dinner as usual, and then let them watch TV for a few hours as I stared at the two little girls who got caught up in some bullshit. I never understood why bitches could never let go when a man didn't want them anymore. Why did Ayana have to be so stupid? I apologized to her because it wasn't intentional. But she still didn't let it go.

Micah came home early, just in time for dinner. "Hey, ma, what you cook?" he asked as he walked in the kitchen. I was getting ready to put the dishes in the dishwasher.

"I just put a roast in the oven, with potatoes. I didn't know you were coming home this early. I would've made your plate."

"No worries. I remember you were not feeling good earlier so I decided to come in, so I can help out with the kids."

"That's sweet of you," I joked.

"Regardless of what you think of me, I am a good man and father."

"Well, I never said you weren't. So quit throwing shots at me. You need to work on being a great husband. All these fake fights you trying to pick with me. You need to let that go. Yes, we're not perfect and we're gonna get into arguments, but you need to not run to the streets or these dirty-ass bitches. You don't see me running out there or cheating on you."

"Man, I feel you, but I ain't fucking nothing else. I put that on my dick."

"Be careful swearing on your dick. That shit might fall off," I joked, but I was damn serious. "Here go your food." I handed him a big plate filled with food that I made with love. I wasn't no fool. I knew if you didn't feed your man, there were twenty bitches lined up waiting to feed him that old nasty-ass food they be cooking.

I sat at the table while I ate. I logged into Facebook, being nosey. I scrolled over to his page. As usual, nothing was going on on his page. I thought he had it where no one could post on his timeline. I knew him too well, and he wasn't no dumbass nigga.

We ended the night drinking and smoking. We then went up to the room and he laid his tongue and dick game on me. I swear, every time, my husband made love to me seemed like the first time. All my anger I had toward him was gone soon, as his tongue touched my clit.

CHAPTER FIFTY

Ayana

Three months later

I finally saved enough money to rent a three-bedroom condo in Lithonia. The day the landlord handed me the keys, I broke down and cried. I tell you, ain't nothing like having your own damn place. Now I could do whatever the fuck I wanted to do.

I immediately contacted the worker to let her know that I got my own place. I had a job, and I could financially take care of my children. She informed me that she didn't think the judge was gonna give me full custody, but more like joint custody. By the time I got off the phone with the bitch, I was too upset to think. I didn't want joint anything with this nigga. I wanted my damn kids.

The social worker did a home visit. I was happy to show this bitch my kids' new bedroom furniture. I watched as she wrote things down in her folder. She then went to examine the kitchen, opening up the refrigerator. Bitch must have thought I was stupid. The refrigerator was packed with food that my kids liked.

"Where do you work, Miss Beasly?" this bitch asked me, then took her glasses off.

"Uh, huh. Does it matter, as long as I got a job?"

"I need to know so I can verify that you work there. The judge needs that information before she can make her ruling."

"I work at Pin-Up Gentlemen's Club."

That caught her ass off guard, because she blinked a few times before she scribbled on her papers. "Have you tried getting a regular nine-to-five job? I'm not familiar with strip bars, but I know they're a dangerous place to work and the hours are not regular business hours."

"Listen, lady, I'm trying my damn best to get my children back. It may not be the best place to work, but it's a job that pays well. If I can remember, the judge said a damn job, not a specific kind of job."

"Miss Beasly, you're behaving like the world is against you. I'm only doing my job."

"Well, do your damn job, and let the judge know I got a place and I got employment."

"I need the address of your place of employment and your hours."

I mean mugged that bitch and gave her the information. I was sick of all this shit concerning my kids.

After I completed the required class and three more home visits, I was given joint custody. It was not what I wanted, but the court was showing favoritism to Ant. The arrangement was the kids would be with him during the week and then come to the house Friday to Sunday. I didn't how I was going to deal with it, but whatever. I also had to agree to visits from social services for up to a year, and the girls and I had to go family counseling for six months. These bitches sure wanted a fucking lot for my damn kids.

The first couple of weeks were very hard. My oldest daughter kept hollering she wanted to go back to her daddy's house.

"Listen to me, you better sit your ass down. Because I've been gone don't mean you won't get your ass torn up."

"I don't want to be here. I want to be with my auntie and my daddy."

Slap! Slap! "Watch your freaking mouth! That bitch ain't your auntie. This is where you belong so get used to it."

She got the picture, because she ran off crying. I didn't give a fuck about no damn tears. That bitch done brainwashed my damn children, having them over here hollering and shit.

After the first few outbursts, everything started running smoothly. He would drop them off, and I told his ass his bitch couldn't come to my house. This was our children, not hers and ours! I hired a babysitter to come to the house to watch them at night when I had to work. I knew the people were on my ass; plus, I didn't want to lose them again to the system.

My relationship with Ant was halfway decent. He wasn't as angry as he used to be. I was still angry at his ass for spitting in my face. I knew how he was: if I acted aggressive toward him, then he would show the fuck out. He was a petty-ass nigga for real.

One day, after he dropped the kids off, I invited him in. "Ay, Ant, I cooked. Can you come in for a little? The girls would love that."

"I don't know. I got some things to handle."

"Please, Daddy! Please," my youngest baby said.

He looked into her big brown eyes, and I knew it wouldn't be able to say no. "A'ight. Just for a little though." I saw when he checked the time.

"Sit down, and stop acting like we're strangers. Just because we're not together don't mean we can't be friends."

"'You,' 'me,' and 'friends,' in the same sentence? That shit don't even sound too good. B, you trippin'." He grinned at me.

"Daddy, come see my new bedroom set," Diamond yelled.

He looked at me. I sensed the uneasiness. "Boy, quit playing, you think we gonna hold you down in here? Don't tell me Tiana got you that shook." I laughed.

"What I told you about bringing up my wife?" he said with a serious look on his face.

"Damn, I'm sorry," I lied and raised my hands up in the air.

He got up and followed Diamond, who held on to him, dragging him toward the back with her. I rushed into the kitchen to pour him a glass of Cîroc Apple Vodka. He was in the room a good twenty minutes when I walked back there.

"Are you hungry?"

"Nah, I'm good. I got food at the house."

"Well, here you go. I made you a glass of Cîroc." I handed the glass to him.

He took it, and stared at it.

"Dang, nigga, what you think I'm going to do with the kids right here? You acting foolishly. I done moved on for real."

He shot me a suspicious look, then took his first sip.

"If I was gonna poison you, I would've done that while we're together. You just paranoid." I shook my head in disgust. I stood there as he took a few more sips. I then eased out of the room to straighten up.

I was digging into the couch when I felt someone walk up on me. "You a'ight?" I quizzed him.

"Yeah, I'm good. Tryin'a see what's up with you though. Your ass look phat as fuck in them shorts." He grabbed my hips, grinding on my butt.

"You tripping! You know you a married man now. I doubt your wife would love this." I played like I gave two fucks.

"Man, you my baby mother. Plus, what she don't know won't hurt her. Come on, let's go to your room." He grabbed my hand.

"Gotcha," I mumbled under my breath, as I followed him toward the back, and into my bedroom.

"I'll be right back." I pulled my hand away and walked out of the room. I walked to the kids' room. "Y'all stay in here. Don't come in my room," I said in a serious tone.

"Why? And where's Daddy?" Dominique asked.

"Your daddy is in my room and it's none of your business." I gave her the look of "don't try it, little bitch." I saw this little heifer was going to try me when she got older. I had something for that ass though.

I closed their door and walked back into my room. This married nigga was butt-ass naked in my bed, with his dick pointed to the ceiling.

"Come here, ma, come sit on this dick for me real quick," he said, while he massaged his dick.

I didn't waste no time. I quickly changed down to my birthday suit. I walked over to him, and gently took his hard dick into my mouth, devouring every inch of his manhood. This was my dick so I knew how to please it. I sucked it just the way he liked it. I peeped at him, and could tell he was enjoying it, just as I was. Within a few minutes, his dick got harder and his veins popped out. I sucked aggressively, and within seconds, his sperm shot out of his dick and into my mouth. I opened my mouth so every drop could flow down my throat. I swallowed and used my tongue to clean up the little that spilled out. I was starving for his dick and I made sure I was filled.

I was getting ready to massage the dick so it could get hard again, but he jumped up off the bed and grabbed me up aggressively. "What you doing?"

He didn't respond; instead, he threw me on the bed, parted my legs, and dug deep into my pussy. I shivered when his tongue touched my pussy. I shoved his head deeper in. I was shocked! I never thought in a million years I would get the chance to feel this nigga's tongue ever again. I wrapped my legs around his shoulders as he pleased my pussy. My body shook as I came into his mouth! He didn't ease up any; he continued sucking on my pussy! I came back to back. I felt like I was about to bust a vein in my head, the way I was feeling.

"Come fuck me, daddy." I tried to pull him up to me.

I loved the feeling I got from the tongue, but I wanted to feel his dick up inside of me! I pulled him toward me. He was latched on to my clit.

"Please, Ant, please give me the dick. My pussy is hungry," I said seductively.

"Damn, ma, this shit is good," he said as he rose up and got on top of me. He parted my legs, threw them on his shoulders, and eased all the way inside of me.

"Oweiiii" I screamed out in ecstasy as my baby daddy, the love of my life, entered my love cave.

First, he eased in and out. I tightened my muscles to grip his dick. He pinned me down, pushing his arm up under my back. He then started going harder, tearing down my wall. I threw the pussy up on him. I was sure his bitch didn't fuck him this good and I knew he missed fucking me, with the way he was carrying on. Even though he was beating the pussy up really bad, I didn't flinch. I lay there taking every inch of his manhood.

"Daddy, it's your pussy. Fuck it, daddy, fuck it."

See, he always loved encouragement. He sped up his thrusts and he sank all the way in. I knew he was about to cum. I threw the pussy on him all extra and shit. He held me tighter. I bit down on his shoulder.

"Aaaaarrrrrrgggggghhhhhhhh," he groaned as he let out his juice all up in my guts. "Damn, your pussy is deadly," he said as he rolled off me onto the bed.

I didn't say anything. I just lay there thinking. I hoped he loved this fuck enough to bring his ass home to me and his children. I turned to say something to him, but this nigga was knocked the fuck out, snoring. Damn, I knew the pussy was powerful, but I didn't think it had the power to literally knock this nigga out.

I jumped off the bed and snatched up my cell phone. I snapped a few pictures of him up close, naked in my bed. See, these niggas be creepin' and shit, but they're careless as fuck. I grabbed my blanket and threw it on top of him. I quickly got dressed and exited the room.

I fed the children, bathed them, and put their asses in the bed.

I decided to call out from work. My man was sleeping in my bed, and there was no way I was going to leave. Matter of fact, I was trying to see if I could get some more dick before he left. I was counting on it, because the date rape drug Ketamine should have been wearing off right about now.

I decided to take a quick shower. As I washed, I massaged my breasts as I thought about the sex we had earlier. I could fuck a million niggas, but only one could me feel the way Ant made me feel. This nigga knew we're good together and he knew damn well ain't no bitch out there could fuck him like I did. I stuck my finger inside my pussy and licked it. I could still taste his cum. I was kind of shocked that he wasn't more careful.

I oiled up my firm body and threw my robe on without underwear. I walked back into the room and noticed he was somewhat awake. I lay beside him and tried to rub on his chest. He grabbed my arm.

"What the fuck you doing?" He looked around, and looked down at his naked body. "Where the fuck am I? And why am I naked?" He let my arm go and jumped up off the bed.

"Calm down, you're here in my bed. You wanted to spend the night with me, you remember?"

"Hell nah! You trippin', B. The last thing I remember . . . I remember . . ." He paused and rubbed his hand through his hair.

"You need to calm down! I know you panicking because it's late, but you a grown man, and that scary shit don't look good on you," I spat.

"Man, shawty, shut the hell up right now." He cut the light on, and picked his pants up. He pulled his cell phone out of his pocket and looked at it. "Fuckkkk," he yelled. He grabbed his shirt, looked at me, shook his head, and opened the door.

So much for getting some more, I thought as I followed him. "What is wrong with you? You're behaving crazy. Are you sure you're able to drive?"

"Stay the fuck away from me, B," he said as he opened the door and disappeared into the night.

"Damn. Sorry, nigga, was only trying to make sure you good," I said out loud.

I locked my door and went to my room. I glanced at the clock; it read 2:35 a.m. "Ha-ha.

Looks like somebody has some explaining to do." It wasn't my fucking problem that her man, with a little help, still wanted me. I straightened my bed up and got in. I was feeling great. I laid my head on my pillow and dozed off.

CHAPTER FIFTY-ONE

Tiana

I twisted and turned all night. I kept calling Micah's phone, texted him, and left voice mails, but still hadn't heard from him. The last time I saw him was when he left with the girls. He was supposed to drop them off and come right back. Baby Micah was with his mother so this was supposed to be our date night.

I was sincerely worried because this was so not him. It wasn't like we were beefing or anything. Actually we were on good terms. I cut the TV on to see if there were any accidents or shootings that happened. I didn't see no breaking news or any new incidents. "God, please protect my husband," I prayed as I laid my head back down.

I didn't want to get his mother involved in what we had going on, but I was a nervous wreck and I knew if anything happened she'd be the first to know. I grabbed the phone and dialed her number.

"Hello," she whispered.

"Hey, Ma, sorry to wake you up. But have you seen your son?"

"No, why, did something happen?"

"No, I just can't reach him since this evening. I thought maybe you seen him."

"No, I haven't. Hold on; lemme try calling him off the house phone." I anxiously waited until she came back on the phone. "Baby, his phone is going straight to voice mail."

"Oh, okay," I said. I was disappointed.

"It's okay, don't worry. He probably out in them streets and his phone went dead. You know how men are. Child, get you some rest. He will come home soon."

"All right, Ma. Sorry to wake you up again."

I hung up the phone feeling worse, because if anything happened his mother would have been aware. My mind started wondering if my husband was laid up with another bitch and forgot to make it home. I quickly shook the feeling. I had no proof he had ever cheated or was cheating on me.

I walked downstairs to make a cup of ginger tea. I walked over to the window and peeped out there. My nerves were torn up. I felt a tear drop from my eye. I quickly wiped it away and walked back up the stairs with my tea. I drank the tea and browsed the Internet. I then logged on Facebook to see if he was online, but he wasn't. I wished I had that bitch Ayana's number, because I would sure ask where my husband was since he left here to go to her house. But I doubted that Micah would be over there with her. He despised that bitch after the shit she put his kids through.

I finished my tea and lay down on the bed, still worrying about the whereabouts of my husband.

I wasn't fully asleep when I heard someone entered the house. I jumped up and sat up in the bed. I had the gun I bought in the drawer close to my side of the bed. As soon as the person hit my room, I noticed it was Micah.

"Where the fuck you been?"

"Sorry, babe, I was with the niggas. My phone was dead, so I couldn't call you."

I looked at this nigga and I could tell that he was on some bullshit. "Really, Micah? Did you forget that we're supposed to be going to dinner and the movie? You really think I believe that shit? Boy, I swear, you're fucking a liar."

"I swear on my life, B, I ain't lying to you. T, why can't you just believe me that I ain't cheating? I'm not, B," he said, damn near pleading.

"I swear, Micah, if I find out you fucking with any one of these old nasty-ass bitches, I'm going to divorce your ass and move the fuck out of this house. I'm about sick of your shit. I could've stayed single if I knew this was how your ass would be acting. Now I see what Ayana was talking about."

"What the fuck you mean, what Ayana was talking about? Don't you ever bring up that bitch's name when we're talking 'bout us. I was a good nigga to that bitch; she was the fucking whore," he yelled.

That kind of threw me off. He'd been mad with her plenty of times, but I'd never heard him call her any kind of names and definitely not a whore. It seemed like he was drunk or something. "Are you drunk? Yo, what the hell is really going on with you?"

"Listen, I said I'm sorry and I promise it won't happen again. I need to take a quick shower." He walked off into the bathroom.

Hell no, I really didn't believe shit he was saying now! When a nigga comes home and rushes to the shower, unless he getting off work I thought the nigga trying to wash another bitch pussy scent off his dick.

I got up and ran into the bathroom. He was already washing off. I picked up his dirty drawers and smelled them. Nothing jumped out at me but sweat. I threw them back on the floor and walked out of the bathroom. I sat on the bed. I wasn't feeling this. Was I overreacting? I was never an insecure chick, but lately my actions were just that.

I crawled back on my side of the bed. I was happy he wasn't in jail or dead. I pretended that I was asleep when he came out of the bathroom. I was still pissed off, but without proof, it was useless to keep on going. I would accuse him, and he would deny it. I knew for a fact whatever was done in the dark would definitely come out in the light!

CHAPTER FIFTY-TWO

Ayana

After Ant and I had sex, he started acting really stank toward me. Whenever he dropped the children off, he barely mumbled, "Hey." Shit I had no idea why he mad though. I really should have been the one who was upset. He fucked me, got up, and went home to his bitch!

I stood outside waiting as he pulled up to drop the kids off. I walked over to his car. "Hey, Mama," they said in unison as they got out of the car and ran toward the house. He was about to pull off when I walked up on his car.

"Yo, what is your problem? You barely say two words to me ever since that night you left here."

"Yo, B, ain't nothing to really say. I don't know what the fuck happened, but I do know I didn't willingly get in your bed."

"Ant, you sound stupid as fuck! You're saying I forced a grown-ass man to get in my bed, suck on my pussy for over twenty minutes, and fuck me? Come on with that bullshit. That might sound reasonable to you, or when you're explaining that shit to your bitch, but not to a normal person. You saw me in my little shorts and you wanted to fuck. Plain and simple. I missed fucking you, so I gave you the pussy. You enjoyed it, just like I did."

"Yo, if it's like you said, why the fuck can't I remember anything? I can only go by what the fuck you're telling me."

"I 'ont fucking know. Maybe you just suppressing that shit, so you don't have to accept the fact that you wanted me that bad," I said with a grin plastered across my face.

"Ayana, you're full of shit. Nice try, but just know we are over and done with. I'm a married man and I'm faithful to my wife." He started the car.

"Yeah, okay. That's not what you're screaming when you was head deep sucking on this pussy." I patted my front.

"I swear, B, I be trying to tolerate your ol' dumb ass 'cause of my kids, but I swear I wish you'd just get the fuck on out of my life."

He backed out and pulled off without saying another word. I bet you that ass was in the car racking his brain as to what happened between us! Silly fool had no idea that I put that date rape drug on him.

I walked back into the house, ready to deal with these bad-ass kids of mine. I sure wished their daddy would stop playing and move back in so he could take care of their bad asses. Especially that Dominique; that little heifer so caught up on her so-called Auntie Tiana, I tried to let her little ass know that she wasn't related to that bitch at all.

I wasn't feeling too good. I was nauseated and feeling weak. I figured it was because I was working hard, and I wasn't eating like I was supposed to. Even though I didn't want to, I forced myself to get up out of the bed. I fixed eggs and bacon with some fried potatoes. I was hoping I would feel better after I ate. False. The minute I swallowed pieces of the food, my mouth gathered water; and I knew that feeling all too well. I ran to the bathroom, and hung over the toilet seat as I vomited up everything I just ate. I hung over the toilet seat until nothing was left to come up but that green nasty liquid.

I got up, brushed my teeth, and washed my face. I stumbled to bed. I knew this feeling all too well, but shit this couldn't be. I lay there, pondering. I recalled when Ant and I had sex a few weeks ago; he didn't use a condom and didn't pull out.

"Oh, shit," I yelled out, but quickly regrouped. Why was I yelling out? If I was pregnant with Anthony's child, this would mean Tiana would be livid. I know that bitch too well, and I was pretty sure she would divorce his ass, which meant I would have a better chance to get my man back.

I ain't goin' to lie, I wasn't sure who the fuck my baby daddy was. Shit, I fucked Daquan, Keyshawn, the fucking Indian man at the hotel, and Ant. I shook my head in disgust at myself. How did I allow myself to get caught up in some shit like this? Fuck it, I wasn't going to stress myself out. As far as I was concerned, this was Ant's baby until he proved different. I knew once his bitch found out, her pride was going to be crushed and she wouldn't stick around.

I looked in the mirror and noticed that my hair was a hot mess. I decided it was time to take out this weave and get a fresh sew-in. I took a shower, and got dressed. I made sure I was on point, because it'd been a minute since I went around the way to the hair salon, and all these messy-ass bitches be around there.

I pulled up at the Beauty Café on Columbia Road. I parked across the street and sashayed toward the store front. I quickly peeped Daquan's car parked at the entrance. I straightened my clothes and put an extra pep in my step. I saw him staring at me as soon as I got closer. "You can stop staring now, boo; it's only me," I said as I stepped in front of him.

"Shawty, go ahead with all that extra shit," he said, looking all nervous and shit.

"Damn, why you looking like you want to take a shit? Your bitch must be somewhere nearby," I said sarcastically.

"I done told your ass, go on now. I ain't wit' this drama shit right now."

"Boy, please, you wasn't saying that when you was fucking and sucking on this pussy."

"Say what?" I heard a bitch's voice said. I quickly turned around to face his bitch. I didn't personally know her, but I knew of her and I'd seen pics of her on Facebook.

His face turned red and he looked like he was about to pull a disappearing act.

"You heard me right. This nigga acting brand new. He damn sure wasn't acting like this when he was fucking me, and sucking on my pussy—"

Before I could finish my sentence, this bitch popped me in my face, knocking me backward.

I dropped my purse and went straight for this bitch's high yellow face. I used my car keys to dig a hole in that bitch's face.

Slap! Slap! "Get the fuck off her," the nigga said as he slapped my face numerous times. That shit hurt, but I wasn't gonna let her ass go. I continued pounding on that bitch.

"My face! My face. This bitch cut my face," the bitch screamed out.

"Yo, bitch, get the fuck up." He snatched me hard and threw me to the side.

"Fuck you, nigga, you and that punk bitch," I said as I held my head. I felt to see if there was blood coming out, but there was none. The pain, however, was intense.

"Bitch, I should blow your fucking brains out right here on this concrete, but I got you another time. Now get your bitch ass up and get the fuck out of here."

I was hurting too bad to respond to this nigga the way I really wanted to.

"Girl, you a'ight? What the hell happened out here?" the old, fake-ass hairdresser bitch said.

"Bitch, get away from me." I managed to stand up. I looked over at the bitch who was bleeding from her face. There were also patches of weave along with that ho hair on the ground below. I looked down on my keys and saw that

I had blood all over them, and also all over me. I thought about calling the police on this fuck nigga, but judging by the injury on her face I was pretty sure I would be locked up as well.

I dragged myself across the street to my car and jumped in, quickly pulling off. My head and my body were hurting bad. I was angry as fuck, but also happy that pretty bitch wouldn't be that damn pretty after all. Every time she took a look in the mirror, she would remember that ass whupping I served her ass.

So much for getting my damn hair done. I knew Daquan wasn't into calling no police; however, I wasn't too sure of his bitch. It's bad enough I had to worry about Tiana's bitch ass snitching on me; now I had to worry about another bitch. *A bitch can't catch a break. Fuck this day.* I decided to go home and see if this headache would go away.

On my way home, my phone started to ring. It was funny; e'erytime some shit pop off, this nigga was the first one to call my phone. "Hello," I answered with an attitude.

"Hello there, Miss Beasly. I'm just calling to check on you, see how you doing."

"Are you having me followed? Because for some strange reason you're always popping up or calling when some shit happens."

"I told you that I won't stop until I bring down that baby daddy of yours. I think you're a smart woman and you know that it's only a matter of time before he and his crew are arrested."

"Okay, so if you know all of this, why do you keep calling me or bothering me about him? I'm not with him anymore, so you need to go bother him and his new bitch." I regretted ever answering his phone call in the first place because he was getting real annoying.

"Why are you protecting this sleaze ball? He don't give a fuck about you and your daughters. He left y'all and shacked up wit' that other girl over in Stone Mountain. I think the best way to get him back is to help us get him off these streets and out of your girls' lives for good."

"You know what, Detective Robinson, you really don't give a fuck about me and my girls; you're pretending. I got to go. I heard enough." I clicked the end button.

Detective Robinson thought I was a stupid bitch, but I was far from that. There was no way I was going to give them anything on Ant if there wasn't any benefit for me in it.

I threw the phone on the seat and cut the music on. It wouldn't be a bad idea to tell everything I knew about all these niggas who did me wrong. Especially that nigga Tahj. I would never forget how that nigga tried to kill me. The last I heard, his ass left town because Ant and his crew was after him. *Ant, Keyshawn, and Daquan better watch their backs.*

CHAPTER FIFTY-THREE

Tiana

It was Labor Day weekend, and the weather was lovely. Georgia wasn't too hot this year; it was just right. It was a weekend so the girls were supposed to be with their mother, but Micah wanted them to go with us to his mother's house. She was having a big cookout for the family. I really didn't feel like socializing, but I didn't want to disappoint her. Some of her family from up North came down so she wanted everyone to meet Micah's wife.

"Y'all ready?" Micah yelled as he walked down the stairs.

"Yup, we ready! Are you driving your car?"

"Yup, come on. Let's go grub on this good ol' food my mama cooking."

I got in the car while he strapped the kids in securely. He got in and pulled off.

He pulled up at his mama's house and parked across the street. The kids were happy, so they jumped out and ran across the street into their grandma's yard. Micah grabbed the baby and I grabbed his bag. We walked over to the house.

"Hey, love. Come on, let me introduce you to the family." His mother kissed me on the cheek. I followed her toward the back yard. I met his uncle and auntie from Baltimore. I also met his cousin; he was my age. They welcomed me into their family. There was all kinds of food and drink. They were really celebrating. I grabbed me a bottle of Heineken and sat down, listening to the family exchanging old family stories.

"So I see you met the rest of my crazy family," Micah walked up on me, and whispered in my ear.

"Yes, I did." I chuckled.

"Here hit this real quick." He handed me a blunt. I looked at him. I didn't like to smoke in front of my elders.

"Girl, go ahead. Hit this shit." I took the blunt and took a few pulls. "See, your ass too damn greedy," he joked.

I took a few more pulls, then gave it back to him. He walked off into the house. I went back to listening to different stories as they remembered them. The music was also blasting, so I sat there just vibing. His mama had my son, just showing him off. She was definitely a proud grandma.

CHAPTER FIFTY-FOUR

Ayana

I decided to go to the clinic on Clifton Road to confirm what I already knew. As I sat in the waiting room waiting, I thought of how I was going to break the news to Ant. I mean, I was fucking other dudes, but I was pretty sure it was Ant's baby!

"Miss Beasly," the nurse called.

"Here I come." I hurriedly walked toward the back.

"Come on in," the nurse practitioner said.

I sat down, kind of nervous for real. Having another baby was definitely not on my agenda. But hey, shit happens.

"Well, you're pregnant! Congrats."

"Thank you," I said, as I digested what she just said to me.

"Do you have insurance? If not, we can sign you up for Medicaid today."

"Yes, I need that please."

After doing my paperwork, I left a pleased bitch. I couldn't stop smiling. I hoped this was the boy Ant wanted. Fuck that son Tiana had. I had his girls, so it was only fair I give him his prince! Shit, it might have even been Daquan's seed or Keyshawn's. Oh, well. A bitch would be paid either way.

I left the doctor's office and started to call them one by one. Ant's phone went to voice mail. Keyshawn picked up. As soon as he heard my voice, he hung up; and Daquan's number was changed. Hmmm, these niggas were playing a dangerous game, but since I was the head bitch, they would soon learn not to fuck over Ayana.

It was Labor Day weekend and I was bored as fuck. I was on the schedule for tonight, but I had nothing to do in the daytime. I sure wished that I had my own little family to throw something on the grill for. So much was missing from my life. I just wished things were different. I thought about taking the kids to Six Flags, since I had a few dollars to burn.

I called Ant's phone. I knew the girls asked if they could stay with him, and at first I said it was cool, but I changed my mind. I didn't want my fucking kids around him and his fake-ass family.

"Hello," he answered like he had an attitude.

"Hey. I was wondering if you can drop the girls off. I wanted to surprise them by taking them to Six Flags."

"Man, we talked about this earlier. You said it was cool for them to spend the weekend. Plus, my mama having a cookout so we over here."

"What the fuck she having a cookout have to do with my kids? It ain't like she fucks with my kids anyways. Like I said, can I get my damn kids?" I blurted out as loud as I could.

"Listen, B, I said no, and that's final." He hung the phone up.

I looked at the phone. *Did this nigga just hang up like I wasn't speaking?* My blood started boiling. See, he done made me mad as fuck. I jumped off the bed and started looking for some clothes. Even though my stomach wasn't showing, I had a little pudge. I grabbed a pair of tights and a little wife beater, which would definitely show my figure.

I took a shower, got dressed, and stormed out of the door. I got in my car and turned the music up.

I sang along with K. Michelle. I was definitely in a zone that scared me. I lit me a cigarette and drove fast down the street. I was on a mission. Anthony Micah Brown was gonna learn today I was not the one to be fucked with!

I spotted his car as soon as I pulled up, but there was no parking space. I drove up the street and parked. I grabbed my purse, which had a can of Mace in it. I was mad I had to get rid of the gun. I had no idea what I was walking up on. I dialed his number. After a few rings, he picked up.

"I'm out here; bring me my kids."

"Yo, A, I already told you no. And you're not welcome at my mama house, you know that."

"You better bring yo' ass out here before I come in there and let everybody know I'm having your baby."

"Say the fuck what?"

"You heard me, nigga. Yes, I'm pregnant and it's your baby. Congrats, Daddy," I said sarcastically.

I saw when he walked to the front of the house. I hung the phone up, and walked toward the front of the house.

"Yo, B, why you tryin'a start some shit? Man, I ain't sleep with you so how you pregnant by me?"

"Boy, stop playing. I'm pregnant for you. I'm pretty sure your wife would love to hear about our little rendezvous."

"Bitch, you think I'm playing with you?" He took a step toward me and grabbed me.

"Micah, don't you hit that bitch," his no-good-ass mama shouted out.

He looked back at her, and shoved me away from him.

"How dare you show your face at my mother-fucking house? What is it that you want?"

"Damn, Mother, I guess I ain't your daughter anymore? Anyways don't none of that matter. I'm here to get my children, but since your son want to be an ass and shit, I think I should tell his lovely wife."

CHAPTER FIFTY-FIVE

Tiana

I was so caught up in listening to these half-drunk people exchanging stories that I didn't notice that Micah disappeared on my ass. I got up to go see where he was at, and also to make sure the kids were not out in the streets. I heard a commotion outside, more like people arguing. I walked hurriedly through the back fence. I walked upon Micah's mother, Micah and, to my surprise, Ayana, just in time to hear her say, "Tell his wife."

"Tell his wife what?" I put my hand akimbo.

"Well, look what we got here, my long-lost sister."

"Babe, go back in the house. She was just leaving."

"Nah, I wasn't leaving. I wanted to tell you I'm carrying your husband's love child." She rubbed her stomach and smiled.

It took me a minute to realize what this bitch was saying to me. I looked at Micah; his black ass was turning red. I looked at his mama; she looked like she wished she was anywhere except here.

"Micah, what the fuck is this bitch saying to me? You been fucking her? Talk up, nigga!" I demanded.

"T, don't believe shit her ass saying to you. She mad 'cause she wanted to come get the girls and I told her ass no."

"Really, Ant? You didn't stay at the house 'bout three weeks ago after you dropped the kids off? Here go my results. Here is my proof; do the math." She shoved the results of her pregnancy test in my face.

"Hell nah, B, you lying. I 'ont fuck with you like that. Man, get the fuck on with that bullshit before I beat your ass."

"Nigga, fuck you! You just don't want T to know the truth."

"So why are you here telling me now? Why didn't you hit me up when he was getting ready to fuck you? Bitch, you're scandalous and you think by you telling me this I'm gonna say I'm done. Well, I got news for you: this is my husband, so get the fuck on, and find your baby daddy." I walked the fuck off.

I walked toward the back and grabbed my child. I wasn't about to cause no drama at this lady's house, so I needed to get away fast. I found my son sitting with his grandaunt in the living room.

"Tiana, where you going?" his mother asked me.

"I need to get out of here, Ma. I need to go before I end up killing your son and his bitch."

"I understand that you need to go, but leave the baby here. He don't need to see his mama hurting. I can't even speak on this shit because I'm shocked just like you. Please don't do nothing stupid. He's my son, but I love you as my own child. I'm telling you this from my heart. Ain't no dick worth you losing your freedom over. Take a ride out to clear your mind and think before you act. You have a baby who needs his mama."

"Thanks, Ma," I said before I kissed my baby on his forehead and stormed out the door.

"Tiana, where you going?" Micah snatched my arm.

"Let me get them keys up off you." I stretched my arm out.

"T, that bitch lying. This is exactly what she wanted. This: for us to split up."

I looked at him with disgust. "Give me the fucking keys. I ain't trying to bring no drama to your mama's house. And, for the record, please find somewhere for you and your children to stay. I don't want you at my house."

"Where the fuck I'm supposed to go?"

"Bitch nigga, I have no idea. Shit go shack up with yo' baby mama! I don't give a fuck," I spat. "Give me the fucking keys." I stepped up on him. Slap! Slap! Slap! I slapped the shit out of him.

He grabbed my arms. "Yo, B, what tha fuck wrong with you, putting your hands on me?" He shoved me.

"Give me the fucking keys, Micah." I gritted my teeth at him.

He looked at me, and mumbled some shit under his breath. He dug into his pocket, pulled out the keys, and handed them to me. He started to say something, but I didn't want to hear that shit.

I looked around to see if that bitch was around, but she was gone. I ran across the street and jumped into his car. I pulled the seat up, fixed the mirror, and pulled off, burning tires as I sped off! That's when the tears flowed out onto my face. I was trying to drive, but my eyes were blurry and I couldn't focus.

Honk! Honk!

I quickly wiped the tears as the horn quickly brought me back to reality. I slowed down a little, but I saw it was too late. I heard a police siren behind me. "Fuck!" I blurted out, as I pulled over on the shoulder.

I took my license out of my purse. I reached over and pulled the registration information out of the glove compartment.

"Hello, ma'am. Do you realize that you were going eighty-five miles per hour in a sixty-five miles-per-hour zone? License and registration please?"

"Here you go." I handed them to him.

"I'll be right back."

I watched as he walked back to his car. I was agitated as fuck. I wished I could just get away from it all. I tried my best not to cry, but my heart wasn't having it.

CHAPTER FIFTY-SIX

Ayana

I tell y'all about messing with these fuck niggas. See, this bitch-ass nigga goin' to stand in front of his bitch pretending like he didn't fuck me and it wasn't his baby I was carrying. I didn't really care about all that shit he was talking. The Kodak moment was when I told his bitch that I was pregnant. It was a script that I couldn't have written better myself. I almost busted out laughing when I saw the hurt plastered across that bitch's face. I saw she got a dose of her own medicine. See, the shit was funny when he up and left me and my kids. I imagined her ass was feeling the same intense burning I felt in my heart.

I grabbed my kids and headed straight home; I was no longer in a festive mood. Even though I enjoyed the show earlier, I was kind of hurt in a way because I saw the hatred in Ant's eyes for me, and the cold look he gave me when he denied sleeping with me.

I threw my purse on the floor and walked into the kitchen. I knew I shouldn't be drinking, but I was mad as hell. Even though I told him I was carrying his child, he still didn't show any kind of emotion. I wish I'd had my gun. I swear, I would have killed this nigga and his bitch for sure this time. I put the bottle to my head and drank it down as if it was water.

I then went into my bed and cried my hurt out. I was sick of this. I swear, I was plain sick of living!

I searched through my phone and found that bitch's number. When Ant spent the night, I'd searched his phone and took out her number. I searched and found the pictures that I took of him being naked, and pressed send, with a message: no caption needed!

I waited a few minutes; then I called her phone. The phone rang without her answering. I was angry that this bitch wasn't even woman enough to pick up the phone. Ol' scary-ass bitch talked all that shit, but she wasn't woman enough to pick up the phone. I decided to send her a message:

I told your ass he was mine. Now do you see who he really loves? That's right, your man was over here sucking on this pussy. I bet you he lied to you about where he was at. Girl, wake up. Ant loves me, my daughters, and my unborn child.

I waited for a response, but none came. I dialed Ant's phone and his phone went straight to voice mail. I threw the bottle into the wall, shattering it. I didn't give a fuck that the liquor left a stain on my brand new carpet. Man, I should've let him keep them fucking kids. I thought if I had them, he'd come to his senses and move back in. Today proved that shit wasn't gonna happen. I stuck with this nigga through all his bullshit and he went and married the next bitch. "I hate all of you bitches," I screamed out.

My damn alarm clock kept going off. I knew it was time to get my ass up. I was still angry about the shit that went down earlier, but regardless of how I was feeling, I had to get to the money. There was no way I was going back to being broke or homeless. I was a bad bitch and being broke was not on my agenda. With that thought, I got up and started sorting through my things. Tonight was a holiday night, and that meant all the big dope boys and jock boys would be coming through. Money symbols went up in my head immediately; that was motivation enough to get my ass dressed. The girls' babysitter arrived and I was out the door.

As soon as I entered the club, all eyes turned to me. I saw a few of my regulars and a few new faces. I was excited to get dressed and get on the stage. I stopped by the DJ booth and let him know what songs I wanted.

"Get That Money" by Lil Durk blasted through the club speakers. I wasted no time popping that pussy and letting it do what it do. Money started flying on the stage and I continued teasing. I used my fingers and stuck them deep into my pussy, later removing them and licking them off. My set was over and I was picking up all my money. I noticed some of it flew off the stage. I walked my butt-ass naked behind off the stairs and bent down to pick them up.

"Yo, shawty, you looking extra thick tonight," Mari said to me as I picked my head up.

I didn't know what to say because this was Lori's man and one of Ant's sidekicks. "Mari, what's good with you?" I said in a very seductive tone.

"Yo, quit playing and come kick it wit' a nigga real quick. I'm over here." He pointed to a table in the back.

"A'ight, lemme clean up real quick and I'll be there." I flashed him a smile and walked off. I put an extra strut in my steps so that nigga could see my ass bouncing.

In no time, I was back sitting at the table with this nigga. See Mari was the kind of nigga who had good looks, and his money was long. He was Ant's right hand, and the nigga who cleaned up all of Ant's dirty work. Truth was, he was the muscle behind Ant's business. "So you tryin'a give me this dance?" he asked.

"What you paying?" I looked at him.

"Shit, whatever your number is, but I want to fuck!"

"Ain't you in a relationship with my ex-friend? You know I don't roll like that."

"Ayana, fuck all that. Lori my bitch, but she ain't here and I'm tryin'a fuck."

"I have one more set then I'm done for the night."

"Bet. I be around."

After my last set, I got dressed and I met up with Mari in the parking lot. I got into his car and we started making out. Before I knew it, his hand was down in my leggings and deep into my pussy. "Awee, awee," I groaned.

I reached over and started to unbutton his pants. But before I could take his dick out, I heard a banging on the window. "Y'all take this elsewhere," the club security guard, Roger, said.

"Fuck! Yo, Lori ass is doing a night shift tonight; let's go to the house for a little while."

"Nigga, you tripppin' right? I'm not fucking with that bitch."

"Man, chill out! I know you 'ont give a fuck about her; plus, she my bitch. Lemme worry about her."

"A'ight. I'm good."

On the ride to the house, a rush of guilt came over me, but it soon disappeared. In my mind, I felt like that bitch didn't fuck with me anyway, so why should I give a fuck about her? I smiled to myself as I recalled the last time I saw that bitch. She was all high and mighty, acting like her pussy was special. Well, look what we had here: her precious Mari was about to beat this pussy up.

The car stopped and my thoughts were interrupted. I looked up and noticed we were outside of the house he shared with his bitch.

"Come on," he said as he parked and got out.

I grabbed my purse and followed him into the house. That nigga walked straight upstairs and into their bedroom. He wasted no time; he started peeling off his clothes. I could tell he was a little tipsy. I started taking off my clothes and we started going at it like two high school kids having sex for the first time. Mari didn't waste any time. He lay on his back and called me. "Come ride this dick. Lemme see what you working wit'."

I was always up for a challenge, so I crawled on top of him. I held his erect dick and slowly slid down it. It wasn't big, but it wasn't small. It was definitely a dick that I could maneuver. I squeezed my pussy muscles together, and worked that dick like I wasn't no stranger to it.

"Daddy, oh, this dick is so good. Oh my God," I said as I ground faster on his dick. I thought I heard a door close. "Did you hear something?"

"Nah, all I hear is your pussy slurping up my dick." He laughed and grabbed my waist pulling me down on his dick. I returned my focus to pleasing him. *Who knows, he might love my pussy so good, he'll leave that bitch.* I could only imagine Ant's face when he found out his right-hand man was fucking me.

I was so caught up in my thoughts, I didn't realize that bitch entered the room until it was too late. "Mari, what the fuck are you doing in my bed?" Lori yelled as the light turned on.

Before I had the chance to grip what was going on, I felt a lamp shatter on top of my head. I grabbed my head, jumped off Mari, and faced this bitch.

"What the fuck? You're the one my nigga is fucking?" That bitch started to throw blows straight to my face. I lost my balance, but then I started throwing blows back. I wasn't going down like this, but that bitch wasn't backing down.

"Both of you bitches cut this shit out!" Mari yelled.

"Nigga, fuck you! How could you do this to me?" she said while pulling my weave out. I needed to get my head out of her grip so I bit down on her hand. "Bitch, you bit me," she said and pulled harder.

"Help meeeeeeeeeeeeeeee! Help me, Mari. This bitch is killing me," I screamed out.

Somehow Mari managed to pull us apart. I immediately leapt across the bed to grab my clothing. I had scratches and half of my hair was on the ground. I grabbed my purse and pulled out my Mace. I leaped toward that bitch, and stretched over Mari, who had her pinned up against the wall.

"Awwwwww," that bitch screamed out as I let the can of Mace go in her face.

"You stupid bitch! You just Maced me too," Mari yelled out.

I didn't give a fuck! Fuck him and his bitch.

"Bitch. I'm gonna kill her! Let me go, Mari, so I can beat this ho's ass." She was kicking and screaming.

"Yes, Mari, let her ass go so she can get some more of this ass whupping." I didn't give a fuck that she ripped my weave out or my body was bruised up. I would have loved to go another round with that ho. 'Cause one thing about it: Ayana ain't never back down from a fight before and damn sure wasn't gonna start now!

I quickly put on my clothes minus my drawers because I couldn't find them and I was too mad to even look for them. I walked out of the room as he stood there apologizing to that ho. I shook my head and exited the house. *Ain't this a bitch*. I remembered that I didn't drive over there and my car was left at the club. "Fuck," I said as I pulled out my cell to call a cab.

I was mad because this old dumbass bitch came and interrupted my nut. To make matters worse, I didn't even have a chance to get my money. As I stood out there waiting for my cab, I saw a big rock on the side of the house. I picked it up and busted her windshield out. "Now, bitch, let's see if you big mad or little mad," I said out loud as I spotted my taxi pulling up.

CHAPTER FIFTY-SEVEN

Tiana

It'd been days that I hadn't eaten. I cried most of the time and slept the rest of the time. I was so hurt by that shit that went down between Micah and Ayana. Micah was staying at his mother's house because I told him I didn't want him here.

I was sure I wanted a divorce after I saw a text come though on my phone from Ayana. In front of me, my husband was naked with dick hanging in this bitch's bed. I brought the phone closer to my face. In my mind, I was in denial. Tears welled up in my eyes when I remembered how much it hurt when I realized this bitch wasn't lying. My husband was fucking her.

He called me every day, begging and pleading. Sometimes I would hang up on him, but then he would call right back. I swear this boy got on my last nerves. I wished he would just give me the space I asked him for.

I just dozed off when I heard my phone ringing. I took a quick glance; it was a blocked number. I picked it up. "Hello," I answered with an attitude.

The person on the other line didn't say shit; they just kept breathing into the phone.

"Ayana, you old scary-ass bitch, why don't you find somebody else to play with?" I spat.

"Ha-ha," the person laughed, then hung up the phone.

The phone continued ringing until I finally cut it off. I swear, I was too grounded for this bullshit. What the fuck did this bitch want? She wanted Micah. Well, she could finally get him.

I realized that this bitch wasn't going to leave me alone. I knew I needed to take things into my own hands. I just didn't know how. I could report her to the police, but I didn't have any proof that bitch was harassing me, aside from the phone calls. For all I knew, that bitch might've called from a prepaid phone.

I was also aware that this bitch tried me the first time, so I kept my gun close to me. I also started going to the shooting range. I wanted to be prepared. See this bitch had no idea that, even though I was quiet, I could be as deadly as her. I was trying not to take it there with her, but I had a feeling she was gonna continue pushing until I reached my boiling point.

***

I finally got enough strength to go to class today. I swear, I couldn't afford to fail. As soon as class was over, and I walked outside, I bumped into Micah. I was pretty sure it wasn't by coincidence.

"Move out of my way," I demanded and tried to walk toward the side.

"T, we need to talk." He grabbed my arm.

"You sure you want to do this out here?" I said looking around.

"Fuck them! You my wife and I need to talk to you."

I snatched my arm out of his grip. I started walking off.

"T, I'm begging you, B. Please just give me twenty minutes of your time. I promise that I will leave you alone after this," he pleaded.

"What do you want to talk about? You fucking your baby mama you claim you hated? Boy, I had enough of you and that stalking-ass bitch."

"Man, T, I don't want that bitch! I swear, she's lying to you."

I dug into my purse and snatched out my cell. I scrolled to my pictures. "Here you go, fool, in black and white." I shoved my phone in his face.

I watched him closely as his facial expression changed. "Where the fuck you got this from?" he yelled out.

"From your bitch; and you should know since that's you lying in another woman's bed, buck-naked." I stepped closer and smacked the shit out of him.

He grabbed my arm and pushed me back. "Man, what the fuck you doing? Yo, B, I know what it seems like but, T, I swear on my seed, I 'ont know nothing 'bout this picture. I wasn't in that bitch's bed."

"Micah, you know what? You are busted. So you can quit lying now."

"T, I'm serious. Please listen to me! We took a vow, for better or worse. I'm asking you to please believe me. I do not know about this. I didn't willingly sleep with this bitch."

I looked at him. I knew my husband. I saw the sincerity in his eyes. But I still couldn't understand. If he was telling the truth, how was he naked in her bed?

"Micah, I'm not no fool and I know pictures don't lie."

"T, I swear to you on everything. I'ma a real nigga. If I was fucking another bitch, and you caught me, I would go ahead and admit it; but I swear, B, I don't know how her ass got this picture."

"Micah, that's between you and her. I want a divorce. I told you before I would leave if you cheat on me. I believed you when you said you were done with her ass. But you and that bitch played me. When did you fuck her? Was it when I'm at the house watching y'all kids? I am such a fucking fool," I cried out. I started running to my car.

"T, hold up." He ran behind me and grabbed me. "Woman, listen to me! I fucking love you! I didn't cheat on you. I swear to you, T. Don't believe this shit. I don't know what happened between Ayana and me. I've been racking my brain, trying to remember anything. Man, I think this bitch drugged me or something."

I wiped my tears, and looked at this nigga. I wanted to make sure I heard him right. *Did this nigga just say she drugged him?* I knew he was desperate, but damn, I never imagined he would sink that low.

"Micah, you trippin'. I don't think you should tell anyone else this crazy shit 'cause you sound stupid as fuck!" I said at him.

"I know how farfetched it sounds. But you know how vindictive that bitch is. This is a bitch who beat herself up and accused me. Like I said, the last thing I remember was when I dropped the kids off, she asked me to come in. I refused, but the kids were begging me, so I did. I was in Diamond room when she offered me something to eat. I said no, because we were going out to eat. She then hands me a glass of liquor. I took a few drinks and I swear e'erything after that is blank. I don't remember anything after that. I swear to you, T."

"So you're dumber than I thought. You go into this bitch house to chill. A bitch who set you up before and who put you through hell with your kids. Nigga, you deserve everything this bitch throw your way. I got to go. I done entertained this bullshit long enough."

I walked off to my car. I blocked out whatever he was saying to me. I started the car and pulled off, leaving him there looking stupid.

This time, I couldn't even cry. I played in my mind everything he just said to me. I actually felt pity for him. He seemed like he lost weight and he looked desperate. Maybe I thought about turning around and going back to him. But the stubborn part of me wouldn't allow me to. I continued driving, even my heart was broken seeing him like that.

My phone started to buzz. I reached over on the next seat and grabbed my purse. I took it out; it was a text message:

You married me for better or worse! Well this my worse, so please don't leave me. I need you.

I threw the phone over on the seat and continued driving. Tears welled up in my eyes. I tried my best not to cry, but it was too much. I did miss my husband. He was my best friend, my everything. But I couldn't get over this. How could I get past this? And now this bitch was talking about having his baby. It was bad. I had to deal with the two girls now. I couldn't deal with any more of her kids. More tears rolled down my face as I realized what a fucked-up situation I was in.

CHAPTER FIFTY-EIGHT

Ayana

I called the nigga Mari to get what he owed me but, instead of paying, that fuck nigga told me to go eat a fat dick! I was furious, because his ass got some free pussy. I dialed Ant's number. At first he didn't pick up so I called right back.

"Yo, what the fuck you want, B?"

"I need to talk to you 'bout your boy."

"Yo, you talking 'bout Mari. I already know he fucked you, ho."

"Ho? What the fuck you mean? Your right-hand man try to fuck me and you don't give a fuck?"

"Ayana, cut the bullshit out, B. Any nigga with money can fuck you. My dumb ass fucked up by having babies with a ho," he lashed out.

"You know what, Ant? Fuck you and your boy. I'm done with you."

"Yo, bitch, I been done with you. Go find you a couple dicks to suck," he said and hung the phone up.

The tone that he talked to me in had me feeling disgusted. I needed to let him feel the pain he inflicted on me. I scrolled through my phone. Maybe it was time to talk to this detective about him and his boy. They had no idea how much shit I could get them in. No idea!

My stomach was growing, and it was getting hard to hide it when I was at the club dancing. I was trying to stock up on money before I had to quit. I thought about having an abortion, but quickly dismissed that idea. This was probably Ant's child growing in me, so there was no way I was going to kill the baby.

I kept calling that bitch's phone. She would pick up and I would sit on the phone giggling. I wasn't gonna ease up on her ass until she got tired and got rid of Micah. A few times she'd go off and then hang up.

One night, I was feeling lonely after drinking a few glasses of wine. I kept calling Ant's phone and he wouldn't pick up. I called the bitch's phone and it went straight to voice mail. I was getting angry; here I was over here carrying his child and he was ignoring my calls.

I got up out of the bed and put on a pair of tights and a wife beater. I tied my head up with a scarf and grabbed my keys. I peeped in the girls' room; they were asleep. I walked out and locked my door. I got into my car. I was heading to this bitch's house. She thought that I didn't know where she stayed at. I had no idea what I was going over there to do, but I knew I was going to cause havoc.

I pulled up to the house. Anger and rage filled my heart as I noticed how nice the house was. I knew his ass bought this house while my kids and I were struggling. I pulled into the driveway, behind her car. I grabbed my car jack and my spray paint, and jumped out of my car. I started beating on the car, and spraying the word WHORE all over it. I also busted out all the windows. The alarm started sounding off, so I ran back to my car, and jumped in, and slowly pulled out. I wasn't sure if anyone was in their window and I damn sure didn't need any witnesses.

I cut the music all the way up as I drove out of the subdivision. I didn't care what I was going through, K. Michelle's CD always gave me life. I didn't cry this time; matter of fact, I was cried out. No tears were left to waste on this nigga or his bitch. I was going to file for custody of my children and, when I got them, I would show Ant who was really in control.

Early the next morning, I made up my mind. It was time to show Anthony Micah Brown and Mari that I was the wrong bitch to fuck over. I scrolled through my phone and hit the send button. I called the number that I'd been itching to call ever since he gave me his ass to kiss. See, I was hoping that things wouldn't come to this and Ant's ass would stop playing, but the more time went by, the more I realized that shit wasn't going to ever happen. Detective Robinson was too happy to meet with me and, to be honest, I was just as excited to finally spill my guts about everything I knew!

I got dressed, and drove to DeKalb County Police Department out in Tucker.

"Hello, I'm here to see Detective Robinson."

"Your name please? And do you have an appointment?"

"Ayana Beasly and yes, he expecting me."

"Hold on a sec—"

Before she could finish her sentence, the detective walked out of the office. "Miss Beasly. Good morning. Come on back here with me."

I smiled and followed him into the office.

"Take a seat! This is my partner, Detective Sewell. So I'm so happy you finally decided to make contact with us. I have to let you know our conversation will be recorded, but your name will be kept confidential. So you have nothing to worry about."

"Before I start talking, I need your help on getting full custody of my girls." I looked at both men.

"I can't promise anything. What I can do is put in a good word for you with the juvenile courts."

I looked at that nigga. This was the reason why I didn't fuck with the police! The only reason why I was up in this bitch was because I knew how bad they wanted to get at Ant and his homeboys! I knew everything about that nigga and the shit he did all over the city. He claimed he stopped hustling but, trust me, the only one he was fooling was that ol' dumbass bitch over there.

I sat across from them and spilled the beans on these niggas. I watched as they sat there looking at me like they just hit the jackpot.

"I'm going to need you to write down all the addresses that you know he sold drugs out of. Also, put that barber shop address down. I want to make sure I hit all the spots at one time. This has been a long time coming for this city."

"Okay. So you're sure my name won't be mentioned in none of this, right? I have kids with this dude; plus, I know what him and his crew are capable of doing."

"I give you my word. Your name will never be mentioned. On the paperwork, it will say 'confidential informant' or 'CI' for short. We would not jeopardize you like that."

"All right. I hope this was enough to get him off these streets."

"It's more than enough! Even with all our hardworking officers, this is the closest we've gotten to him."

I got up out of my chair. I hated to be around them. I wasn't doing it for them; it was for my own personal reasons. I walked out without saying a word. I just hoped that these bastards kept my name out of that shit.

CHAPTER FIFTY-NINE

Tiana

What is a woman to do when she is cheated on but she still loves her husband? After seeing Micah, and listening to him, I swear I believed what he was saying to me. I couldn't explain what happened because I had no idea, but it was possible that bitch did something to him. I still blamed his ass for putting himself into the situation.

I decided to go to his mother's house today. I was feeling a little better; plus, I missed my son. I tried to dig deep and pull out my inner strength. I got out of bed, and took a long, much-needed bath. I needed to relax my mind and soul. I got dressed in a nice sundress with a pair of Michael Kors sandals. I brushed my hair in a ponytail. I turned the AC on because I didn't want to come back to a hot house.

Shocked would be an understatement when I stepped foot outside the door. I noticed all my windows and my front door were busted out. I walked around my car to further investigate; my car had a long scratch from the front to the back. The word WHORE was written all over it. All four of my tires were flattened. "Oh my God!" I yelled out as I saw the damage that was done to my shit.

I grabbed my cell phone and dialed Micah's number.

Ring! Ring! Ring! "Hello."

"You need to come over here now! Somebody done fucked up my car," I cried.

"Calm down, T. What are talking about?"

"My car is fucked up. I'm about to call the police."

"On my way around there."

I hung up the phone and immediately called the police.

I sat on my steps waiting for Micah and the police. I knew that it was either that old dumbass mother of mine or Ayana who did this. These bitches were cowards, coming over here and fucking up my car like this.

I saw a police car pulling up to the house. I got up and walked out to the driveway.

"Hello, ma'am. I'm Officer Stewart, and I'm here to take a report about vandalism."

"Yes, Officer, I'm Tiana Caldwell-Brown. I just came out of the house to get in my car and this is what I saw: my car, all messed up." I pointed to my car.

"Around what time was that, if you can remember?"

"Umm, I would say around ten-thirty a.m." I watched as he wrote in his notepad.

"Are you the only one who lives at this residence?"

"No, I live here with my husband. However, he wasn't here. I think I know who did this. His baby mother been harassing me for a while, calling my phone and not saying anything."

He continued writing things down. I gave him that bitch's name and also my mother's name. I was sick and tired, and even though I didn't like the police this bitch needed to stop for real before I ended up hurting her.

The officer took my statement and left. I called my insurance company and reported the situation. They told me they would handle the situation. I was pissed as fuck. I took pictures of my car and popped my trunk so I could take out my belongings before the tow truck came.

In the midst of taking things in the house, I realized that it had been over an hour and Micah hadn't shown up at the house. I put Baby

Micah's car seat in the house along with a few other things, and then I called his phone. It kept ringing. I was about to redial when I saw his mother's number coming through.

"Hey, Ma, how are you?"

"Baby girl, you need to get around here now! The police just busted in my door and they have Micah and his friends in cuffs. Baby, get around here; it doesn't look good."

"Whattttttttttttttttttt?" My heart sank! What the fuck was going on! Handcuffs? "Micah, what the fuck have you gotten yourself into?" I said as I jumped online to find me a cab.

"Can you hurry up please?" I said to the Yellow Cab taxi driver.

"Ma'am, I'm going to speed limit," he said in broken English.

I breathed hard. This motherfucker was barely going forty-five, and we were in a fifty-five miles-per-hour zone. "God, please wrap your arms around my baby," I whispered as I closed my eyes. I was trying to calm myself down.

Finally, he pulled up to Micah's mother's block. Police cars blocked the street off. "Ma'am, I can't turn on that street." He sounded scared.

"How much is it?"

"It's thirty-four dollars, ma'am."

I took out forty dollars and gave to him. I didn't wait to get change from him. I jumped out of the taxi and ran onto the street. My heart was racing. First things first, I needed to make sure my son and the girls were okay. Then I needed to know what was going on with my husband.

I was stopped by a big, burly cop. "No one is allowed any closer. The police are conducting a search."

"Tiana, come over here." I heard his mother's voice coming from across the street.

I gave the officer a nasty look, then ran across the street. I picked my son up and hugged him. I noticed the girls were on the side playing. I let out a long sigh. "What the hell is going on over here? Where is Micah at?"

"They have him and his friends in the back of the police cars. They had search warrants, and the damn dog tearing up my house."

"What are they looking for? And why would they come up in your shit?" I never cussed in front of her, but this was not the time to be politically correct.

"I have no idea. I was in the kitchen, fixing something for the children to eat. Micah and them was on the balcony. All I heard was the front door breaking down. By the time I rushed to the front, guns were pointed in my face telling me to get down. I was too scared for my son because of all the police shooting going on around here lately."

"Did they find anything on Micah?"

"I saw they took a gun off him. I don't know if they found anything else."

"Fuck," I yelled out. That alone just crushed me. The gun was illegal. I just prayed to God there was no body on it. This shit was crazy as fuck. "I'm about to call the lawyer I used for him before. He was pretty good."

"Well, I see we meet again, Miss Caldwell."

I immediately recognized the voice. It was the overbearing detective from the hospital. The same one who called himself warning me about Micah.

"Well, hello, Detective! I see you're still harassing my husband and me." I turned around to face him.

"Ha-ha. Harass? No, dear. We actually have your husband on different charges. I tried to warn you that he was bad news, but no, you didn't listen. He will be gone for a very long time."

"So you say. It's called innocent before proven guilty," I snapped on this punk-ass nigga. I was about sick of his sarcastic ass. I could see the happiness gleaming through his eyes.

Your Man Chose Me 399

I walked off, and dialed the lawyer's number. I wished I could talk to Micah. I could get a better idea of what was going on.

After speaking to the lawyer, I walked back down to where his mother was at. The detective was gone and the police cars were also pulling off. "I just talked to the lawyer. He said he is on it."

"I have a bail bonds number. But we have to wait to see if he has a bond first."

"This can't be happening. Where is all this coming from? I think they're framing him." I started to cry.

"I know, baby. Let's go over here. Get these kids out of the street. All these motherfuckers out here with their nosey asses."

We walked over to the house. It was a shame how they tore that lady's house up. I watched as she started crying. It was a damn shame. I walked over to her and hugged her. "It's gonna be all right. I'm gonna help you clean this mess up."

We tried to clean up the things that were broken and put everything back into place. I mopped the floor while she cleaned the kitchen up. They'd opened flour, sugar, and rice. I knew they were looking for drugs, and whatever else they thought he had up in here.

***

It was 5:00 p.m. when I called the jail.

"Hello, DeKalb County Jail. How may I help you?"

"Umm, I'm calling to see what Micah Brown is charged with and how much is his bond?"

"Hold on a second. How do you spell his first name?"

"It's M-i-c-a-h," I said.

"He is charged with distribution of cocaine, conspiracy to distribute cocaine, possession of a firearm, possession of a weapon during the commission of a drug offense, and maintaining a drug premises. Looks like he doesn't have a bond."

"What the hell you mean, he doesn't have a bond? Y'all acting like he committed murder."

"Ma'am, I'm just telling you what is on the monitor in front of me."

I hung up on that bitch before I went off on her ass. *How the fuck she means he doesn't have no bond?* I couldn't stop the tears from flowing.

"Is his keys in here?"

"They are on top of the fridge."

"I'm about to go to the house. I need to get my head together. I'll take the girls with me. I hope the lawyer find out something fast."

"All right, baby. You know the kids could've stayed with me."

"I know, but I miss my baby. I need him close to me right now. I will call you if I hear anything."

"Okay, love you."

"Come on, kids, let's go."

I grabbed Baby Micah's hand and we all left the house. I got them in the car and pulled off. I felt bad for Miss Debra. You could see she was hurting. Micah was her pride and joy.

"Hey, Auntie, why did the policeman take my daddy in cuffs?" Dominique asked me, interrupting my train of thought.

"Baby, I have no idea, but don't you worry about that. Daddy will be back real soon."

"Is it because of what Mommy was telling that detective man on the phone the other day?"

"Huh, what?" I managed to say.

"The other day, I heard Mommy telling somebody she called Detective that she was handing Daddy over to him and they can lock him away forever. She didn't know I heard her, but I did. I ran to my room and cried. Because I know my daddy gonna be in trouble."

"Baby, no, I don't think that's what your mommy was talking about."

I couldn't believe what she just said out of her mouth. But I knew this wasn't something a child would just make up out of the blue. I knew there was more to what she was saying. I just didn't want her to know how important this was.

I started to feel nervous the closer I got to the house. I wasn't sure they didn't break down my door also. I swallowed hard as I turned on my street. I breathed easy as I pulled into my driveway. I noticed my car was gone. *The tow people must've picked it up.* I looked around as I hurriedly took the kids out of the car and got them safely into the house.

I washed them up, fed them some ravioli, and put them in the bed. I needed a minute of quietness so I could get my thoughts together. I poured a glass of Taylor's port wine and gulped it down. I needed that. I wished I had a blunt right now; it definitely would've helped to relax me. I dialed the lawyer's number, but it kept ringing. I called right back; still there was no answer. I was irritated as fuck. I needed to know something.

I must've dozed off, because I heard my cell ringing. I looked over to the side and saw that the number was unknown. I thought about not picking it up, but then I wondered, *what if it's Micah!*

CHAPTER SIXTY

Ayana

News traveled fast as hell; plus, one of my old nosey-ass homegirls called me and told me to turn on the TV. The five o'clock news was on, and it was breaking news. I stared into the face of my baby daddy as they dragged him out of his mama's house in handcuffs. I also recognized his boy Mari. I wonder what his bitch-ass girlfriend Lori was saying. I knew they were building a case. I just didn't know it was going to be this soon. I cut up the television so I could hear every word this news bitch was saying!

"I just spoke to Detective Robinson from the DeKalb County drug task force, and he told me this was one of Georgia's biggest drug busts. He also told me that he and his team have been trying for years to bring this crew down, but have not been successful until today. I tell you, Ross, the police department is being praised for bringing down this drug empire. In the next half hour, I will be showing the viewers some of the drugs and guns that were seized in this operation. Jenise Scoot reporting for Channel 2 News. Now back to you, Ross."

I was not shocked at what I was hearing at all. I knew from the day I laid eyes on him he was moving major paper. His old lying ass claimed he wasn't hustling anymore! That old dumbass bitch might've believed that shit, but not I!

I was up bright and early. I called the jail and found out Ant didn't have bail. That was great news for me. I bet his ass would sit there and think about all the shit he put me through. I took a long shower to revive myself. Last night was the best I'd slept in ages.

I quickly got dressed. I had to go get my children from this bitch's house. I knew she didn't think I was going to leave my fucking children over there.

I got in my car and drove to her house. I hoped this bitch just let me get them without a hassle because I had zero tolerance for this shit. I pulled up at her address and I parked. I walked my fat ass up the driveway and rang the doorbell. There was no response, so I rang it again and again. I knew that bitch was in there because Ant's Charger was parked in the driveway; plus, I saw lights on in there when I peeked to the side of the window. I put my head close to the door and heard movement! *That bitch better open this fucking door because I am not leaving without my kids!*

CHAPTER SIXTY-ONE

Tiana

I was so restless. I waited up half the damn night thinking Micah was going to call. Every time the phone rang I jumped and grabbed it, thinking it was him, only to be disappointed. I was also pissed off that his lawyer didn't hit me up. Best believe his ass was going to hear about it as soon as I saw his ass this morning. I let out a long sigh and got up out of the bed.

The girls were already up, and I knew it was only a matter of time before they started asking for something to eat. I dragged myself downstairs and started making pancakes and eggs. My mind was so clouded and I was feeling helpless. I hoped they gave him a bond this morning, 'cause God knows I couldn't go through with this. I hated the fact that we were not on speaking terms when this shit happened. I wished I could hold him.

Ding! Ding! Ding! The chiming of my doorbell startled me and interrupted my thoughts. I swear, I had a bad feeling about this. I hoped to God it wasn't the fucking police showing up at my door. I panicked. I had no idea if Micah had anything illegal in the house. I tiptoed over to the door, and glanced through the peephole.

"Is this bitch for real?" I whispered to myself.

"Bitch, open the motherfucking door! I know you in there. Give me my damn kids," she hollered.

I leaned against the door, thinking whether I wanted to entertain this bitch or call the police on her ass.

Bang! Bang! Bang! She continued showing her ass off.

I had enough of this shit! I unlocked the door and stood there looking at this deranged bitch! "What the fuck is you at my house banging for? Bitch, I don't fuck with you."

"Bitch, I'm here to get my damn kids. I suggest you send them out before I drag your ass on this concrete."

I stepped out of the door, and down to the pavement. "I whupped your ass once before; please don't let me do it again. I done told yo' ass I ain't wit' all this kiddy shit. You know what the court order said. Now get the fuck off my property, before I drag you in this house and tear you the fuck up." I took a step back and walked into my house. I slammed the door behind me.

I wanted to go off on this bitch, but I knew I had to keep my calm. Micah was already in a fucked-up situation and he needed me to be out here to handle things. I walked into the kitchen and realized I'd left the stove on, and the pancakes were burnt to the point where they were black. I cut the stove off and put some water in the pan. I poured me a glass of water, and drank it down to help ease my level of frustration.

"Auntie, I'm hungry," Diamond ran into the kitchen yelling.

"Baby, you have to eat some cereal. Auntie accidentally burnt the pancakes."

"Oh, man," she pouted.

"I'm sorry, baby! Auntie will make it up to you," I said while I choked back tears.

I poured her some cereal, and went to clean up the kitchen. I knew I had to hurry up, because I had to be in court this morning.

CHAPTER SIXTY-TWO

Ayana

This bitch lost her damn mind! Who the fuck did she think she was, denying me my damn children? I was one second away from jumping on her ass, but for once my common sense kicked in. I wanted to do it the right way so I could be assured the state didn't take them back, or Micah's ass didn't beat his case and take the kids away from me.

"911, how may I help you?"

"Hello, ma'am. I need an officer. This lady has my children in this house, but won't let them out."

"Ma'am, what is your name? Are these your biological children or do you have custody of these children?"

"Yes, I do," I snapped on this bitch. I ended up giving her the address. I was irritated because this bitch was behaving like she didn't understand me.

"Okay, ma'am, I am dispatching a unit to meet you over at the address you gave me."

Without responding, I hung up on that bitch. I really wasn't in the mood this morning.

I walked back to my car, and sat in the seat with the car door open. Twenty minutes later, a police car pulled up. I got up, and closed my door and walked over to him.

"Hello, ma'am. Are you the one who called the police?" the young, sexy officer said. Damn, if it was a different situation, I would definitely be flirting with him. But I wasn't in the mood for no dick right now!

"Yes, that's me. My name is Ayana Beasly and there is a custody arrangement between the children's father and me. However, he was locked up yesterday in that big drug bust out here in Stone Mountain. So I'm trying to take my kids home with me."

"Did you knock on the door?"

"Yes, and the bi . . ." I caught myself fast. "The lady said she is not giving them back."

"Okay, please stay here. I'll talk with the homeowner." He walked off toward the door.

I wasn't trying to hear that shit! I walked up the driveway behind him. I stopped at a fair distance. I didn't want the cop to say anything smart to me. I saw when he banged on the door. The bitch opened it quickly and he started talking with her. I tried to listen, but they were damn near whispering. I had no idea what that bitch said, but the officer stepped inside and closed the door behind him. By then another unit pulled up. *Hmm, this bitch might be joining her baby daddy in jail.*

The door suddenly opened and the officer walked out alongside my youngest child. A few seconds later Dominique walked out screaming and hollering. "I don't want to go. I want to stay with my Auntie Tiana. Please, I don't want to go home," she screamed, and tried to reach back into the house.

"You better bring your ass." I grabbed her arm and slightly pulled her toward me. I was careful not to cause a scene because of the police presence. "Thank you, Officer," I said before I walked down the hill, pulling on this little bitch who was resisting.

"Get in the car," I said to Diamond. I then threw Dominique's overgrown ass into the back seat.

"I don't want to go! I hate you. I want to stay with my auntie," she screamed.

Slap! Slap! "Shut the fuck up, you little bitch! You're going home whether you like or not. That bitch is not Mama and you better get used to it because this is the last time you gonna see her ass," I blurted out. I didn't give a damn right now! I was tired of her shenanigans and her behaving like that bitch spit her out of her pussy! "Now buckle your damn seat belt and shut the fuck up."

I walked to the driver's seat. I was ready to pull off before the officers walked over here. The last thing I needed was another accusation of child abuse. I looked in my mirror as he pulled up from behind.

He stopped beside my car. "Hello, ma'am. Is everything okay?"

"Yes, Officer. Thanks again for helping me." I smiled at him.

He nodded and pulled off. I watched as the other unit pulled off in the other direction. I was happy because my tag was expired; plus, I ain't pay the insurance. I waited a few seconds and then I pulled off.

I cut up the radio so I could tune out all the crying this little heffa was doing. God knows that I would have to push my foot up her ass soon. I was not the one to be fucked with and she would find out soon enough.

CHAPTER SIXTY-THREE

Tiana

I locked my door and fell to the ground. My heart was broken. The tears streamed down my face as I gripped my chest. I was hurting for me, but more so for that little girl. She'd been through more than enough and what made it sad was that bitch Ayana didn't really want them. She was doing that shit to get back at Micah and me. I swear I didn't want to let them go, but the officer explained to me that this was between Micah and Ayana and, unless I took her to court and won, I had no legal right to the children. As much as it hurt my heart, I understood completely.

I sat on the floor crying about everything that was going on in my life. "God, please wrap your hands around my family! They need you. I need you," I cried. I wasn't the most religious person on this earth, but I swear I needed help from

God. Everything just spiraled downhill and out of control. I didn't know what to do, or where to even start. I continued crying as I poured my heart out to the Man Above.

I heard my phone ringing upstairs. I wiped my tears and ran up the stairs. I grabbed the phone. "Hello," I said, all out of breath.

"Hey, babe, it's me. Are you on your way yet?" Micah's mama's voice echoed in my ear.

"On my way?" I stuttered.

"Yes, to court. You know Micah has court this morning."

"Oh, shit! Yes, I'm on the way," I lied.

I hung the phone up and threw it on the bed. I stripped down in seconds and jumped in the shower. I took less than five minutes to make sure I washed my arms and my pussy. I jumped out and dried off. I rushed to my closet and pulled out a pair of jeans and a nice dress shirt. I quickly got dressed and rushed out the door. Court started in twenty minutes, but knowing the traffic in the morning I was definitely cutting it close.

I was lucky there was no backed-up traffic this morning. I got to the courthouse about five minutes before court was scheduled to start. I parked and walked hurriedly into the court-house. As soon as I walked through the metal detector, I spotted his mother. "Good morning, Ma. Sorry I'm late."

"Hey, honey." She kissed me on the cheek.

"Is the lawyer here yet?"

"No. I didn't see anyone in the courtroom except the bailiff."

"I had the worst freaking morning. They came and took the kids."

"Who took the kids?" She looked at me for clarification.

"Ayana knocked on the door, asking for the kids. I told her no, and closed my door. Next thing I know the police was knocking on the door. I thought about not opening up the door, but the last thing I need is to get locked up."

"Are you fucking serious? Please excuse my French. That bitch not gonna stop until I beat her ass. She keeps fucking with me and my damn son. I have a strong feeling she the one who set them people on Micah. I told his ass long time ago to stop fucking with her ass," she said in a high-pitched tone. She started crying.

I moved closer and wrapped my arms around her. She held on to me. I could feel this lady's pain because I was hurting also. I knew I had to remain strong, but right now I didn't know how!

I looked up and saw the lawyer walking toward the courtroom. "Mr. Pocasso." I let her go and called the lawyer over.

"Good morning, Mrs. Caldwell-Brown."

"Good morning. This is Miss Debra, Micah's mother. I tried to reach you all yesterday, but I got no response. I even texted you a few times."

"Yes, sorry about that. I was handling a heavy workload yesterday. But I did make it down to the jail to talk with Mr. Brown."

"So what's going on? 'Cause I'm lost."

"Well, the state claims they have an enormous amount of evidence against him. I've yet to see what they're talking about. I also learned there was a confidential informant who is working closely with the drug force. I will be filing a motion for discovery to get a better understanding of what evidence they have against him."

"They ain't got shit. I know my husband and I do know he wasn't in them streets anymore. They're trying to frame him for real."

"We have to go in the courtroom right now, but we'll talk some more after court."

I nodded and followed him into the courtroom. Micah's mother followed closely and rubbed my back as we walked into the room. I took a seat right behind the attorney. I wanted to hear everything that was going to be said.

I was looking down, trying to keep my emotions under wraps. When I finally lifted my head up, I saw the bailiff walking Micah out. He spotted me as soon as he walked in. He looked at me and mouthed, "I love you."

"I love you, babe," I mouthed back. My husband didn't look like himself! He looked stressed out. I wished I could hug him and let him know it was going to be all right. I hoped!

"All rise, the district court of DeKalb County, Criminal Division is now in session. The Honorable Judge Preston is residing. Please be seated," the bailiff said.

"Your Honor, calling docket number 456783: State of Georgia versus Anthony Micah Brown. Five counts of possession with the intent to distribute, drug trafficking across state lines, possession of a firearm during drug trafficking, maintaining a drug dwelling, conspiracy to distribute crack cocaine."

I stopped listening, because it was becoming a little too much for my mind. I lowered my head and breathed slowly. I tried to tune out everything. I didn't want to hear all the lies that were being told about my husband.

"Bond is denied," definitely got my attention.

"What do you mean, no bond? He has a family, and he ain't trying to run anywhere," I stood up and blurted out.

"Ma'am, please be quiet. Bailiff, if she doesn't sit down and remain silent, please remove her from the courtroom."

Micah's mother grabbed my hand. I looked at Micah. He looked at me and shook his head no. I knew he didn't like what I just did, but I swear, I couldn't take it anymore. I grabbed my hand away from his mother and ran out of the courtroom. I didn't stop running until I got to my car.

I collapsed onto the seat, crying uncontrollably. I couldn't believe they denied bond. My husband wasn't no criminal. I knew this man; they didn't! I laid my head on the steering wheel and just let the tears flow loosely.

Bang! Bang!

I lifted my head up, quickly wiping snot from my nose. I noticed a thick-ass female standing by my window. My first instinct told me she was a bitch Ant was fucking. I swear I wasn't in the mood. Nevertheless, I let my window down. "Yes," I said in between sobs.

"Hi, my name is Lori. I was in the court. Mari is my boyfriend and he is Ant's codefendant."

I looked at her like, "Okay, so what the fuck you want?"

"I never met you, but I've heard so much about you. I was wondering if we could talk for a few."

I thought about it, then agreed. I grabbed a tissue out of my bag and wiped my face. I opened my door and stepped out. I was still being cautious because I didn't know if this bitch was a friend or a foe. "So what you want to talk about?"

"I want you to know I know exactly what you're going through. Mari and Ant are good friends. Anyway I used to be friends with Ayana and—"

"I don't want to discuss that bitch, so if she sent you I don't wanna hear that shit." I turned to get back in my car.

"No, wait." She grabbed my arm. "I think you'll want to hear what I have to say."

"You got five minutes." I turned back around and folded my arms.

"Like I said, Ayana and I were friends. A few months ago, we're talking and she blurted out how she tried to kill you."

She definitely grabbed my attention with that statement. I'd suspected that she did it, but up until now I had no proof. "So why are you telling me this if she's your girl?"

"A few weeks ago, I caught her fucking Mari in my bed. We fought and she was angry. It's kind of strange that all of a sudden Ant and his crew is locked up. They did a huge bust even at spots that no one outside of me and Ayana knew about. I know damn well I didn't tell nobody, so that leaves her."

As I stood there listening, something that Dominique said to me the day her daddy got locked up played back in my head.

"Are you okay?" She touched my arm.

"Yes, just thinking about something."

"Well, like I said, I don't think it's coincidence. I swear that bitch better not let me catch her ass. Mari suspect it's her ass too."

"You really think Ayana is that evil?"

"That bitch is scandalous. She is obsessed with Ant and will do any- and everything to get him back. I think she is over the edge because she see that she can't break you and him up. I don't know you, but I think you should be careful. Watch your back at all times."

"Let me ask you a question, woman to woman; and I need you to be honest with me."

"Sure, what's up?"

"Was my husband still in them streets? Did he do all that shit they're accusing him of?" I looked at her.

"Well, you know, Mari kept me out of his business, but yes, Ant still was the head nigga in charge. He wasn't doing hand to hand after he met you, but he still call the shots. I know they were out there heavily. I can't say they did all that and I can't say they didn't."

"Thank you. I needed to know the truth."

"Ant loves you and maybe was just trying to protect you from all of this."

"Listen, I got to run, but put my number in your phone. Call me if you need to talk."

I got into my car and pulled off. Everything I thought about that bitch was confirmed. The hardest part was finding out my husband was lying to me. Now it made sense, all those late nights and early mornings. I thought he was cheating on me, when all along he was still running around in them streets. I was hurting because he deceived me.

It was time to pick up my son from daycare. It broke my heart that I couldn't bring his daddy home. What would I tell my son? I took a long sigh and pulled into the daycare.

The next day after I dropped Baby Micah off with his grandma, I made my way to the DeKalb County Jail. Luckily it was Micah's day to get visitors. I put on a little makeup to kind of take away the dullness from my face. I also made sure my hair was done. I didn't want him to see me looking like hell. It was bad enough he was in that hell hole. I'd never been to jail before, but I'd heard enough horror stories. I was kind of happy that I was getting the chance to see him.

I needed some sort of explanation to all this madness that was going on!

I parked and walked into the lobby. I hated being here, but a bitch had to do what she had to do. I swallowed hard and walked up to the front window to show my identification. I took a glance around. I noticed there were a bunch of females along with children seated, waiting for their names to be called. I shivered inside as I silently prayed this would be my one and only time going through this.

"Hello, I'm here to visit Anthony Brown."

"Your ID," she said with an attitude.

I pushed the ID in front of her. I didn't give a fuck if this bitch was an officer; she needed some damn manners. She examined my ID, then gave it back. "Have a seat and listen for your name to be called."

I took my ID up and walked away. I hoped she didn't mind that I didn't say thank you for nothing. I sat in the nearest seat available and tried my best to tune out everything that was going on around me.

Names after names were called. I was feeling anxious. I wondered what was taking so long for them to bring him out.

"Tiana Caldwell-Brown."

"Here I go," I said as I jumped up like I just won an award. I walked into the visiting area and anxiously looked around. I spotted my husband all the way toward the end. This shit was crazy. I couldn't even touch him. He was behind glass, and we could only talk on the telephone. I walked over to him and grabbed the phone.

"What's good, ma?" He looked deep into my eyes.

Without saying anything, the tears started to flow out. "Hey, boo," I whispered in between the sobs.

"Damn, ma, you know how much I hate that! Yo, you killing me right now!"

I tried my best to control the tears. I then wiped my eyes. "Micah, what the hell is going on?" It was my turn to look him dead in his eyes.

"Ma, you know I can't even talk to you the way I want to. But, I assure you, these charges are bogus."

I didn't say anything. I was good at reading people, and I was good at telling when my husband was lying to me. Only this time I couldn't tell. All I saw in front of me was a broken man. That broke my heart more. I wished I could tell him it was going to be okay, but I couldn't.

"Ma, listen to me! I need you to pay the lawyer and I want you to take care of you and little man.

Please know your man is G, and I got this. You look like hell, so I know you been up worrying yourself to death. You need to chill out," he said in a stern voice. "So how the girls and little man doing? I hate that they had to witness this shit the other day."

I forgot he had no idea that bitch came and got the girls. There was no easy way to say it. "Ayana called the police and they came and got the girls," I blurted out.

"What the fuck you mean, they came and got them?"

"You have shared custody with her, but you are locked up. I'm not related to them, so the police told me to hand them over."

"Fuck! I'ma kill this bitch," he yelled out as hit the wall.

"Boy, you better calm your ass down. Sitting up here talking like that."

"Yo, B, my girls and my son are everything to me. This bitch keep playing with me. I'm already tight as fuck 'cause of that stunt that ho pulled the other day."

"I understand all that, but you need to keep a level head so you can figure out how to get out of this case."

"Man, these people ain't got shit on me, B. I swear, that fuck nigga Detective Robinson been trying to pin some shit on me and my niggas for a while now."

"I tell you what, you need to stop worrying about these niggas. You got your family; that's who you need to be loyal to. For real," I spat.

"Ma, chill out, a'ight?"

"Chill out? Do you have any idea how bad this shit is? You're facing a lot of time, possibly life. And you telling me to chill out. I told your ass from day one I wasn't with this shit." I started to cry again.

"Ma, listen, I didn't mean anything by that. Tiana, I love you and this shit is killing me, just seeing you hurting like this. Ma, please wipe them tears. I know this don't mean a lot, but I want you to know I didn't do anything to intentionally hurt you. I love you, ma, and truth is I have no idea how this shit going to turn out, but I need you to know that I love you with everything in me." A few tears dropped from his eyes. He didn't even try to wipe them away. Instead, he just them flow.

Seeing him like this did something to me. I knew he was hurting inside and, as his woman, I felt helpless. "I think Ayana switched on y'all!"

"What make you think that?"

"Because I do. I can't say a lot right now, but I think so."

"Visitation over," I heard a guard yell.

"I love you. Please take care of yourself out there. Don't trust none of these niggas or bitches out there. These motherfuckers are grimy as fuck."

"I love you too and I already know that."

"Let's go," another guard yelled.

"A'ight, ma. Kiss my li'l man for me."

I walked off in a rush. I swear, I couldn't take it anymore. Something had to give!

CHAPTER SIXTY-FOUR

Tiana

I lay on the carpet in the living room, finishing up my sixth glass of Moscato. That visit earlier did a number on my heart. My chest tightened up on me as I wept silently. Just a few months ago, my life was not perfect, but it was somewhat normal. I should've known that things were not going to stay that way for long. As I lay there thinking and indulging in self-pity, I couldn't help but think about the bitch who started it.

Yes, that bitch Ayana. This bitch shot me and now I knew she was bragging about it. I also bet my life on it that she was the confidential informer they talked about. My body temperature started to rise and my hatred for that ho intensified. I took one last gulp of the wine. Wicked thoughts were invading my mind. I tried to block them out but I couldn't. I thought about killing myself to stop the pain, but I couldn't leave my baby without a mother.

"Micah, I need you, baby! I swear I need you," I cried out.

I slowly got up and walked up the stairs. I was about to grab my gun; instead, I ran to Micah's drawer. I wasn't sure, but I thought he'd always kept a gun in his drawer. It was my lucky day; there was a .380 up under his underwear. *What else this nigga has in the house?* Now wasn't the time to go snooping. I grabbed my oversized sun hat and a pair of my Gucci glasses.

I then ran down the stairs and looked around. Micah kept a gasoline can. I found it and grabbed the lighter.

On my way to this bitch's house my mind was blank. My cell phone kept ringing, but I didn't want to talk to anyone. I was on a mission.

I parked by the curb and looked around, grabbed the gasoline can, and then I got out. I ran up the driveway. I almost stumbled. I was drunk, but that didn't stop me from making my way up the driveway. I knocked on the door, and waited.

"Who is it?"

"It's your neighbor from three houses down. I need to talk to you about a few break-ins in the neighborhood," I said in my best elderly voice.

"I didn't hear about no brea—" She opened the door.

"That's right, bitch, there are no break-ins." I pushed the door with all my might. I almost fell on my face.

"Bitch, what the fuck you doing at my house? You must come for another ass whupping." She took a step toward me.

"Back the fuck up, bitch!" I pulled the gun out of my purse and pointed it to her head.

"Hold up! What the fuck you think you're doing? Put that shit down, bitch."

"See, that's your problem, Ayana; you always think everything is a joke. No, bitch, this ain't no joke." I took a step closer to her.

"Man, T, we sisters, boo. You goin' to let dick come between us? This me, T."

"Bitch, you ain't my motherfucking sister. Matter of fact, you ain't shit to me for real." Slap! Slap! Slap! I slapped her across her face three times with the butt of the gun. That bitch grabbed her face and fell to her knees.

"No, get up, bitch! I begged you to leave me and my man alone, but you kept bothering us." I used my foot to kick her ass dead in the face.

"Oh my God, you trying to kill me! I swear, bitch, you better not let me live. I'm going to beat your motherfucking ass," she said through clenched teeth and leapt toward me, knocking me to the ground. I regained my footing and aimed the gun at her.

"I didn't plan on it!" Pop! Pop! Pop! I squeezed the trigger and fired into that bitch's face and torso. In that split second, I went from being a wife and mother to a cold-blooded killer!

"Help me," she managed to say before falling backward, knocking a lamp to the ground. "Help me, sister," she said while gasping for air.

I stooped down beside her. "Nah, bitch, the only person who can help you is God." I stood up and put the gun to her forehead and squeezed the trigger.

I quickly grabbed the gasoline can and started sprinkling gas everywhere. I was nervous, so my hand was trembling. I tried not to get any on me. I then walked into the living room and sprinkled some on the couch and the carpet. I checked her pulse; she was dead. I threw the rest on her. I then lit the fire. The smell of flesh burning quickly illuminated my brain. I needed to get out of there.

I nervously opened the door and slowly walked down the hill and got into my car. I slowly eased off her street; then I picked up the pace. I looked in my rearview mirror and I could see fire and smoke spreading. I should've felt nervous, but no, I felt relieved. I felt like a big weight had lifted off my shoulders.

The saying was true: "I'm no killer, but don't push me." Because I had to end that bitch's life and let her know who the man chose!

As soon as I was far away from her condo, I pulled over and took my shirt off because spots of blood and the smell of gasoline were all over it. I pulled over by an abandoned building, and lit the shirt with a lighter. I stood there as it burned. I think I was trying to bide time to figure out my next move. I was a bit sobered up and reality was setting in.

EPILOGUE

I got back into my car and pulled back on the street. I was crying as I tried to figure out what I was going to do. I wished Micah were here to hold my hands, but the reality was he wasn't here and I was all by myself. I had to put on my big girl panties and figure it out. I had some money that Micah had in an account for our son, or an emergency. I needed to go home and pack some things and get my son from his mother.

I pulled onto my subdivision, and an eerie feeling came over me. The closer I got, the queasier I felt. I saw a crowd of people standing outside. I drove closer and saw that there was a raid going on at my house. I didn't stop. I kept driving as the tears flowed heavily. I pulled out my phone and called Micah's lawyer.

"Mrs. Caldwell-Brown, I've been trying to reach you."

"About what?" I nervously asked.

"I got a tip that the police were going to raid your home and I wanted you to get out of there."

"What are they looking for?"

"They got a tip that most of the drug money was up in there."

"Really? Well, thank you. I got to go." I hung up the phone and turned it off. I decided to grab my son from his mother's house.

I looked around as I got out of the car. I was nervous because I knew by now Ayana's body was found and they would be looking for her killer.

"Hey, baby," Miss Debra greeted me.

I fell right into her arms crying.

"What's wrong, baby?" She hugged me tight.

"Ma, I need to go! I did something to Ayana," I cried.

"Baby, go, don't worry about the baby. Your mama got you. Do what you have to do, then call me one day when you feel like it's safe. Go up North; we have family up there. I'm going to call my brother now and he will be there waiting for you. Do you need money?" Before I could respond to her question, she started talking. "Be careful of these phones. I'll talk to my son when he calls. Just be careful and trust no one outside of my brother. You hear me?"

"No, I'm good, and I understand you," I said and walked toward the back, where my son was sitting down watching television. I knelt down beside him and broke down. I took his hand and just cried. He was my world; how would I leave him behind?

I left for Landover, Maryland, and stayed there for a while. Being away from my son was killing me slowly. I followed Micah's case slowly and, exactly eight months later, he went to trial. He was convicted of possession of a firearm, but was found not guilty on all other charges. The state's main witness was found murdered and they had no physical evidence against him. Mari stepped up to claim the drugs and guns that they found in the house. They offered him a plea for fifteen years, which he gladly accepted. His lawyer told me Detective Robinson wasn't too pleased with the plea deal.

I jumped for joy the day his mother called me from the courthouse. Later that night I got a call from him.

"Hey, babe," he said sounding like the Micah I met in the beginning.

"Yes! You did it!" I couldn't contain my excitement.

We ended up talking until the phone was cut off. I was genuinely happy for him, but I wondered if the police would be looking for me. I stayed in contact with the lawyer, but nothing was mentioned. I kept a low profile, spending the money Micah had stashed in our son's name.

He was sentenced to five years for the gun charge, but that was nothing compared to what he was facing. I knew someone was watching over my family and for that I was grateful. Lori and I became close friends and we keep each other motivated.

I made Maryland my new home; after all, I needed a change. My son was growing up, and Georgia's streets were not safe. What can I say but the man chose me and that bitch Ayana did not get him. In the end, our love for each other kept us grounded.

31901061172666